The
Monumentals

Zac'cia

Lorca

Huggard

Kalicut

The
Waiting
Lands

Old
Ocean

Verret River

Baglan

Blue River

Isle of
Lily

Rocky
Harbor

Port Marshall

FONTANIA

Eastern Isle

J
17.95
Ingram
4/15

Books in the Tales of Fontania series
*The Traveling Restaurant*
*The Queen and the Nobody Boy*

www.TalesOfFontania.com

Book 2 Tales of Fontana

First American edition published in 2013 by Gecko Press USA,
an imprint of Gecko Press Ltd.

A catalog record for this book is available from the US Library of Congress.

Distributed in the United States and Canada by
Lerner Publishing Group, Inc.
241 First Avenue North
Minneapolis, MN 55401 USA
www.lernerbooks.com

First published in 2012 by Gecko Press
PO Box 9335, Marion Square, Wellington 6141, New Zealand
info@geckopress.com

Text © 2012 Barbara Else
Cover and illustrations © 2012 Sam Broad

© Gecko Press Ltd

Design by Luke Kelly, Wellington, New Zealand
Printed by Everbest, China

ISBN hardback (US) 978-1-877579-49-3

**For more curiously good books, visit www.geckopress.com**

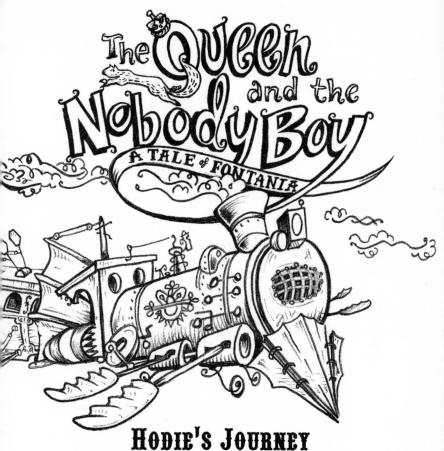

# The Queen and the Nobody Boy

## A Tale of Fontania

### Hodie's Journey

(IN FIVE PARTS ALL ABOUT BAD CHOICES)

BY BARBARA ELSE

~ WITH ILLUSTRATIONS BY SAM BROAD ~

GECKO PRESS

# DEDICATION

to good companions

Once upon a time, the world was rich in magic. It was used wisely, not wasted on anything selfish or mean-spirited. It was saved for important things like making sure babies slept safe in their cribs, that people had enough to eat, and that the world was peaceful. There were dangers, as there always is with magic. But there was also common sense. Some people began to experiment with science and machines, and that was all right. You see, everyone thought somebody was in charge.

— Polly, *The Traveling Restaurant*

# CONTENTS

## PART ONE
## HOW TO LEAVE THE
## CITY OF SPIRES

## PART TWO
## HOW TO CROSS THE
## STONES OF BEYOND

## PART THREE
# HOW TO TRAVEL TO Um'Binnia

## PART FOUR
# MANY SHOCKS AND MANY TEMPTATIONS

## PART FIVE
# WHAT TO DO WHEN YOU'VE ESCAPED BUT ONLY SO FAR

PART ONE OF HODIE'S JOURNEY

# HOW TO
# LEAVE THE
# CITY OF SPIRES

# HOPING FOR TOAST

Hodie trudged past the elephant house (which hadn't smelled of elephant for years) and the army barracks (which smelled of gunpowder and sword polish). He took the path through the Grand Palace herb garden (lavender, sage, and thyme) and sat on the kitchen step where he smelled porridge.

If the cook was in a good mood she might give him some leftover toast. There might be some bacon. Maybe there'd be a poached egg with a broken yolk that the cook hadn't liked to serve to King Jasper or his sister, Queen Sibilla. Of course, sometimes there was nothing at all.

Whatever the servants might bring out would be cold by now, but Hodie couldn't remember eating anything that wasn't. A hot egg would probably taste awful.

He picked at a new hole in the side of his boot then made himself stop it. When these ones fell apart, he'd never find another pair.

Chickens argued and scratched in the dirt. Through the

window came the voice of Mrs. Emily, the housekeeper, scolding the staff while she had a cup of tea.

"No more of your gossip where the little Queen can hear. She was upset when she came down to breakfast."

Pots and pans clattered about. "They're all sailing for the Eastern Isle today and she'll be nervous." It was the cook. "Any girl in her shoes would be on edge."

"It's nothing to do with the Eastern Isle," snapped Mrs. Emily. "She heard someone complain she wasn't trying hard enough to be Queen. Thank your lucky stars that Lady Helen didn't hear of it. There's no fury like a mother guarding her child."

Could that be true? Hodie had no idea.

"Why are they going to the Eastern Isle anyway?" asked the new footman with the whiny voice.

"Oo," said a maid, "they're searching for the missing Ties."

"The Ties?" said the footman. "What Ties?"

"They're some treasures that are all to do with magic," said another maid. "They must be like a golden harness. Oo, for when the King and Queen ride the Dragon-eagles."

"Did you hear what I said about gossip?" Mrs. Emily clashed her tea cup.

"Their journey's overdue, my granddad reckons." It was the burly footman this time. "We need The Ties now, before Um'Binnia declares war on us."

"Oo, true," the first maid said. "My auntie says we'll need the help of a lot more magic before we can stand with —I mean 'withstand'—Um'Binnia."

"Get on with the royal packing!" said Mrs. Emily.

Hodie stopped listening. He was only the odd-job boy, so their talk was none of his business. But he'd still like a bite of breakfast.

He'd just nerved himself to stand up and tap on the door to ask after scraps when he heard someone marching into the kitchen with a military jangle of equipment.

"Message for the royal parents, Mrs. Emily." (Hodie recognized one of the officers.) "I'd prefer you to take it up, if you'd be so kind. It's from Um'Binnia."

There was silence. It meant everyone was watching the housekeeper open the message. Hodie wished the window was lower so he could see, too.

"Greetings to the royal family of Fontania..." Mrs. Emily let out the sort of shriek that meant it would be wise to keep out of her way for several hours. "The Um'Binnians are coming to stay! They'll be here in thirty minutes! The Emperor, the Princessa, the Commander, and a dozen officers! The message says, 'A Friendly Visit!'"

"Splitting my sides laughing," said the burly footman. "Friendly Um'Binnians?"

"Today?" said the cook. "Without any warning?"

"And I have to tell Their Majesties and their parents!" cried Mrs. Emily.

"Dr. Ludlow's at the wharves, stocking up the *Royal Traveler*," said the whiny footman.

"We know that, you silly egg! He's Their Majesties' father. He still has to be told." Mrs. Emily began to rattle out orders.

The Grand Palace erupted with the crisis of finding

enough pillows and good towels. Hodie heard the muttering of the cook working out what to do about lunch for all those extras. He actually had to jump aside when King Jasper's fiancée, Lady Beatrix, came dashing out the back door with a face like thunder to fetch a carriage.

"You should have found The Ties years ago!" she shouted up at a second-story window. "I'm going on the *Royal Traveler* anyway!" She gave a sarcastic curtsy, then blew two fat kisses that you could tell she meant—one would be for the King and probably the other was for his sister, Queen Sibilla.

Everyone heard King Jasper slam down to his workshop.

Hodie also heard that the King and Queen's mother, Lady Helen, actually said the Royal Swear Word. (It's in very tiny letters at the end of the book. Nobody must see you look at it.)

All it meant for Hodie was today he wouldn't even have a slice of toast.

—

## BREAKFAST AGAIN
## A WEEK LATER

Hodie waited on the kitchen step again. The chickens nattered and the Palace cats lazed, ears twitching. The Um'Binnians were still here, so this week the royal scraps had been delicious.

He'd only seen the Um'Binnians from a distance: one portly Emperor, who waxed his ginger mustache into a new design each day; one Princessa, who was a full-grown woman and wore jewels on her slippers; and Commander Gree'sle, a skinny man with a pencil-thin mustache who kept a smile on all the time although it never looked sincere. Mrs. Emily had told Hodie to stay out of sight because it wasn't a tidy thing, an odd-job boy.

He heard her now through the open window. "King Jasper refused to sit at breakfast again this morning. He whisked a bowl of oatmeal off to his workshop. Lady Helen is being so polite to the Um'Binnians it makes my teeth ache. Poor little Queen Sibilla looks bored beyond death."

Hodie didn't think Sibilla ever had much fun being Queen. One time he'd seen her pick her nose and Lady Helen had growled at her. It was much better to be an odd-job boy with no parents. The only risk was irregular meals. He tried to see it as a daily sort of adventure.

A puff of wind pushed his bangs out of his eyes. The pair of scruffy gray squirrels chittered in the walnut tree. One leaped onto the roof of the King's workshop, sat for a good scratch under both front leg pits, then spotted Hodie. It scooted down the drainpipe and ran over to nibble the new string he'd fastened around his boot to hold it together.

"Careful," Hodie said. "You'll tie your guts into a parcel."

A door banged in the kitchen. "More bacon for the Emperor of Um'Binnia!"

"That's his third helping on top of porridge!" cried the cook. Bacon on a bowl of porridge? No one had ever given Hodie that across the doorstep.

"I found out why he won't use normal spoons," said Mrs. Emily. "When he looks in them, his reflection is all askew."

"The vanity!" The cook clattered dishes and pots.

"And they still haven't said what day they're leaving," the housekeeper growled.

"That's the top-most rudeness in a guest," the cook replied.

If you asked Hodie, Emperor Prowdd'on was top-most in many of the ways to be selfish and rude. Hodie had overheard a lot around the Palace. He'd also seen Commander

Gree'sle and his officers poking about in all sorts of corners, and that was definitely not good manners. Hodie suspected they were snooping to make sure a war with Fontania would be worth it.

"Er," said one of the maids, "that boy's on the doorstep."

There was a pause, a quiet curse, and the back door opened. The cook frowned at Hodie. She dropped a bruised banana on his plate and a burnt slice of toast with no butter. The skinny housemaid poured a splash of milk into Hodie's mug. It didn't even fill it to halfway.

"Thank you," said Hodie clearly. If he mumbled, the cook might think he'd said "silly old goat" or something worse and there'd be no dinner.

The cook gave an irritated sigh. "You can't expect to live like this for ever. The Palace needs a dozen odd-job men, not one half-grown boy." She shut the door.

Hodie's heart felt as if it had been punched. Living in the Palace grounds was the only life he could remember.

~

He sat in the shadow of his lean-to behind the elephant house, peeled the banana, and ate it in three bites. Hodie's father, Dardy, had been the odd-job man until he disappeared. A vanished odd-job man is no good. A vanished father is even worse—the thought made Hodie's throat feel as if it had a furball.

The thought of being thrown out made the furball seem bigger. But facts were facts, so he should think in a practical way. He could see it as a chance to better himself.

After all, he could do with some bettering. But what would he do? Where could he go?

There were four possible directions. Behind the City of Spires were cold high mountains. That would be no good without warm clothes and leak-proof boots.

He would not go north, to Um'Binnia. First you had to cross The Torrent on a terrifying bridge—the Bridge of Teeth. Then you had to find your way through the Stones of Beyond. Lately, he'd heard, the Um'Binnians had begun using wind-trains to travel through them. Even if Hodie dared cross The Torrent, he'd have to find his way to the Depot, the wind-station for the trains that took you over the Stones. Walk for more than a day, then climb into something that carried you through the air? Hodie would never be that stupid. Breakfast or no breakfast, he would throw up.

Third choice would be sailing east upon Old Ocean. But Hodie had no money to buy a ticket on a steamship or a sailing ship. He could offer to be an odd-job boy in a ship's crew—no, they might send him into the rigging where he'd absolutely definitely throw up.

Last choice was…The second gray squirrel hopped up and eyed Hodie's toast. *Tck-tck?* Hodie grinned. The squirrel took the crust with a bow and another *tck-tck*!

Where had he got to? Last direction. South. Green fields, open sky, waving corn, sheep, cows… A job on a farm! He'd learned a lot about animals from Dardy. As well as being the odd-job man, his father had been the elephant keeper before the elephant died of old age.

Until Dardy had disappeared, he'd been a good father. And he had been very good with elephants (one elephant, anyway).

Hodie's eyes turned watery. He was utterly sick of the Grand Palace and all its gossip. "Oo, babies not sleeping safe? We need stronger magic." "Oo, Fontania needs a royal family that pays more attention to its magical abilities." "Oo, what can the King be doing in his workshop? I hope it's magical experiments."

*Magic!* he scoffed to himself. How could magic exist in a world where a boy's father was here one day but gone the next without a word? How could it exist in a world where a boy didn't know a thing about his mother? Well, he'd learned to live without parents, and he didn't need the Grand Palace either—especially if the Palace didn't need him. It was high time he left here. He would go south.

~

On a hook in his lean-to hung Hodie's jacket. There was a blanket on his mattress. Dardy's clothes were in the box at the end of the bigger mattress—just his satchel and jacket were missing, that was all, because the day Dardy never came back he had said he was off to the market.

In a box under Hodie's bed was a drawstring bag full of Hodie's mother's stuff. It was like any other old bag that gathered cobwebs till it was tossed into the trash. He hauled out the box, pulled open the drawstring bag, and looked at the junk. There was a battered metal cup and a wrench that was good for long thin spaces. Hodie remembered playing with it when he was three or four years old. His father had been annoyed so Hodie had used it in secret after that and not very often. The only other thing in the bag was a soft pouch containing some rough old beads. They might be worth something if they could be polished, but somehow Hodie doubted it. For a moment, though, he wished he could remember his mother. For just a moment it seemed sad that all she'd left him was useless old stuff.

He hung the bag on a hook in case he decided to take it with him. Right now he had to find a stronger bag that would hold as much food as he could scavenge from dinner. He'd do some odd jobs till then. For instance, the hinges of the side gate needed oiling and the faucet outside King Jasper's workshop window was dripping. Then tomorrow he'd be off.

—

# A NUMBER OF BAD CHOICES

Hodie had almost finished fixing the faucet when Queen Sibilla, in striped leggings and a frilly blue tunic and with her fair hair flying, hurtled down the back steps of the Palace. She took no notice of Hodie (why should she? She was the Queen) and rattled the handle of the workshop door.

"Annoying little sister, go away!" the King called out.

"How did you know it was me?" She stood on tiptoe and peered in the window. "Let me in. I want to hide from Princessa Lu'nedda. She's been making jokes at breakfast about your beard. She said for the fifteenth time I should wear my hair in ringlets like she does. They dangle like black sausages." The little Queen made a strangling sound. "*Ergh.*"

Hodie wiped his nose to hide a snort. The little Queen was famous for unruly hair. Lady Helen had promised her that having hair that showed your mood could be a sign a royal child would sooner or later come into magical ability. Hodie knew nothing about mothers personally, but he believed they sometimes lied to make their children feel better. Lady Helen's hair behaved oddly too, but where was her magic?

"What are you making?" Sibilla called to her brother. "I can see little golden screws…tin snips…"

"Go and sign the royal correspondence!" Jasper shouted.

"It's your turn!" Sibilla bashed the window and ran off.

Hodie tested the faucet. Perfect. He decided the next job should be to clean up down by the barracks. He trudged through the herb garden with his tools.

The pair of squirrels flitted onto the barracks roof. Queen Sibilla appeared from somewhere and called up to them. One skittered down to say hello. She crouched in the dusty path and rubbed its chin. Its tail looked full of burrs and dirt as usual. They were the ugliest little animals but good-natured and very loving to each other. Hodie would be sad to leave them when he set off south.

Footsteps sounded behind Hodie. He dodged out of the way of the Um'Binnian Emperor Prowdd'on and Commander Gree'sle. Today the Emperor's ginger mustache was waxed into spears that stuck straight out toward his earlobes. Prowdd'on stopped behind Queen Sibilla—she was tickling the squirrel's belly now and didn't notice—and held a hand out to Commander Gree'sle who fetched a gold flask from a pocket and gave it to him. Prowdd'on smiled at his reflection in the side of the flask, unscrewed the cap, and had a sip.

Princessa Lu'nedda hurried down from the Palace, too.

The diamonds on her slippers twinkled through the dust. Her shiny black ringlets dangled just like the Queen had said. "Little squirrel!" she cried. "May I pet it?"

Queen Sibilla stood up with the squirrel in her arms. "Let it get used to you first," she began, "then take it gently…"

Emperor Prowdd'on pushed his daughter aside. "I am best with bird and animal!" He grabbed the squirrel and stroked it hard.

"Be careful, please," said Queen Sibilla.

"Emperor, it is very ugly rodent," said the Commander.

The Emperor was squeezing the squirrel far too hard. Its black eyes were full of fear. The Queen's hair had started to crinkle. She reached for the squirrel, but Emperor Prowdd'on held it higher. Hodie couldn't do a thing. He was just the odd-job boy.

Sibilla held both hands like a cradle to show Prowdd'on how. "Gently. Please," she said again.

The Emperor laughed. "Not many little girls play game with Emperor Prowdd'on of Um'Binnia!" He whirled himself around then stopped. "*Ugh!*" He let the squirrel fall into the dust and brushed his hands.

For a moment, Hodie thought the squirrel must have pooped on the Emperor's waistcoat. But the ugly creature didn't move—it didn't breathe. Sibilla didn't move either.

Hodie heard a harsh little gasp above his head. On a branch the second squirrel stood staring down, quivering.

"Father! You squeeze much too hard," Lu'nedda said.

Prowdd'on waved his daughter away. "How foolish,

Lu'nedda. The rodent was sick. Little Queen was very wrong to encourage me to play with faulty rodent."

Hodie's head jerked up. "It was you!" He couldn't stop himself. "There were only two squirrels and you killed one!"

Commander Gree'sle's hand grabbed for the hilt of his sword, but visitors weren't allowed to wear weapons in the Grand Palace so his hand actually groped at his empty scabbard.

Emperor Prowdd'on folded his hands on his purple waistcoat. "This is very bad behavior to important guest. In Um'Binnia, anyone who shows moment of disrespect to Emperor is sent to tend Ocean Toads. It is long and painful death with no escape."

He stalked away around the gardens. Commander Gree'sle narrowed his smile at Hodie then hurried behind. The Princessa took a step toward Hodie as if she wanted to ask something then shook her head and ran after her father.

The little Queen picked up the bundle of tatty gray fur and held it for a moment, her head lowered. Hodie saw her pointy chin quivering. Her hair was tangled as tightly as a bird's nest. One of her tantrums might be coming on.

"Boy," she said to Hodie in a husky voice. "Please bury her."

Hodie bowed and took the squirrel gently. Queen Sibilla turned away. As he carried the squirrel to place it under the walnut tree, he saw her march up the steps into the barracks. It would be the nearest place to hide sobs and screams of rage.

~

While Hodie dug a little hole, the second squirrel, with puzzled cries, crept down to watch. Hodie finished the burial and stroked the grieving animal. Then he went to sweep near the exercise yard and get rid of any horse droppings.

Corporal Murgott was scaring the new recruits into marching in step. This was difficult with three dwarfs, four trolls, and five ordinary men of all shapes and sizes. But Murgott was perfect for the job: he had once been a pirate (and was also a cook). His ears looked like scorched cauliflower from many sunburns years ago at sea.

The more a corporal shouted and bullied, the better a man he made of you (so people said). "Hand-to-hand fighting," Murgott roared now. "Copy me! Raise right foot, so! Swivel left foot, so! Kick right foot, hard! And the other bloke's flat on his backside!" The new recruits tried it and all fell over.

Then Murgott made them begin bayonet drill with rifles. "Your rifles are not bleedin' fairy wands!" he roared. "Run round the practice yard twice! And while you're runnin', chant out loud: *We're all useless little runts and we will improve!*"

Hodie figured it would be wise to take himself and the broom out of Murgott's sight in case a burst of cursing came his way.

He rounded the corner. There on the barracks' back veranda was a stool. The Corporal's best boots were under it and there was a notebook sitting on top—that must be his too. It was easy to tell Murgott's boots. There was a tiny skull and crossbones on the left one. Nearby was a pile of horse droppings. Hodie rested his broom against the wall. He had just found the shovel when he heard an angry scream—the little Queen was storming onto the veranda in a definite tantrum. She lunged for Murgott's boots, flew down the steps, whacked their toes and heels into the droppings, then saw Hodie. She dropped the boots in the horse-pile and jumped back just before Murgott, leading the squad of recruits, appeared round the corner.

For a moment the Corporal stood speechless.

Then—"My boots!" he roared at Hodie. "You horrible scum!"

Hodie shot a look at Queen Sibilla and took a step forward. "I'm sorry, sir!"

The Queen opened her mouth then closed it slowly. Hodie didn't blame her. The recruits were goggle-eyed. It would be dreadful if Murgott realized Queen Sibilla had ruined his boots. It would be worse if her mother learned of it. And Princessa Lu'nedda had just popped her head back around the side of the Grand Palace, looking this way.

Murgott's face would curdle porridge. "You wait, boy," he growled. "Wait in your hut while I consider whether to keelhaul you or make you scrub every stone in the exercise yard."

From the corner of his eye, Hodie saw Queen Sibilla edge away and then hurry for the back door of the Grand Palace.

—

# AND SEVERAL MORE,
# POSSIBLY WORSE

In late afternoon, even inside his lean-to behind the old elephant house, Hodie heard ructions from the Palace kitchen. "The potato peelers are broken!" "The knives are blunt!" "The banquet's due to start in sixty minutes!"

He would have left for the south at once before Murgott came up with a punishment. But he had to take food. There should be excellent scraps after the banquet.

Hodie snuck to the barracks and searched in the cupboard on the back veranda. It was used to store things like the soldiers' odd socks, which were in a big old satchel. He stacked the socks on a shelf but kept three especially long ones to use as bandages. He'd probably need a bandage at some point. The satchel would be useful too. Then he crept up through the gardens with his cracked platter for tonight's dinner. He hoped he'd find enough leftovers for tomorrow's breakfast, lunch, dinner, and, with luck, something to start him off the day after.

A housemaid saw him coming and slammed the door.

He sat on the step. There was whispering inside. The window opened and Corporal Murgott's bald head appeared—he must be helping with the pastry.

"Boot-wrecker!" The Corporal's eyes were wet—from crying?

The window banged shut.

"It is just a pair of boots. Try scrubbing them," Hodie muttered.

Sounds of polite merriment floated from around the corner on the evening breeze. He stole down the side path. Through the gauzy summer curtains of the Grand Banquet Hall glowed hundreds of candles. A hundred guests, important people of Fontania, as well Emperor Prowdd'on, Princessa Lu'nedda, and Commander Gree'sle, chattered, checked that their fingernails were clean (sucked them a little bit if they were not), and waited for food.

At the head of the table near the open floor-to-ceiling window sat King Jasper, his silver chair back shaped like a Dragon-eagle's feather. Jasper stroked his short black beard. He looked kingly but bored already. He'd be missing his fiancée, Lady Beatrix.

In the queenly dining chair beside her brother, Sibilla was in a blue silky dress and pearl coronet and she wore her favorite gold pendant around her neck. Her hair was only untidy at the ends. She reached down to scratch her ankle, still in the stripy leggings she'd had on that morning. How ridiculous everyone was, hoping that a girl who had tantrums would gain magical ability. If it were true, it would be highly dangerous.

Hodie crouched in the shrubbery to wait. The first course was served: onion tarts, melon cubes, and crumbed fish nibbles.

The Um'Binnian Emperor had his usual charming smile and kept checking it in the little flat gold spade he used instead of a spoon. His mustache was waxed into a circle with the ends meeting over his chin and other little circles all the way around. He would have to aim each forkful of his dinner exactly right to get it in.

"Are you enjoying your meal?" asked Lady Helen.

"Very pleasant onion tart!" the Emperor shouted. "Very nice fish nibble! I have bigger fish and bigger onion in Um'Binnia!" He smiled again at his reflection.

Queen Sibilla firmed her pointy chin and stabbed a napkin with her fork. Hodie spotted half an onion tart under the table. With luck when the feast was over he'd crawl in and grab it.

Princessa Lu'nedda wiggled her ringlets. "You were busy today, King Jasper? You did great feats of magic in royal workshop?"

"Thank you for your interest," Jasper answered. "I'm just building a few bits and pieces."

The Princessa gave a roguish laugh. "I think perhaps you make new treasures because you lose old ones."

"We hear rumors about The Ties and your Dragon-eagles," said Commander Gree'sle with a narrow smile and narrow eyes.

If The Ties were actually harness or ropes, Hodie didn't think they would be much use. But he understood why the

Um'Binnians were interested. The lost Ties must be very valuable.

With a polite nod, Jasper leaned back. "I'm sure you have huge rumors in Um'Binnia."

"Perhaps King Jasper makes magic cage for dragon bird!" said the Emperor.

The King's hand flexed, but he spoke calmly. "The Dragon-eagles are free, Emperor. No one can own them."

The shrubbery prickled Hodie's neck. He noticed a potato near the little Queen's feet. Could he sneak in and snaffle that?

Lu'nedda fiddled with another ringlet. "Forgive us for teasing. We do not have magic. Um'Binnia is very happy with machines. We are most progressive country."

"Very true." Emperor Prowdd'on pursed his lips so the mustache circle turned into an oval. "We have wind-vehicles and you do not."

"Don't wind-trains keep crashing?" Jasper said. "Besides, they can't fly when there's no wind."

Prowdd'on behaved as if he didn't hear. "And everyone is rich in our great city!"

"How rich?" Queen Sibilla asked. "How much do you pay people?"

Lady Helen frowned at her daughter, and shook her head.

Prowdd'on spread his hands and smiled. "Why should I pay? Everyone very proud to work for me."

"You mean they're slaves? That's not progressive," Sibilla said.

Hodie felt like yelling out that the Fontanian royal family had never paid his father. They didn't pay Hodie either, not even with regular meals.

"Our people are happy. My father has wonderful progressive Zoo. Many fine creatures!" The Princessa batted the air with imaginary paws. She was older than King Jasper—too old to pretend to be cute, if you asked Hodie.

"And once you had middle-sized elephant." Commander Gree'sle looked extremely narrow now about the eyes. "Who looked after it?"

The wind rattled the leaves in the shrubbery. Sibilla had her teeth clenched as if she was trying hard not to explode. She turned her head and looked right at Hodie in the shadow. She started and frowned down at her plate. The Commander's question went unanswered because the next course arrived.

Hodie backed deeper into the prickly shrub. The wind skirled again, and the candles in the banquet chamber wavered. Queen Sibilla bent down, scratched her ankle, and glanced at her mother. Then she snuck a whole potato into the napkin on her lap. She dropped it and, under the table, flapped a hand in Hodie's direction.

Heart racing, he stayed in shadow until, in a flurry of servants carrying trays heaped high with roast chickens, he could sneak toward the banquet table. Lu'nedda's eyes glanced over him. He hoped she didn't remember that he'd spoken out against her father.

The Emperor shouted, "I have chicken with more drumstick in Um'Binnia!"

Lu'nedda turned toward him, and Hodie took the chance to duck under the table.

Down the far end were three sausages, more potatoes, and five bread rolls (some of them buttered). He avoided boots and shoes and high-heeled slippers. When he crawled back to Sibilla's end, there was a whole roast chicken wrapped in a napkin on the floor. He had no idea how she'd managed that, but he was thankful.

The satchel was almost full. He slipped from under the table and back to the shadows of the shrubs. Had anyone noticed? Lu'nedda was looking toward the window, frowning again. Commander Gree'sle asked her something. She ignored him. Gree'sle's smile stayed on, meager and grim.

An Um'Binnian officer entered a side door and spoke quietly in Commander Gree'sle's ear. Gree'sle turned and whispered to the Emperor. Prowdd'on smiled so the circle mustache opened up like elaborate pincers. His fingers drummed the belly of his gold waistcoat.

"Announcement!" he cried at last. "Tomorrow we hurry home! For our farewell now, we have treat of Um'Binnian Cream. My officers whip it with huge beater. Frothy, very sweet with crunchy sprinkle!" He grinned so the mustache ends stretched well apart. "Wait two minute for one last whip, then we enjoy!"

The officers served bowls of the pudding and stood back. Hodie noticed that none of the Um'Binnians at the table touched it right away. He supposed if they ate it often they must be sick of it. Did he have any chance of a leftover treat?

Sibilla put a small amount to her lips. The Emperor clapped his hands as if he was trying to encourage a two-year-old. Sibilla looked as if she really would explode. He clapped his hands at her again. Suddenly she stood and grabbed a whole bowlful of the Cream.

"Everyone should taste it, Emperor Prowdd'on!" She pushed through the Um'Binnian officers, stepped outside, and thrust the bowl into Hodie's hands. He was so surprised he nearly dropped it.

He gave a bow—Gree'sle and Lu'nedda were both staring at him now—and stepped backwards into more prickles.

Lady Helen shoved her chair back and strode to Sibilla.

"My dear, excuse yourself," she hissed. "Please go to your room."

The little Queen swept a magnificent fake-polite curtsy to all the guests and marched out, her back stiff as a pillar.

Hodie sped off around the corner and down to his lean-to, the full satchel bouncing and his arms clasped tight around the Cream bowl.

~

The first mouthful tasted like nothing, but the second was very sweet. When Hodie had finished, he yawned so hard his jaw clicked. He listened till he thought the banquet was over and the guests gone then crept up the garden. He heard the mournful chitter of one lone squirrel lying by the tiny grave under the walnut tree.

Just as Hodie put the bowl on the kitchen doorstep, the side gate squeaked. Lucky he hadn't oiled it today after all.

He ducked behind the trash cans in case it was Murgott. But it was King Jasper and (even though she'd been sent to her room) his sister, the Queen. Hodie stayed well out of sight.

His father had warned him about eavesdropping: *You shouldn't really do it but it can sometimes save your life—and other people's.* He had never explained what he meant, but Hodie felt it had something to do with why Dardy had become elephant keeper in the first place.

King Jasper yawned. "I wonder what the message was to Prowdd'on?"

"I don't care, if it means they're going," said Queen Sibilla. "They're horrible. They don't think I should be Queen."

"Nor do you," said Jasper. "And our mother sent you to bed."

"Shut up," said the Queen.

King Jasper chuckled. "I thought I shouldn't be King." He yawned again. "But sometimes things turn out better than you imagine."

"They won't for me," said Sibilla.

"Magic takes its own time," King Jasper said. "Don't try to push it."

Hodie nearly scoffed aloud. But they were coming nearer. He crouched further down behind the bins.

"Now listen. Tomorrow I'll give you a present," Jasper continued.

"Not another talking coat hanger!" said Sibilla.

"It was useful," said the King. "It told you when to get up and what to wear."

"It broke," said Sibilla.

"Accidentally-on-purpose," Jasper said. "Go on, admit it."

"I don't want any presents. Just leave me alone! I hate everyone and everything!" Sibilla ran up the back steps.

"For goodness sake…" King Jasper started to follow her, but a sudden breeze lifted a skein of leaves into the air.

The King tilted his head to the midnight sky. The wind seemed to beat like giant wings, and a warm sort of scent came to Hodie. He tried to see over the trash cans in the shifting moonlight. A huge winged shape had settled on the herb garden. It had a crown of feathers which glowed a faint silvery-green. Its silver feather-scales rustled in a quiet metallic chime.

King Jasper held out his arms. "Dragon-eagle!" His voice was hushed but happier than Hodie had heard it for many months.

~ *Take care of your sister* ~ said a voice that seemed like a soundless echo.

"Of course…" began Jasper.

~ *Take care of the Guardian of The Ties* ~ the voice continued.

"My father and Beatrix are searching for them." Jasper spread his arms again. "We hope this time…"

~ *The Queen must come into her magic before I die* ~ The green glow of the Dragon-eagle's coronet dimmed almost to nothing. The great hooked beak lowered to the ground.

"Die?" King Jasper took a step forwards.

~ *I grow old too fast from the wounds I suffered* ~ said the soundless voice. ~ *And my companion has been captured* ~

The side gate gave another squeak. The visiting Um'Binnian officers straggled through it.

The breeze gusted. Leaves and grit dashed around, and the officers turned and ducked to save their eyes. When Hodie looked though his shielding fingers, it was as if a silvery bird-shaped cloud with the paws of a lion soared into the dark sky. A last chime of words floated down. ~ *Find The Ties* ~

The King stared after it. The wind surged and whistled around the garden and died down. The sweet perfume disappeared.

"Unsettling weather in Fontania," groused one of the Um'Binnians.

Another noticed the King, nudged his friend, and saluted. "Pardon us, Your Majesty."

"Of course," said Jasper, cool and King-like, as if nothing had happened. "I'm off to bed. It's your last night with us, and you should be tucked up too. I hope our barracks have been comfortable." He gave a polite half-salute to the men. Back straight, he passed the trash cans without seeing Hodie. But as the King went up the step he staggered as if weariness and sorrow tried to lower him.

Keeping in shadow, Hodie followed the Um'Binnians down to the barracks. They nudged each other as if they knew something they weren't telling.

Hodie was feeling very strange indeed. That Um'Binnian Cream might have disagreed with him. He'd seen—and heard—a Dragon-eagle for the first time. He'd heard it speak in a voice like a strange song. But parrots could talk.

So could magpies and budgies. It meant nothing about magic. Anyway, Hodie was getting out of here tonight.

The officers straggled onto the barracks veranda. One of them knocked something to the ground. "Oops," he said. "Clumsy Um'Binnian, cannot be trusted." The others muffled their laughter and stumbled inside.

Hodie crept up to see what had fallen—the stool and Murgott's notebook. It was a common sort of notebook around the Palace, the kind people used to jot down chores and write their birthday wish lists. Everyone knew, but never said, that Murgott used his to write poems. Murgott had been a stinker to Hodie, but if the book was left out all night the dew might spoil it.

A wave of tiredness pulled at Hodie and he found himself inside the lean-to, the Corporal's book in his hand, without quite knowing how he'd got there.

Moonlight came through the little window. He put the book down, took his jacket from its hook, and tucked it into the top of the satchel. Then he tied his blanket to the satchel with a piece of string. The old drawstring bag with his mother's stuff hung there in the moonlight. Would he bother to take that with him? Well—it wasn't heavy. He may as well.

He tucked Murgott's notebook through the loops of the bag so he wouldn't forget to put it back on the veranda, yawned, and sat on his bed while he tied a fresh piece of string around his boot. He wanted to lie down for just a minute.

~

The moonlight disappeared and Hodie told himself to stand up and get moving. He must have fallen asleep—the blanket of the night seemed wrapped around him.

There were soft footsteps, and people gave puzzled whispers and scuffled about. Then it was quiet. Hodie remembered the nothing-taste then sweetness of the Um'Binnian Cream, and sleep came over him again. It was a sleep laced with an uneasy dream where he waded in a vast dish of hot pudding with little Queen Sibilla trudging beside him. Even though he was asleep, he told himself it was definitely a dream. And that was just as well because it was a dream in which he and the Queen were heading north to the Bridge of Teeth, to the boundary of Fontania.

～

# DANGEROUS CHOICE

A ray of sun poked through the window of the lean-to. When the sun came through like this, it was midmorning.

Hodie tried to put a hand over his eyes, but the blanket was wound around him. Dardy used to tuck him in this way when he was little, so tightly the mattress folded up like a canoe. It had made Hodie laugh. But he remembered tying the blanket to the old satchel last night. And he couldn't have tucked himself in.

He wriggled free. His head felt blurry and he was still in his clothes—even his boots. He staggered out into the yard.

A small figure ran from the back door of the Palace and sped from the herb garden to the laundry lines and back. It was Queen Sibilla in dressing gown and bare feet. "Where's everyone?" she called. "What's going on!"

The barracks door slammed open. Corporal Murgott lurched onto the veranda in his socks. Hodie stayed where he was by the lean-to.

"Murgott!" The Queen came running through a flurry of chickens. "Murgott. Everyone is sound asleep."

The Corporal saluted. "Your Majesty, Lady Helen and the King must be tired after the banquet."

"I mean everyone!" cried Sibilla. "The cook, the servants—but not the Um'Binnians. Thank goodness, they've gone like they promised."

Murgott nodded. "The officers are not in the barracks, and they've left their beds in an awful mess."

"Well, my mother won't wake up. And Jasper's snoring. I thought only old men snored," said the little Queen.

"Er..." Murgott finished buttoning his shirt. "There's nobody but me awake down here."

Neither the Queen nor Murgott had glanced at Hodie. If he gave a meaningful cough, would they notice?

*Er-hrmph?*

They didn't.

"Your Majesty," Murgott said, "let me make pancakes for you. It will cheer me up to toss 'em. With honey and lemon..."

"I don't want breakfast!" Sibilla shouted. "I'm saying everyone seems drugged. Even the servants."

"Everyone?" Murgott scratched his forehead. "That would use up a lot of my belief, Your Majesty, and believe me I have plenty of belief."

"I bet it was the pudding," said the Queen. "Everybody gorged on it but me. Did our soldiers have that pudding?"

"The men dived at it," said Murgott. "Everybody does, when something's free. There was bowl after bowl and then more bowls. I'm the only one down here who couldn't face it." At last he turned to Hodie with a sunburnt scowl.

"Ruined boots sit heavy on a soldier's mind."

The Queen looked startled and her face went red.

Hodie's throat filled with the bubble of a laugh. He stepped back into the lean-to. He buckled his jacket to the satchel, bulging with food from the banquet—he could have sworn he'd fastened it there last night. For the second time he folded and tied his blanket. Now, where was Murgott's notebook? He'd toss it at the Corporal and step whistling down the side path…

Hodie saw the hook where he had hung his mother's bag. The bag was gone. So was the notebook.

He looked on the floor, in every corner—there was no sign of the drawstring bag, nor of the notebook. Had the Um'Binnians stolen the bag when they left in the night? And nicked off with Murgott's poems too? One of the Um'Binnians must have taken the time to tuck Hodie in after stealing his mother's old rubbish. What very strange people.

Still, why should he care about that stuff of his mother's? He'd never even known her.

Hodie jammed a cap on, slung the satchel on his back, swung outside, and crashed the door shut. He bowed at the Queen, nodded at Murgott, and strode off for the side path.

"Come here!" called the Queen. "Did you eat that pudding?"

Hodie kept walking.

"The Queen spoke to you!" said Murgott.

Hodie stopped. He had to admit his heart was jumping. He turned around but didn't bow. Queen Sibilla went red again. The ends of her hair twitched.

"Your Majesty," said Hodie. "Thank you for helping me last night at the banquet. But I have to tell you now, I'm not one of your subjects."

"Of course you are," said Queen Sibilla.

"Learn some responsibility," said Murgott. "First you ruin…"

The little Queen held up her hand and blushed even harder. "I was going to tell you, Murgott. It wasn't the boy who wrecked your boots. I'm afraid it was me. I'll buy you a new pair as soon as my mother gives me more royal pocket money."

Corporal Murgott's face went purple-red. His mouth stayed open but he made no sound. A door banged in the barracks and a troll soldier staggered out. A servant opened a window in the kitchen.

"Now, boy," began the Queen.

Hodie's heart jumped more than ever. "Your Majesty, the Grand Palace never paid my father. I suppose he might have worked for you to pay some debts. But I came to the Grand Palace with him when I was small. I didn't have much say in it. Now I do."

Sibilla blinked but Hodie continued. "I don't know where I was born, but I do know it wasn't Fontania. And I have a name. It's actually Hodie. And I've had enough of being ordered around and not paid and not fed properly. So I'm off, Your Majesty."

His heart was racketing about, so Hodie put a hand on his chest to help him speak calmly. "And by the way, your guests stole something that belonged to me. It might be wise to be more careful who you have to stay."

He left the Queen standing there as if she couldn't believe her ears.

"Your Majesty?" he heard Murgott say. "You let the boy take the blame? For wrecking my boots? If I may say so, Queen Sibilla, that was not well done."

As he marched around the side of the Grand Palace, Hodie heard the first scream of another tantrum.

⁓

# VERY LITTLE CHOICE FOR LUNCH

In wooden barrels outside the High Street shops, marigolds and sky blue pansies danced in the breeze. A steam-tram puffed at an intersection, brakes squealing to be let off. Merchants were sticking up new *Bargain* signs in their windows. Groups of noisy school children straggled down to learn about the wharves and lined up for the museum.

Hodie was so happy to be on his way that he marched right past the first crossroad south without noticing. It didn't matter. He could stay on High Street going west. Out of the City it turned into the High Way. Eventually it turned into the Low Way and headed north, but he'd turn south at another crossroads. His feet sidestepped a sign for the daily paper that said: *Lucky Escape. No War with Um'Binnia.*

In only an hour the bustle of the City of Spires was behind him. Ahead was parkland with well-groomed trees, sweeping lawns, and ferny gardens. He walked with a hop and a jink and imagined saying what he liked to Emperor Prowdd'on or laughing in Commander Gree'sle's sour face.

THE QUEEN AND THE NOBODY BOY

If he was following them to claim his mother's stuff, that's just what he'd do. But why should he care about a mother he couldn't remember?

He began to whistle one of Murgott's marching songs. When he stopped to take a breath, he heard footsteps pattering behind him. He glanced around. A boy, smaller than he in a floppy cap, gray shirt and trousers, and a jacket tied by its arms around his waist, waved at him. Hodie didn't want company and strode faster.

The boy caught up, puffing.

"Boy!" said the boy. "I knew I'd catch you!"

Hodie's mouth dropped open. It was the Queen. Over her shoulder she carried a bag with a silver feather embroidered on the side. He recognized the cap, an old one of King Jasper's and big enough to hide all her hair.

"I've run away too," she said. "I should have done it months ago. I can't bear it!" She gave a little laugh, though her eyes were red and teary.

Hodie's head was a thicket of thoughts. Which one to say first?

"It's all right," she said. "Talk to me as if I'm normal."

She strode on and he caught up, still struggling with words. She smiled at him, a sheepish glimmer.

"You don't know how awful it is, everyone watching you, waiting, when nothing is ever going to happen!"

Did that mean she knew magic was nonsense? That must make things very complicated for her. Hodie didn't blame her for running away—though he didn't want her to think she could travel with him.

She flung her arms out and took a deep breath. "This is much better."

Hodie had to do another hop to keep up with her. "It's actually a really bad idea."

She smiled again. "The Um'Binnians were terrible guests. But they were my guests. If they've taken something of yours, I should help you get it back."

"But I'm going south," Hodie said. "I'm heading south."

"It's nice there," she said.

"I'm not going to Um'Binnia!" he said.

"No, but you can catch up with the Emperor first. We'll turn south then." She stopped and faced him. "I owe you a kindness. I was awful to let Murgott blame you about the boots. I've told him the truth."

"I heard," he said.

She shuddered to show it had been a difficult moment. (It served her right.) "He said such behavior was to be expected if you were a pirate. But that everyone must learn to do better and I have to make amends." She made a face. "He didn't really say that last bit. I realized it myself, when the tantrum passed. I'm actually pretty sure it's my last tantrum." She let out a sort of sob-chuckle. "Anyway, making amends is what he meant and what I've decided."

"Your Majesty, you helped me at the banquet so we're even."

"I'm coming to help, and that's that." She walked on fast.

Soon they'd reached the end of the parkland. Under a tree with shimmering leaves was a stone seat for weary travelers. Hodie hoped the Queen would sit on it.

Surely she'd start whining for a coach to carry her home?

Instead she gave Hodie a bright smile and went on faster.

Maybe he should say something about what he'd seen and heard last night—the King and the old Dragon-eagle. Even if she didn't believe in magic, she might scurry off. Then Hodie could forget her.

Apparently when Queen Sibilla was a toddler she hadn't talked much. Now she started rattling on without a pause. "Princessa Lu'nedda pretended to be nice, but she was spiteful. My mother says spiteful people are really unhappy. Do you think she was spiteful or just bumbling? I mean, Lu'nedda is a grown-up, but her father treats her like a badly trained spaniel—a big spaniel with ringletty ears. If everything in Um'Binnia is so wonderful, why did the Emperor bother to visit us? I suppose just to show they don't want war."

Hodie let her chatter. Queen Sibilla might be selfish and spoiled, how could she help it? She was basically good-natured, and she was a beautiful little Queen with sparkly eyes and long blonde hair that fell straight when she was content and twisted in various mad ways when she was not. People couldn't stop themselves from spoiling her. She needed to be protected. But Hodie didn't intend to be the boy who did that job.

~

They passed a few coaches, some carts, and a steam-truck. Nobody recognized the Queen under the big cap and in those clothes. Hodie thought Sibilla enjoyed pretending to be ordinary and a boy. One man on a plodding horse began to ask something, but the breeze kicked up a flurry of dust. The man rode on, hunched into his coat, muttering about silly boys too far from home.

Lunchtime came and still no crossroads. A stream rippled beside the road. Some yellowy grass made a place to rest, though hardly a nice one if you were royal. There was torn newspaper and ants crawled over two apple cores and a crumpled napkin with a golden edge. Hodie guessed the Um'Binnians had picnicked here for breakfast and left their litter.

Sibilla screwed her nose up but sat down and took off her shoes. "Oo," she said. "Spongy bits."

"They're blisters," said Hodie.

She poked her toes. "How interesting."

Hodie didn't want to look at royal blisters. He brought one of the baked potatoes out of the satchel, broke it apart, and offered her half.

She crinkled her lip as if to say *What's that?* then gave a chuckle. "Oh," she said. "Thank you."

"Don't mention it," Hodie muttered.

She sat on the bank of the stream, munched the potato, and swished her feet in the water. After a while she frowned.

Hodie hoped she was ready to give up. "You really shouldn't come with me."

"Of course I should," she said. "The Um'Binnians will listen to me and you'll get your stuff back."

"It doesn't matter," Hodie said.

She stiffened her jaw. "Of course it does, and I'll tell Prowdd'on."

"The Emperor didn't listen about the gray squirrel." That was mean—he wished he'd kept his mouth shut. It had reminded him as well.

She splashed her feet as if she'd like to kick him. Hodie edged back. But Sibilla just dried her toes on the crumpled napkin and put her shoes on. "Thank you for lunch."

"My pleasure," Hodie mumbled. By now he'd rather have let out a string of curses.

~

They trudged further along the Low Way. A steam-cart overtook them slowly (which wasn't difficult for it). Sibilla ran up and took hold of the back rail—her blisters must be hurting, though she wasn't letting on. Hodie jumped up too. They bumped along in its dust (and chugging steam) to the crossroads where the steam-cart turned south. Thank goodness. Hodie clung tight.

But Sibilla jumped off and fell on her hands and knees. Hodie nearly leaped down too, in case she was hurt. But why should he? She would learn from a few mistakes. As the steam-cart carried him away, he watched her climb to her feet and dust herself down. She looked very alone and very small.

The cart came to a bend in the road. In spite of himself, Hodie let go and slipped off. He watched as the cart disappeared from view and the chugging faded. Then he straightened his satchel and jogged back to catch up with the Queen.

"I'm not going to Um'Binnia!" he said.

"Nor am I," said the Queen. "It would be horrible."

"As long as that's clear," said Hodie.

"Do stop going on about it." Sibilla set off north.

She didn't talk any more at first. The silence worried him. But when she started chattering again, he found it annoying.

"How long have we traveled since lunch? I mean distance, not time. It would be useful if this pendant of mine was a watch, but it's just my lucky charm. I'm not supposed to wear it in case I lose it, but it always turns up. That's why it's lucky. Murgott has a naval anemometer with four little cups that whizz round to show how hard the wind blows. That's not much use either. If the wind is blowing, you know how strong it is, don't you?"

"Yes. At the moment, it's Force Three, Light Breeze," Hodie said. "The scale goes from nought to twelve. It starts at Calm, then it's Light Air, then Light Breeze, Gentle, Moderate, then Fresh, then Strong Breeze. After that it's a Near Gale, then a Gale, then…"

She stopped walking and stared at him.

"What?" he asked.

"You actually seem clever." Immediately she reddened—she must know she'd been insulting.

Hodie didn't waste breath on a reply. He'd listened to soldiers, and sailors. He'd also sat underneath the Grand Palace schoolroom window, pretending to garden. And Dardy had told Hodie a few things over the years. Not many. But enough for him to know what would happen if the Queen tried to cross that bridge over The Torrent.

By now the sun was gliding down behind the hills. In front of Hodie and Sibilla was the turnoff to the river.

There was only one small grove of trees. Some had leaves but some looked dead. Then the stony road led down to the Bridge of Teeth. At each end of the Bridge stood tall iron pillars. From this side it looked like an ordinary bridge. The planks across appeared ordinary too. On the other side against one of the pillars was the machinery—a set of complicated-looking gears and lots of levers. Dardy had said that if you could pay the toll or knew the password then the Bridge wouldn't show its teeth at all.

From here, the Stones of Beyond didn't look too bad either in the soft rays of late sun.

They reached the grove and Hodie stopped.

"What are you doing?" asked the Queen.

"Is there anywhere else we can wait till morning?" He settled on scratchy brown grass under the trees.

"You mean all night?" The little Queen looked alarmed for a moment. Then she shrugged, sat down, and took her shoes off. Sibilla didn't let him see her feet this time. He bet they were very bloody.

There were signs of another picnic. Um'Binnians again from the amount of trash left about. There was also a damaged cartwheel with grass growing through it and a few rusty bits from years of broken carriages.

Sibilla started chattering again. "The Um'Binnians would have been embarrassed when they realized what their pudding had done."

"I bet Emperor Prowdd'on doesn't know what embarrassment feels like." Hodie kicked a rusty metal bar. He remembered how the officers had chuckled and nudged.

"They must have put a sleeping drug in the pudding on purpose. How could you do it by accident?"

"Oh, they wouldn't…" Sibilla frowned. "Boy," she began again. "I'm sorry—I mean Hodie. What exactly did they take of yours?"

"Nothing much." He didn't want to talk about his mother or father.

"But why would they bother? That is…" She blushed again.

He didn't answer. He knew what she meant—an odd-job boy couldn't own anything valuable. Well, he didn't. But one day he might, after he'd found work in the south and bettered himself.

Sibilla glanced at the setting sun and the growing darkness over the Stones of Beyond and gave a shiver. He felt sorry for her—only a bit—and pulled two chicken drumsticks out of the satchel.

"There are many bigger drumsticks in Um'Binnia," he said.

She let out a laugh. Hodie thought this must be rather like having a friend, though being the friend of a Queen would have many awkward moments. Tomorrow he would set off on his own.

—

# HOW A QUEEN SAYS GOODBYE
## TO THE SOFT LIFE

The last of sunset faded from the clouds. The little Queen shivered again and pulled on her jacket. Hodie put his on too and passed her the blanket. "You'd better have this."

It smelled of oil from the odd jobs with an ancient whiff of elephant. But she wrapped it around herself and lay with her back against a tree. He settled down as well but had to move a bit so he wasn't lying on yet another rusty bar from an old carriage.

Suddenly the Queen sat up. "What about you? We'll share the blanket."

"It would be very rude of anyone to hog the only blanket from the Queen," he said.

She gave a tiny laugh. "But I'm allowed to hog the blanket? The wind is getting up. It's ridiculous not to share."

He felt very uncomfortable but shuffled beside her. She wrapped the blanket more or less around them both.

"We must look like a condiment set," she said.

"A what?" he asked.

"Salt and pepper shakers," she told him.

"Oh. Yes." That had made him seem stupid. He knew about such things even though he'd never used them.

"How are the blisters?" he asked after a while.

"They don't hurt when I'm not walking," she said.

"That's the way with blisters," Hodie said.

He was tired after the long day. The wind wasn't really cold, more like something breathing now and then to remind him it was there. The night deepened. The river growled and muttered over rocks. From the Stones of Beyond he heard a distant howl that sounded mechanical. It must be a wind-train approaching the Depot. The Emperor would get on it if the Um'Binnians hadn't set off on one already. Hodie bet Queen Sibilla hadn't thought of that. He grinned to himself. She'd realize tomorrow how hopeless it was to try to catch up with his mother's stuff.

Around the tree the wind still blew like something breathing. He heard the Queen swallow hard and realized that, like him, she wasn't asleep—and she was trying not to cry.

He shifted to give her more blanket. "It's all right. We're safe tonight."

"It's not that…" She gave a really juicy sniff. "But it is so awful everyone expecting me to do something special. I'm really ordinary, like you… Oh, that didn't come out right." She covered her head with the blanket and shook with sobs.

This was far too embarrassing. Hodie scrabbled to his feet and walked around the tree to settle down with just his jacket.

He didn't expect to doze. For a while his head felt gritty and cross. But then he opened his eyes and the first glimmer of dawn showed over the Stones. High up in the tree the leaves were rustling.

"What's that?" whispered the little Queen on the other side of the trunk.

"A bird probably." Hodie scrambled round to her and opened his satchel. "Here. A stale potato from your own banquet."

"Thank you." Her hands were dirty. Her cap was askew. She looked very ordinary now.

The potato he chose was floury and tasteless. Hers couldn't be nice either. But she ate without complaining and then put on her shoes. He stole a look—the blisters seemed better.

The sky was clear and the sun began to warm them. Wind rattled small bare branches through the grove, and above them the leaves kept rustling. Down below The Torrent looked peaceful.

"You know about the Bridge of course," he said.

She looked torn between scorn and a chuckle. "It goes from one side of the river to the other. You thought that I'd give up before we got here."

It was clear she didn't know about the Bridge and still thought she could catch up with the Emperor. All right, Hodie wouldn't argue. He'd simply show her. He'd race down to the Bridge ahead of her, put one foot on it, and she'd realize how dangerous it was. Then they'd set off back to the crossroads. She could hitch a ride home alone from there on another steam-cart.

He licked the last crumbs from his fingers, stood up, and stumbled for a moment over one of those half-buried rusty bars. Sibilla stuffed her hair back into the cap.

"Um," Hodie said. "If you want to, you know, go to the bathroom, why don't you go behind that bush?"

Sibilla muttered thank you and hurried off. He rolled up the blanket. But she came back before he'd strapped it to his satchel. Blast.

Above his head leaves rustled again, just on one limb.

"Is something up there?" Sibilla reached to grab a branch.

"Don't!" said Hodie.

"Why not?" She hoisted herself up and clung to the trunk.

"You might fall," he said.

"I just want to see." Her trousers snagged. "You come up too." Her feet disappeared into the leaves.

"Stuff's dropping in my eyes," he called. "Come down!"

She laughed. "Are you scared?"

"Of course not!" His voice came out so sharp it must be obvious he was fibbing.

There was more rustling and this time a squawk. "It's a strange bird," called the Queen. "Ouch…" There was a ripping sound. "It's very tame, it isn't moving… I've got it. Hodie, it's made of metal."

She slithered down, hands scratched and clothes torn, and held out something shiny. The bird's head was round like an owl's, with dark eyes. Its tail feathers were like spikes, some of them bent.

Hodie stared. "I saw King Jasper making that. I didn't think it would actually fly and it got this far!"

"He said he was making me a present…" She turned it in her hands.

Hodie felt relief swell in his chest. "The King put a lot of work into that. Some of it's gold. You'd better take it home before it gets broken."

The bird squawked again, then chirped. Queen Sibilla held it to her ear. Hodie heard a few words, faint and garbled. Then there was a soft whirring as if it caught its metal breath.

"There," Hodie said. "It told you to go home."

Her eyes sparked with mischief. "It said that you were a bit afraid of the Bridge. Race you across!"

She grabbed her bag and started running.

—

# EARLIER BAD CHOICES
## LEAD TO . . .

The bird had said nothing of the sort! Hodie looked around for something that might help, wrenched one of those rusty metal bars out of the dirt, and hurtled after her.

Loose stones skidded under his boot, but he righted himself and reached the road. Ahead was a squawk—the metal bird was flying above the Queen's shoulder.

Hodie pounded on. *But can't you sneak across quietly?* he had asked his father. *No*, Dardy had answered. *You have to run for it. Run for your life.*

He slipped again but found his balance. The little Queen had nearly reached the first set of iron pillars. Now Hodie was near enough to see tiny spikes of metal on the planks. Sibilla set foot on the Bridge, and a loud yell came from underneath. It was the bridge-troll.

The river churned and frothed as the troll lurched to the machinery on the far side. "Oi! Say me the password!" It grabbed the levers.

Sibilla hesitated—good, Hodie would catch her in time,

he might not need to use the metal bar after all. But then she tossed her head and started across.

There was a shriek of steel. The metal spikes along the planks shot up. The Queen screamed and dodged. The troll heaved on the levers to make the spikes jab up and down.

Hodie reached the pillars and ran on. A spike scratched his calf. He nearly dropped the metal bar, juggled it, and had to leap because another spike stabbed up.

Ahead the little Queen scrambled and dodged too, screaming. Three spikes jabbed for him at the same time—somehow, he jumped them all. At last he saw a gap between the planks and jammed the metal bar down into it as hard as he could. With a terrible screech, the machinery stopped.

Hodie leaned on the railing, chest heaving. Blood dripped into his boot. The little Queen was half way across, hands on her hips.

The troll kept tugging the levers. "You break the mechi-nism!"

The little Queen's voice rang out. "All we want to do is walk across! You don't have permission to stop us!"

"The Um'Binnians put him there," called Hodie.

"Bad boy break mechi-nism!" The troll waded back into the river, tugging its hair and grumbling louder.

"One side of the river is Fontania," Sibilla shouted down to it. "But nobody owns the river, and nobody owns the Stones of Beyond. There is an agreement that we share the Stones with Um'Binnia!"

"But they don't want to share! They don't let everybody in!" Hodie limped toward her. "And Fontania has never done a thing about it."

"Because we don't like arguments!" Sibilla cried.

"You're arguing now!" he yelled.

Sibilla stuck her chin out. "If Emperor Prowdd'on says he owns this bridge, he's wrong."

"There was nearly a war because Fontania won't stand up for itself," Hodie shouted. "Um'Binnia thinks it can own everything because it's so much bigger."

The troll let out a roar. "I just does what I is paid for! Even if I isn't paid much!" It disappeared from sight, but Hodie heard furious splashing. Then, to his horror, he saw the troll's fingers gripping the edge of the planks. It was starting to climb.

Hodie had a quick look at the cut on his leg—not very deep. If he could grab the Queen and haul her back into Fontania… But the troll's foot heaved up onto the railing. With a desperate groan it pulled the other leg up, rolled over with a thump that shook the Bridge, and stretched across to yank out the metal bar.

"Run!" Hodie tried to shove the Queen. She wouldn't budge.

Hodie saw the metal bird dive sharply. There was a squawk, a peck, a yell. The troll clapped a hand to the top of its (very ugly) head, toppled back over the rail, and sank completely.

Sibilla walked on to the end of the Bridge. Ahead of her were the Stones.

Spluttering, the troll surfaced, clambered onto the river bank, and started wringing out its shirttail. "Bad boys with hard hearts!" it roared. "One big bad boy, one little one."

Hodie's leg hurt, but he ran to catch up with the Queen. "Stop," he panted. "Go back…"

"Wasn't that interesting?" She settled her cap. "The bird saved you."

Hodie wanted to burst with rage. "Stop!"

This time she did. "I suppose the bird was really saving me. It saved us both."

He took a deep breath. "You say you're not really a Queen, that you're ordinary." She nodded. "But you spoke to the troll as if you were a Queen." She nodded again. He was so angry the words nearly jammed up. "You can't have it both ways. Just go home to your mother and brother. Leave me alone."

Sibilla's chin stuck out. Her gold pendant glinted. "Hodie, I know you want your things back, you don't have to pretend. But the Um'Binnians will never listen to you. I'm behaving like a Queen because it will help."

She set off again.

"If it makes you feel better," she called over her shoulder, "let's just say we happen to be traveling in the same direction."

‿

# HOW TO CROSS THE STONES OF BEYOND

## CHOOSING TO GO ON

The little Queen strode in the dust toward a grove of stunted trees. The bird squawked and whirred after her.

Hodie limped back to the river to rinse the cut on his leg. The troll was still sniveling and Hodie felt sorry for it. The cut wasn't deep, but he pulled one of the spare socks out of his satchel and tied it round the wound. Maybe he should have offered the spares to the Queen. She couldn't like having to wear yesterday's ones all stiff with goo and blood. Lady Helen would be furious when the Queen returned so filthy, dressed like a boy. That was one reason Hodie was very happy to have no parents—no scolding. And now he didn't have to listen to any more from Corporal Murgott.

He stood up. The little Queen was out of sight. The metal bird was no protection for her—it was just an interesting gift, bound to smash itself on a rock before too long.

*One more hour,* Hodie thought, *one more, she'll be ready to cross back home, and this time the troll won't stop us.*

Hodie hurried past a few skimpy, leafless trees and up a gravel path between walls of rock. Ahead he saw the bird crash-land in the dirt and Sibilla marching on. The bird whirred up again.

Back over Fontania the sun still sparkled. But here the sky was gray like the bathwater those times Mrs. Emily made Hodie come and use the servants' bathroom and clean himself properly. He reached a rise in the dwindling path. Ahead lay the Stones—a desert of canyons and craters and gray boulders. Nobody owned them, as the Queen had said, and who would want to? Here and there stood leafless trees (gray) and little plants (gray) like the fuzz when the older soldiers hadn't shaved for several days.

Panting and limping, he caught up with the Queen. "Your Majesty," he began.

"Please," she said, "use my name. I'll use yours. Hodie."

"Er. Sibilla." He nearly choked on it. "You see, this is the situation."

"What is?" she asked.

"Well," said Hodie, "I know you used to daydream when you should have been listening to your tutors."

Her jaw firmed as if she might whack him, but she didn't stop walking.

"The thing is," he continued softly, "we should be quiet."

"Why?" she asked.

"There are things around…"

"Yes, rocks," she said. "And more rocks. Look over there, stones and rubble."

He had to keep his temper. "No—I've heard there are rabbits that aren't the soft and cuddly sort."

"Where?" she asked.

"In the Stones," he said.

"I mean, where did you hear about them?" She was hobbling, and it was clear she felt impatient.

This could be awkward. "I listened underneath your schoolroom window."

She stared at him. "You got free lessons?"

In the circumstances, what was wrong with that? "You can see it as payment for the odd jobs."

She blushed. "I'm also helping you get back whatever the Um'Binnians took from your hut."

He settled his satchel on the other shoulder. "Look, it was just some old stuff of my mother's. And Murgott's poetry, by accident."

"What! Why?" She nearly tripped over the metal bird having one of its rests.

"Because I shouted at the Emperor, I think. When… you know…the squirrel…" He glanced at her warily.

Sibilla's eyes filled with tears. She cleared her throat. She had that look that meant someone's going to try changing the subject. "I remember your father and the elephant. He let me ride on it when I was small. Then he was very good at all the odd jobs. I'm sorry he didn't get paid."

"Thank you," said Hodie.

There was a moment when she didn't say anything. Then—

"Your mother's stuff. No wonder you want it back."

He shrugged, clenched his jaw, and hiked on.

"What was she like?" Sibilla asked.

He'd never been asked before. It came as a shock. He stopped walking. "I don't remember."

"Nothing? What about the color of her hair?"

He had no idea. Even if he could have said—his throat choked again.

The sun was hidden by low clouds that streamed in the wind. Here and there were signs of travelers: a horseshoe, a mangled glove, a few bones. Hodie hoped they were only lunch bones left by humans. The metal bird still circled over the Queen's head, squawking now and then. "Ho-ome. Quee-een, ho-ome!"

The further they walked, the more upset Hodie felt and the more he actually missed Dardy.

The sides of the canyon grew steeper. As they struggled past a small crater, whispery crackles sounded from an oily puddle in its depths. The path kept on rising. Hodie looked up and saw gray fuzzy movement—with luck, it was only bushes in the wind. Then the canyon seemed to end in a tumble of rocks.

"This is it," Hodie said. "Wrong turning. We have to go back."

"For goodness' sake, you give up easily." The little Queen started to clamber over.

"Come back!" But it was no good. She was scrambling on, and he had to follow.

Around a huge boulder a steep slope of pebbles led down to a shallow valley. Deep canyons rayed out in all directions. Dust spiraled and ghosted. In the middle of the valley was a long low building—the Depot. The Um'Binnian crest blazed on its side: a yellow sunburst with a purple coronet. At one end of a wooden platform were pulleys and hoists—Hodie supposed they must be to lift the wind-trains up to catch the gale. Two carriages waited but no engine.

His heart felt sore on Sibilla's account. She looked frightened, and he understood why. The Um'Binnians had extraordinary machines. King Jasper would never make anything big enough to match them, though it was no wonder he wanted to try. The thing was, if the world had such amazing machines, what was the point of magic? What was the point in being Queen of Fontania?

—

# GOING ON BY MISTAKE

It was obvious the Emperor and Princessa would have left on the previous night's wind-train. And Hodie had never expected—or wanted—Queen Sibilla, in her gray shirt and trousers, to simply stride along the platform and say, "You vain pig, Emperor Prowdd'on, give the boy's bag back at once." Still, he felt oddly disappointed.

Sibilla's bird gave a creaky whirr.

"What are we waiting for?" She'd clamped both hands on her cap, so her hair must be trying to frizz.

Hodie opened his mouth to say in a short sharp sentence that they must turn back. But there was a creeping sound, like paws. From the corner of his eye he saw a little blur of animal launch at them. It landed on the Queen's cap, she screamed, and the animal leaped at Hodie. Sibilla slipped and started plunging down the pebbles. He lurched after her. The sock-bandage dangled off his leg—he tripped on it and slid in a clatter and jangle of stones. At the foot of the slope the Queen crumpled onto her knees, clamped both hands on her cap, and let out the Royal Swear Word.

Hodie dragged her toward the Depot—she kept slipping and so did he—but at last he shoved her up the steps onto the platform.

The metal bird rattled down beside them. "Quee... Sib...Quee!" it croaked. It had lost all but one of its tail feathers. Sibilla grabbed the bird and stuffed it in her bag.

Heart still thudding, Hodie looked at the creature that had chased them—a small squirrel, scruffy and gray. It crouched below the platform steps, the metal bird's tail feathers in its mouth. It was extremely ugly, like the ones who had adopted the Grand Palace. This one also looked disappointed in the metal feathers.

Sibilla turned a furious look on Hodie.

"I was scared it was one of those rabbits," he began. "But you ran first."

"A rabbit!" said Sibilla.

"Or...or a toad!" he continued. "But toads are later, at the other end of the Stones, I mean. They need water." He knew it wasn't a terrific explanation.

The little Queen wiped the smears of dust and dirt on her face, which made them worse. Ignoring Hodie, she hitched the waistband of her trousers, sat down, and eased her feet out of her shoes. She peeled her socks off very carefully. "Oo," she murmured. "Ouch."

A number of soldiers in Um'Binnian uniforms milled at the far end of the station. Hodie didn't like the look of them.

A station guard came out of a door and marched over. "No beggars," he said. "No boys who do not have minder."

Sibilla opened her mouth. "I happen to be the..."

Hodie nudged her, then smiled at the man. "*He* wants to see the Emperor. Emperor Prowdd'on."

"Excuse *me*!" cried Sibilla.

Hodie elbowed her again.

The guard grinned. "Two dressed-in-rag urchins? See the Emperor? Very big joke. He arrive last night and take first wind-train. He throw everyone off and leave these extra carriages so he travel faster. Passengers all hopping mad." He jerked a thumb over his shoulder at the soldiers. "And look. Boys must think sense. Enough problems here for me without stray urchins. Clear off, and you are lucky I am not swearing."

"Er," said Hodie. "Can...my little brother!...can he wash his blisters first?"

The guard looked at Sibilla's bare feet. "Oh yes. Wash nasty toes. Then, on your way. Boys safer at home..."

Hodie stared after the man—he was sure he'd heard, "*safer at home until Emperor declare war on Fontania.*"

Sibilla's mouth looked a bit trembly. "I was trying to help. But the Emperor's gone. I should have thought harder."

"Behave like a boy. Stay in disguise," Hodie hissed. "Did you hear what he said? Um'Binnia might declare war after all."

She kept her chin up, glanced at the soldiers, then put both hands to her cap.

"Leave it on!" he said.

"My hair is trying to throw the cap off! They haven't declared war yet and I won't give up. You can't give up either.

I'll get your mother's stuff for you. We'll take the next wind-train."

He couldn't help noticing how her hands shook, though her smile tried to be bright. "I've told you all along," he said, "I want to go south! Besides, the guard would stop us and we don't have tickets."

Her smile dropped. "Oh—you don't have money." She forced another smile. "I'll pay."

Hodie groaned.

"Except…" She bit a thumbnail. "I didn't bring my pocket money. Maybe they'll take a check… No. I don't have one. Anyway, my mother has to sign them till I turn twenty."

What a relief. Now the Queen would realize she had to go home and…

"New message!" squawked the metal bird inside her bag. "New mess-*awk*!" Sibilla jolted the bag. The bird shut up.

If only the Queen would listen to her brother's present, she might realize the trouble she was in. She didn't even seem to realize how lucky she was to have a brother, let alone parents.

By now people with suntans and in sunhats had crowded from the waiting room. They stared at their watches, tapped the dials, and tapped their boots and walking sticks on the platform. On the Depot walls posters said: *Dare the Open Air in quaint Fontania! Sun and surf on the Beaches of Summerland!* Other notices said: *Protect Um'Binnia from rebels. Tell on your friends.*

Hodie grabbed the last odd socks from his satchel. "Use these for your blisters," he said to the Queen.

"Thank you…" began Sibilla in a royal way, then she stopped with a tiny real grin. In a little boy voice she said, "Don't boss me round, oink bruvver." She snatched the socks and took them to a drinking fountain where she dampened the top of one and started cleaning up her feet.

Hodie sat at the top of the platform steps, head in his hands. The squirrel had dropped the metal feathers. It picked up a yellowy pebble, tried to chew that, dropped it and looked pathetic.

"Hungry?" Hodie asked.

The ugly thing stared at him and waved its tail like a tattered banner. Could it be the one from home? Surely not. And he didn't mean home anyway—he meant the Grand Palace.

He fished in his satchel and rolled a small potato down the steps. The squirrel grabbed it and started nibbling. Then it stopped, sniffed the pebble again, and batted it closer to the step. It was Sibilla's pendant along with its chain.

Hodie scrambled down and picked it up. The Queen came back. She'd rinsed her face as well as her feet, but the torn trousers and big cap still made her look like an urchin. He handed the pendant to her.

"Oo, I didn't know I'd lost it." She stuck her top teeth over her lip like a cheeky brother ragamuffin. "Fanks! I'd better keep it tucked away." She threaded the chain round her neck and under her collar.

They sat in silence for a moment. This whole place gave Hodie the creeps. The wind blew dust from one end of the valley to the other, then another gust blew more dust, like gritty ghosts rank after rank. Behind him most of the long building looked as if it was used for storage. That's what "depot" meant, of course. It was better to say Depot than something boring like "coal shed" or something that would give the game away like, "where we keep the weapons to overrun Fontania and steal all their stuff." Hodie had not trusted the Emperor and Commander even as far as their mustaches reached across their faces.

"How long before the next wind-train?" asked Sibilla. He'd known she couldn't stay quiet for more than a minute. "I'm starving. But I'm tired of stale banquet. I hope there'll be something to eat on the wind-train…oh, I'll have to pay for food as well. Like ordinary people."

"We're not going on the wind-train," Hodie said.

Sibilla rolled her eyes. "You give up far too easily. We'll stow away."

He buried his face in both hands.

"We could climb a pylon and hop on at the last minute," she continued.

Climb the pylon? The height was bad enough, but the top was swaying. When the heavy wind-train was slung between the towers… Hodie went cold and sweaty.

"My father used to reckon that something always happens in the end," he managed to say. "We just have to wait." Even before the words were out, Hodie wished he hadn't spoken. For one thing, why had he said anything about waiting? For another, now she'd ask again about his father.

"Where did he come from?" Her eyes were bright with curiosity.

What did that matter? Dardy was gone—disappeared, or even dead. Now Hodie wanted to disappear as well—just not into Um'Binnia.

This was ridiculous. He jumped to his feet. He would march off at once, back the way they had come.

But far to the east, in the direction of Summerland, a flicker showed among the Stones. With it came a faint howl, thinner than the wind and more metallic. Hodie decided it wouldn't hurt to wait and just look at the wind-train.

Railway workers hurried over to the two stationary carriages and began hoisting them out of the way with hooks and pulleys.

The squirrel gave a low *chk-chk* and stiffened, looking up the rocky slope behind the platform. Suddenly it vanished into a crevice between two rocks. Over the rise, where Sibilla and Hodie had tumbled down, a horse's head appeared. Another head appeared, wearing a hat. Then Hodie saw six legs appear: four for the horse as you'd expect, two for Corporal Murgott, whom Hodie had not expected. But he was pleased. Now the Corporal would take charge of the little Queen. Hodie was free.

Murgott wasn't dressed in uniform and had a big duffel bag over his shoulder. He stopped on the top of the slope and brought a sandwich out of his bag. Chewing, he stood and scanned the Depot—he spotted Hodie and seemed slightly puzzled when he saw Queen Sibilla. Her little boy disguise must be very good if it could fool Murgott.

The Corporal shoved the rest of his sandwich back in the bag. He and the horse walked sideways down the slope.

Neither horse nor Corporal looked happy.

The squirrel pounced out of the crevice and headed for Murgott. It was small, but it was tough. It scrabbled up the Corporal's trousers and up his jacket. Murgott dropped the horse's reins, and the horse reared and heaved itself up back the way it had come. Murgott rolled yelling down the slope in a flurry of claws and scruffy tail, duffel bag and second-best boots.

Hodie ripped open his satchel and yanked out a sausage. "Here!" he cried.

The squirrel looked up. Hodie slung the sausage as far as he could. The creature gave a high hissing scream and pelted after it.

Murgott stumbled to the steps, hand to his ear where the squirrel had tried nibbling. "That sausage is off," he growled at Hodie. "I can smell it from here. Are you trying to poison yourself and your tatty little mate… Skull-and-crossbones! It's the Qu–" He creaked up the steps. "In the circumstances I won't bow, Your Mm—ah—nor even speak your title. I can't say how relieved I am to see you in disguise. I have news. In fact, several pieces."

"I'm not going back with you," Sibilla said.

"Please take her back immediately," said Hodie.

—

# ONE WAY TO MAKE
# A SQUIRREL SICK

Hodie hitched up his satchel and opened his mouth to say goodbye. But Murgott's hand clamped on his shoulder. "Boy," he began.

The little Queen put her hands on the hips of her torn trousers. That chin of hers went more pointy with determination. "Before you say anything else, Murgott, do you have food with you?"

He eyed her under bristly eyebrows. "I'm not giving any out right now."

She began to speak again, but he talked over her. "And, Your Mm—ah…you and the boy must not eat anything else from that old satchel."

"But…" said Queen Sibilla.

Something nearby began to give disgusting coughs. The squirrel, perched on a boulder near the steps, was trying to be sick. That was proof the banquet leftovers had gone bad.

"Boy," said Murgott, "I apologize. I should have known you were not the kind of boy to wreck a man's boots."

Sibilla reddened but her jaw went determined as well.

"That's all right." Hodie began to step down from the platform.

"Now boy," Murgott continued. "Bury any other food you have. At once."

Hodie sighed but saw it as one last odd job. He started to pry up stones to make a hole.

Another metal howl came from the east.

"Now, the news, Your Mm—ah…" Murgott looked past Sibilla at the crowd on the platform. He lowered his voice, but Hodie could still hear him. "The King sent a message to hurry back to the Grand Palace. Did it arrive?"

"I missed it, did I?" She blinked at Murgott with those blue eyes.

Hodie couldn't stop a grin. The Queen's words were not a lie because she'd simply asked another question.

The metal bird squawked inside her bag. She jostled it into silence again.

Murgott frowned at the Queen as he must have done before his pirate ship went into battle against twenty others—resolutely, but not with much hope. "So it's as the King suspected. You need another copy of the message. It's spoken. By me. *Er-hem*: 'The old Dragon-eagle visited the King. King Jasper and your mother Lady Helen need you to hurry home at once.'"

The Queen's eyes were troubled. "I'm really fed up and sorry, Murgott. But I'm no use at home. I'm helping Hodie."

Hodie opened his mouth to say he didn't need help, there was no way he was climbing on a wind-train, and all he wanted to do was head south! But Murgott spoke again firmly. "The bad news is that the young Dragon-eagle has been captured. We don't know how or why or who has got it. The worse news is that King Jasper says the other Dragon-eagle is very ill and dying. Magic is at its lowest ebb for ten years. Very soon the old Dragon-eagle will need the King or the Queen and most definitely will need the missing Ties."

Sibilla clutched both hands in fists over her heart. Murgott's voice was a low rumble. "The very worst news is what we have always known—if The Ties are not found in time, it is the end of the Dragon-eagles and the end of magic."

Hodie bit down a snort of disbelief and stomped the last scraps of stale banquet into the hole he had dug. He stole another glance and saw Queen Sibilla's eyes glisten with tears. She held them back but she was trembling.

"And the other worst news is that Um'Binnia still intends to declare war, ma'am." Murgott almost saluted but scratched behind his ear instead.

Sibilla wiped her nose on her sleeve. "But we let the Emperor and Princessa Lu'nedda stay with us for a whole week. Not even he would be so mean as to declare war after sitting in our chairs. Eating our porridge and bacon. Sleeping in our beds. And they already have the biggest and best of everything. Why would they want Fontania?"

Hodie stood up and dusted his hands—he couldn't keep quiet any longer. "Because they're greedy. They spent that week snooping and spying. King Jasper knew. He asked me to fit new locks on his workshop door and…"

"Boy, your observations are not needed," Murgott growled. "Her Mm—ah…somebody has important duties back in Fontania, so we'll say goodbye. Her Mm—ah… somebody and me will sneak off without being noticed. We might catch up with that horse." He glared at the squirrel. It squinted back then turned to chase a flea through its ratty tail.

*Please stop chattering and arguing*, thought Hodie. *Just go and I'll make my own way however I like!*

The little Queen stood as tall as she could (not very) and looked straight ahead, which happened to be at a sweat stain in the armpit of Murgott's jacket. Hodie saw her eyes take on a strange unfocused stare. It must be a trick royal parents taught their children very young.

"Very well," Sibilla said. "I'll go home. But Murgott, Hodie is brave, setting off on his own to face the Emperor. He's been kind and done his best to protect me, though I didn't need it. So I'll do one last thing for him. Hand over all the food you've brought. I don't want a bite myself. Hodie must have it."

The Corporal put both arms round his duffel bag. "I made the picnic with my own hands. I'm not…"

"And give him money for a ticket," Sibilla said. "We'll see him onto the wind-train and wave goodbye."

—

## NOBODY SHOULD DO THIS

Hodie's pocket clinked—with ten dolleros! He'd never had one dollero in his life, let alone ten. His satchel bulged with the Corporal's entire picnic: bacon and egg pie, six fresh cold sausages, several slices of chocolate brownie, a blue glass bottle of lemon cordial. The smell of the pie made his stomach gurgle. Murgott was the best cook in the Grand Palace, even better than the actual cook—perhaps he scared the ingredients the same way he got the best out of new recruits.

"Thank you." Hodie was careful not to bow. He stepped back and walked away along the platform. He couldn't wait to eat one of those sausages but knew the little Queen would be as hungry as he was. It was kinder to wait till she couldn't see. Besides, it had better look as if he was going on the wind-train, or Murgott might demand the picnic back.

Hodie leaned on a crate against the Depot wall. A nearby poster said, *Tell police and army at once about any rebel.* Over it someone had scribbled, Tell rebel about police

**and army too**, and penciled a sign like the sunrise crown lopsided over a snooty face and spiky mustache.

Corporal Murgott looked like an uncle, the Queen like a small nephew in a big cap explaining about his sore feet. It was astonishing how Queen Sibilla hadn't whined about the blisters. Nor had she moaned about having to eat stale banquet or not having a bathroom. Poor her—now she had to set off without lunch, back to a country that was protected only by fragile magic. If you believed in magic. Which of course Hodie didn't. He'd seen a bird sort of thing in the garden, late at night. That bird with a body and paws rather like a lion's, covered in feathers that rustled like leaves made of metal. But that was nothing to do with magic. It was very likely all a result of the drugged Cream. If King Jasper thought the thing had spoken to him, that was the King's business.

The wind strengthened, and Hodie felt splatters of rain. The people on the platform stared at the sky and down the dark canyon to the east. More people crowded from the waiting room, listening for another howl from the wind-train. The Um'Binnian soldiers and station guards shifted from foot to foot. If Sibilla didn't leave soon, it was more and more possible someone would recognize her. She turned now and gave Hodie a smile.

Wind thrummed in the pylons. Dust flew harder and faster from the east.

Then came the long metal howl. In the canyon mouth, Hodie saw a bright blur. The next moment a wind-train shot out of the canyon and snaked above the valley floor toward the Depot. Lamps shone at the front. Four large swiveling wings on the engine made it shift this way and that to catch currents of wind. Larger wings were spaced along three carriages, one of which looked like a dining car, the other a car that must be for luggage. Concertina metal cages linked the carriages.

The wind-train slowed, hovered for a moment, then swooped to land beside the platform with a grinding roar (and several bumps). It rolled for a moment as a grille at the front scooped up trash. Hodie guessed that was to stop stuff being sucked into the engine. All kinds of trash stuck there: shreds of plants, feathers, food wrappings, something with a green glint, even a hat.

The wind-train came to a stop. Valves in the engine puffed and gasped. The whole train was brass and wood, dulled with the buffeting of grit and sand. Along the sides were dents where it must have bashed against canyon walls. A window slid open in the engine. The Um'Binnian driver poked his head out, looked back along the wind-train, reached up and pulled a handle. A high whistle sounded. Carriage doors began to open and passengers piled out to stretch their legs.

Railway workers unhitched the luggage car, and pushed it far back so the two carriages Emperor Prowdd'on had left could drop down from the pulleys to link up behind the dining car. More workers scrambled onto the carriage tops to check the wind-sails and do repairs. Hodie squinted at the sails, held in place by brackets, hinges, and metal ropes, and at how the sails themselves were different shapes depending on where they were along the train: triangles, hexagons, rectangles.

Sibilla and Murgott still hadn't moved off—but then they hadn't seen Hodie climb aboard yet. This could be tricky.

The Corporal said something to the little Queen, ran up to the engine, and hopped down beside the metal scoop. He straightened and shoved the glinting thing into his bag. Was it a satin slipper? One with emeralds that Princessa Lu'nedda had worn in the Grand Palace? They certainly made big slippers in Um'Binnia. With a slightly red face, the Corporal sauntered back to join the Queen.

The waiting passengers were trying to pile in now. The station guard kept shouting. "Be orderly in lines! Show tickets! Not to shove!" The crowd didn't pay a blind bit of attention.

Murgott and Sibilla still stared at the wind-train. Dodging elbows and luggage, Hodie moved further up the platform, hoping it would look as if he was trying to climb aboard. He made sure the Queen noticed him again. Now how best to wriggle backwards through the crowd? He would hide behind the Depot till the train had gone and so had Murgott and Queen Sibilla.

A man carrying a long and awkward piece of luggage had struggled off the wind-train. "Carriage to border!" he cried through his Um'Binnian mustache. "Where is transport? By order of Emperor!"

The long piece of luggage swiped Hodie's shoulder. "Ow!" He rubbed the bruise.

An Um'Binnian officer forced through the crowd. "Are you scientist?" he called. "Show me Silver Medal of Discovery."

A woman with more pieces of strange-shaped luggage joined the man. She wore a medal on a coat with button-down pockets.

"Yes, yes, I am Master-Professor Glimp," the man said. "And here is Madame-Professor Winterbee. Is Fontania invaded yet?"

Hodie listened so hard he almost felt his ears expand.

"King Jasper and Queen Sibilla are not yet in our control," the officer said. "Emperor's plans have…" He put a finger to his lips and lowered his voice.

Down the platform, Sibilla began to turn her head. The officer was still talking.

"…and King Jasper has sped from City of Spires on flagship-steamer, *Excellent Eagle*."

Hodie felt himself being pushed along by the crowd. He edged back to catch the officer's next sentence.

"…telegraph not working at moment. The wires very tangled by the storm. Urgent to fix it. Moment it is A-OK again, war will be declared. Then you examine little Queen for magical ability." The officer clicked his heels and marched back into the Depot.

A scary sense of duty tried to grip Hodie. But none of this was his problem. It really wasn't.

"Typical kerfuffle." The Madame-Professor tapped her fingers on her luggage. "We interrupt our vacation to rush over, but there is no war."

Master-Professor Glimp sucked on his mustache. "We will go to City of Spires as Emperor ordered. Find good hotel. Then wait."

Hodie found he'd shuffled closer to hear more.

"Remember, we will each win Gold Medal of Discovery in next Imperial Honors List." Glimp looked very pleased with himself.

"*Hmph*," said Madame-Professor Winterbee. "What if rebels get rid of Prowdd'on in meantime? What if rebels become new government while we are examining little Queen?"

Rebels? Yes, the rebels against Emperor Prowdd'on! Hodie wanted to give a cheer. He kept on listening.

"Then we say we examine royal Fontanians for honor of new government. There is always very good answer in science." Glimp heaved up various bits of baggage and struggled off across the platform.

The Madame-Professor glanced at Hodie. He pretended he was on a quest for earwax (and actually found some). She took a notebook from one of her pockets, scribbled a few lines, looked at him more closely, then spoke to him. "Boy, are you Fontanian or Um'Binnian? Little brother here is definitely Fontanian."

Little brother...? Sibilla was at his shoulder! Hodie made a go-away face at her. She wiped her nose on the back of her hand and grinned like a small boy being curious. Down the platform Murgott was looking in his duffel bag at something.

The scientist scrawled a last line and showed Hodie and Sibilla the sketch. "There! Fontanian ethnic rags, all very quaint."

She had drawn two ragamuffins with dirty faces: a taller

boy with straight dark bangs sticking out under a cap, a smaller boy in a huge cap with no hair showing. Both urchins stared wide-eyed at the wind-train (there was a hint of a carriage and one sail to give the idea). The scientist had also drawn the pendant peeking out from Sibilla's collar. What's more, she had written a caption: *Fontanian urchins agog at Um'Binnian progress while their royal family undergoes Um'Binnian examination and investigation.*

"Examination?" Sibilla asked—luckily in a high voice that could belong to a little brother. "Investigation?"

Winterbee nodded. "To track and trace magical ability. Myself, I doubt they have it. But scientist keep open mind." She tucked the notebook away. "If it is true, we discover how to make stronger abilities in Um'Binnia." She picked up her luggage.

"Excuse me?" Hodie said. The Professor stopped. "Are you going to hurt the—um—Queen?"

Madame-Professor flicked a hand. "Pain cannot stop progress of Um'Binnia. Little Queen is most interesting because she is just at age of twelve when abilities appear— if there are any. Her, we will examine very hard."

~

Sibilla stared after the Madame-Professor, blood draining from her face, then dashed off to Murgott.

Hodie watched as the two scientists loaded their boxes and bags into a carriage on metal runners (so that's how carriages managed over the stones), hopped in, and set off with a crunching of gravel.

At the far end of the Depot, a bunch of soldiers were

being given polishing cloths. Big double doors were hauled open behind them. Inside Hodie saw rows of army carriages bearing the crest of Emperor Prowdd'on. There were brass and iron cannons on sleds too.

Thank goodness any moment Hodie would be heading south to a job on a farm with quiet sheep where the most scary thing would be a friendly cow.

Something chittered. The ugly gray squirrel crouched at his feet. It blinked at Hodie.

"All aboooaard!" cried the station guard.

The ropes that held the wings began to tighten. Station workers at the pulleys fitted enormous hooks to the engine and carriages. When the wind caught the sails, the whole thing would take off. The height of those pulley towers sent a chill through Hodie's lungs.

Sibilla and Murgott were near the last group of passengers, obviously arguing. Hodie put his bet on Sibilla winning. She looked scared and angry, and who could blame her? Hodie would refuse to go home now if he were royal.

"Oi!" called the guard to the driver. "Have you good supply of Toad Oil to safely land all extra carriages?" The driver nodded. "Enough food for extra passengers?"

"No," the driver shouted. "But no matter, because there is no cook."

Passengers popped their heads out of the windows. "No cook? No cook?" They sounded like a row of fussy poultry. "I will complain to Emperor!" a plump man cried.

More passengers popped their heads out. "Must have cook! Must have cook! Big appetite! Cook! Cook!"

Sibilla bashed Murgott on the back and waved at the driver. "Oi! Over here! This man's a cook!" She whirled around and beckoned Hodie. He saw fear and relief in her eyes. "Us boys is the cook's two helpers!"

Hodie felt as horrified as Murgott looked. Climb on a wind-train? The very thought made Hodie's knees weak. But now everyone had noticed him. They'd think it very strange if he didn't give a goofy grin, trudge over, and look excited.

"Train already is at overload!" shouted the driver.

"Cook!" the passengers roared. "Must have cook!"

It looked to Hodie as if the engine driver said a bucketful of strong curses. "Close windows and shut up! I will take cook and one boy only!"

"Hodie has to come!" Sibilla grabbed Hodie's arm and hissed at him. "You can get your stolen stuff!" He felt her shaking—she was terrified. Again how could he blame her?

Murgott strode over and spoke to her through clenched teeth (very spitty, and it landed on Hodie). "The boy's belongings are not your problem. Your safety is at stake. I am carting you home to your mum."

"But I'll be examined by a scientist!" she hissed back.

"I have orders from the King," insisted Murgott.

She began behaving like a naughty little boy. "Raise right foot, so!" She grinned at the passengers, acting like mad. "Swivel on left foot, so! Kick right foot! So!"

She pretended to kick Murgott, tangled her legs deliberately and fell over. The passengers laughed through their windows. Murgott closed his eyes and clenched his fists, and Sibilla scrambled up and leaped in the wind-train.

Murgott opened his eyes. He let out a piratical curse (to do with bilges) and jumped after her. Hodie cursed like mad in silence and stayed where he was.

Along the carriage Sibilla stuck her head through a window. "Hodie! Hurry up!"

"All aboooaard!" The guard slammed the door.

The pulleys strained and graunched. Wind whistled over the Depot roof and stung Hodie's eyes. The wind-train lifted high above the ground.

The guard came up beside him and spoke kindly. "Urchin-boy, you are better off here. They head into Force Nine gale."

The ugly squirrel was crouched on a crate. Gusts parted its scruffy fur this way and that, no doubt whisking fleas to goodness-knew-where.

There was a crunching noise, and Hodie turned. Down the hill behind the Depot, the scientists' carriage came sledding back. It skidded to a stop and out jumped Professor Glimp. "Stop!" he called. "Stop wind-train!"

"Blimmin' civilians," muttered the guard.

"Boy with big cap!" shouted Glimp. "He has Queen of Fontania's pendant around neck! He is thief or Queen Sibilla in disguise!"

The guard turned to Hodie, mouth open. Hodie yanked his cap down over his ears.

"Not him!" the scientist cried. "Little boy. Big cap. Torn trousers. Runny nose."

The guard pointed up to the wind-train. "He is cook's assistant!"

"Stop him!" the scientist shouted.

"Too late!" cried the guard.

"Send message ahead! Alert army!"

The guard pointed his arms in all directions. "But telegraph is down!"

Could the passengers hear this? Hodie could see that the windows on the wind-train were closed. But Murgott and Sibilla might be captured at the next stop. The Queen would be examined and all for nothing because magic was nonsense!

Three Um'Binnian officers were running over. The pulleys had wound the wind-train almost to the top of the towers.

Hodie took a step back—this was nothing to do with him. Then he took a step forward and another. Clammy with fear, he set a hand on the first strut.

"Oi!" cried the guard. "Oi! Boy!"

"Oi boy, yourself," muttered Hodie. He took a deep breath and started scrambling, two rungs, three...

"Come down! You will kill self!" yelled the guard.

The officers and station workers clamored too. Hodie, hands slippery with sweat, scrambled up another level. He heard his own voice clearly in his head: *Another half-minute—I have to warn the little Queen.* But his satchel snagged and wouldn't tug free. The rolled-up blanket had hitched onto one of the struts. The pulley still groaned on its last turn.

"You will be stowaway!" the guard cried. "Will be arrested!"

Hodie nearly lost his grip. He glanced down and saw an officer set foot on the first rung.

He yanked the satchel again. The wind roared, and along with the roar was the high hissing scream of a squirrel dashing full-scamper over the platform and up the pulley tower. It hauled itself up Hodie's leg (sharp claws!), onto his head (ouch!), then disappeared above him. For all Hodie knew it had toppled off the other side.

The pulley thrummed in the blast of wind. Hodie yanked the satchel a third time and it pulled free. He felt something tumble out, but he didn't dare look in case he followed. Then just as the pulley hooks released the wind-train, Hodie jumped. His jacket snagged, but he grabbed a bar on the side of the luggage car and kicked around to find a step. He hauled himself up, found the strength to slide the door open, and squeezed inside.

~

# HOW TO TRAVEL TO UM'BINNIA

# TOO LATE TO CHANGE YOUR MIND

Hodie lay on the floor of the luggage van. What a stupid thing he'd done. He was a stowaway. If he was discovered, he'd be tossed into the Stones.

He crawled around to see through a crack in the door. Down was a very long way. He went clammy all over again. He glanced up and glimpsed yellowish sky, the shade he felt when he'd tasted something nasty by mistake.

The wind-train rocked from side to side and swerved without warning as it took advantage of the wind that channeled through the canyon. It sped so close to the rocky walls that Hodie saw birds squabbling in their nest. A creature with long ears but slinky as a rat crept up a crevice. When he dared glance down again, he saw craters of oily water strung along the canyon floor.

He huddled against a pile of luggage and faced the main fact right on the nose—every second, he was being whizzed further and further north instead of south to a nice calm life. The next fact—each second whizzed him closer to his mother's stuff. But he didn't want it! He felt deserted by her. That might be silly, but that's how it was.

The third fact? Now he was here, he'd better finish the job and warn Sibilla about what he'd heard. As soon as the telegraph was fixed, the Um'Binnians would send word ahead. Then when the wind-train stopped, that would be that for Queen Sibilla.

Wind howled through cracks in the van. Fact four—he had to get from here along to the dining carriage while the wind-train hurtled through the air.

He began to push through bags and boxes. Most things had labels: the biggest all said *Property of Emperor Prowdd'on.*

The wind-sails sliced the gale and he heard something scratch on the roof. Slivers of light showed the outline of a hatch and a shadow moved across it. A scary rabbit? The scratching came again. Something chittered, like a question. Rabbits didn't chitter—perhaps it was just the ugly squirrel.

He moved a box to stand on, fiddled with the catch, and the hatch slid open. The squirrel dropped and shivered on the floor like a heap of dust. After a moment it sat and perked its ears at Hodie's satchel. *Tck-tck*?

Hodie was surprised to find he nearly chuckled, but then his heart plummeted. A buckle on the satchel had torn open. His blanket had disappeared and so had the food. His jacket pocket was torn too. He'd lost ten dolleros.

The squirrel crept over and peered in the satchel.

"There's a smell left, if you want it," Hodie said. "Oh, no—one small sausage. It's all mushed up. You have it."

The squirrel scoffed down every morsel and a few bits of dirt by mistake. It spat out the grit. *P-tah!*

"My pleasure," Hodie said. He rubbed its neck. It looked very much like one of the squirrels from the Grand Palace. It was just as tame, anyway.

"Look after yourself," Hodie said to it. "Bye now."

He steadied himself in the rocking car and wondered about leaving the satchel. But the buckle still worked, more or less, and you never knew if you'd need to carry a few things. So he kept it just in case.

~

In tipping, turning darkness split with slivers of yellowish light, Hodie fumbled to the front of the luggage car. He tugged the door hard and it rolled open. He didn't like the look of the concertina grille that linked the car to the passenger carriage. There were several missing bars and scary gaps. Below and around, air swirled with dust. A billow of gray steam surged up from the canyon. It smelled worse than soldiers' laundry day back at the Palace.

*The Queen*, he told himself. *Get to the Queen.*

He stepped out on the grille, grabbed a safety bar on the back of the next carriage, and began to shut the car door.

The squirrel appeared there, bright-eyed. *Chrr-tuk!* It clambered out and up onto the roof.

The wind-train lurched. Hodie bumped against the carriage door. The lock and handle were a sort he hadn't come across before, but he didn't dare let go to use both hands. He clung on tight. The wind whipped at him. It was so cold it froze his sweat. The yellowish light was disappearing as night fell. Gusts of steam and ashes tried to smother him.

Something tugged his hair. He squinted up.

The squirrel clawed down into the grille. It put its nose close to the door handle then patted a little button on the lock. *Tck-tck!* With a flick of its tail it vanished again into the gloom.

Hodie finally dared let go with one hand and pressed the button. The door swung outwards and nearly swiped him off through the gaps in the grille. Hodie wobbled, gave half a scream, and snatched hold of a bracket. The wind-train whizzed into another canyon. And as it made the turn the grille folded up and nearly squashed him. Just when he thought he would die if he couldn't take a breath, the train straightened up again and the grille let him go. At last he hauled himself inside and shut the door.

Shaking, still gasping, he stood at the end of a long passage. On the left was a row of closed compartments with little windows, most of them curtained and dark. He heard snores as he crept along and someone slurping as if he ate a plate of dream spaghetti. When he reached the last cubicle, there was a glimmer of light and the murmur of voices.

Hodie put a hand on the door at the end of the carriage then realized what he'd just overheard. A man had said something about his holiday on the Beaches of Summerland. Something about how if you were Um'Binnian it was a treat to bask in sunshine.

Hodie's heart chugged like an engine. The words had sparked a sudden memory of his mother. He tried to shake it away but it grew brighter…

Her light brown hair was pinned into a knot on top of her head. Curly bits of it dangled, and her earrings were bright green. He was a baby on her lap, twisting his fingers in the curls while she sang a rhyme—something about going up a hill in sunshine to see the dragon-bird. They'd been in a room lit with lamps, and he didn't know what she meant by "sun." Then a man came in wearing a long velvet jacket with silver buttons. He had an Um'Binnian mustache. Hodie's father.

~

Hodie jerked the carriage door open, slammed it behind him, and huddled out on the next grille. Wind and foul steam dashed around him. He clung on with one hand and pressed the other over his eyes. When Dardy was the odd-job man, he'd had no mustache. He'd worn old overalls in Fontanian denim with his head covered in a faded cap. The man in the memory—was it Dardy? Was his father an Um'Binnian but his mother Fontanian? If his father was an Um'Binnian who wore silver buttons, why had he become the odd-job man at the Grand Palace? Had Dardy been a spy? Hodie tried to make sense of it, but another turn in the canyon was coming up. Before he got squashed a second time, he wrenched open the door of the next carriage.

—

# HOW TO TREAT A PRESENT
# FROM YOUR BROTHER

Hodie bumped open the door to the dining car—at last—
and slid it shut behind him. There were bolted-down tables
and chairs and brass poles for hanging onto. The little
Queen, in a stripy apron, carried a tray of salt and pepper
shakers, and tried to keep her balance. Behind the counter
of a tiny kitchen, the Corporal flipped pancakes. The wind-
train jolted, the salt and peppers clattered to the floor,
Murgott jumped, a pancake spun out of the pan onto the
burner and—*whoosh!*—it was in flames.

Sibilla screamed. Hodie yelled. Murgott threw the frying
pan into the sink, trod on a salt shaker, skated into a
cupboard door, tripped, and Sibilla fell on top of him.
Pancake batter streamed down the cupboard doors. Batters
in pans—one smelled oniony, the other like berries—
slopped on the burner together.

Hodie flung himself at once behind the counter. He
banged open a window and used tongs to toss the burning
pancake out. The air was thick with smoke and stink.

Coughing, Sibilla dived over to flap the smell away. The gale whipped off her cap. She lunged for it and crammed the small haystack of her hair well out of sight.

Murgott slammed the window hard. "How the devil did you get on board, boy?"

"I grabbed hold. Scary." Hodie hoped he wouldn't throw up now in a reaction. "I came to warn you. The scientists recognized the Queen's pendant. They know who she is. When the telegraph is fixed, she'll be in danger. Get off. Hide. Quick."

"How do we get off a moving wind-train?" Murgott growled.

"Then pretend like mad you're just a cook!" cried Hodie.

"I've cooked on a pirate ship. I've cooked in the army. I'm as good a cook as…" Murgott wheezed in the pancake-smoke. "Just watch it, boy. Don't push me. Since you're here, you can make yourself useful." He threw Hodie a spatula to scrape up the batters—they were stuck all over the stove. The Corporal crashed cupboard doors open. "Bread. Cheese. The provisions are pitiful."

"Is there nothing else? Nothing at all?" Sibilla buttoned her collar up to hide the pendant.

The Corporal's mouth moved as if he chewed a slice of curses. "A bag of tomatoes, all spotty. Cheese, not very moldy. Five loaves of bread. I can manage toasted sandwiches. Where's the proficiency in that? Where's the skill?"

"I'll grate the cheese," Sibilla offered.

She'd probably grate her fingers too, if you asked Hodie.

Murgott scowled. "Smile, the pair of you. You'll put the customers off eating. The best disguises for you both are waiters' aprons."

Hodie figured Murgott was right. Anyway, he had to stay till he had another chance to get away. Why, why had he jumped on the wind-train at all? Now he'd remembered a bit about his mother, all he could think of was that she must have sent him away when he was little. It felt like a clamp around his heart.

"Is something else wrong?" Sibilla asked him.

He lowered his face to hide under his bangs, tied on an apron that matched Sibilla's, and scrambled to fish the salt and pepper shakers out of corners. He wouldn't think about his mother. But if his father was an Um'Binnian spy, should Hodie help the Queen at all? He decided yes. Hodie liked King Jasper, and sometimes Queen Sibilla wasn't too bad. He knew hardly anything about Um'Binnia except it had a vain and cruel Emperor, a silly Princessa, and its spies made dreadful parents. Dardy had stuck with Hodie for longer than his mother, but in the end he'd snuck off without leaving a message. He could at least have written something fatherly like, *Off on a Spy Trip. Don't forget to brush your teeth.*

The little Queen was looking at him strangely. "Don't answer me then," she said. "Murgott, Hodie can set the tables."

The Corporal pointed at Sibilla with a butter knife (had it been a sharper one, it would have been treason). "Don't give orders to the cook. At the moment, you're no more than the cook's assistant. Now, you two, pay attention."

Murgott's scowl was as black as the bottom of the ocean, black as thunderclouds at midnight, blacker than soot. "If war is declared, I'll be the superior officer here because the Queen is not Commander of the Army—King Jasper is. So in the kitchen, and at war, both the Queen and the odd-job boy take orders from me." He whipped out his pocketknife, flicked open the miniature saw, and started slicing the tomatoes. "Wash your hands before you touch food. Keep those aprons clean."

A passenger's head popped round the door from the front carriage. "What time is dinner?"

"When it's ready!" Murgott roared.

The passenger's eyebrows flew up, his head popped back out of sight, and the door slammed.

"It's ready now," said Murgott. He glared at Hodie. "Boy, if you betray the little Queen, I'll have you skewered and fried. Orright?"

Hodie thought the safest choice was to shut up and simply nod.

Murgott jerked a thumb at the big brass dinner button. "Then orright, boy, give it a jab."

The button made a sound like ogre bees in a monster jar. King Jasper would be interested in such a good mechanism—Hodie remembered the metal bird in Sibilla's bag. Broken, but it might still chirp. What if it said "Hello, Queenie!" while passengers were licking melted butter from their fingers?

Before Hodie could ask where she'd stowed her bag, the door from the front carriages slid open again. Two men tumbled in, steadied themselves against the poles, sat down and called for menus.

"It's toasted sandwiches or starve," Murgott announced. "Because of the weather."

"Weather is always bad over Stones of Beyond," one of the men objected.

"Sometimes is worse than others," said his friend. "There is forecast for terrible storm. Train might tip over and fly backwards!"

They roared with laughter. Hodie had overheard such talk in the barracks. They were trying to scare each other and show how brave they were themselves. These men were actually scared sick. So was he.

The little Queen wiped her nose on the hem of her apron, checked her cap again, made sure her pendant was buttoned away, and put on her normal-little-boy expression. A flash of blue lightning made her jump (Hodie too, to tell the truth).

"Weather," Murgott called. "Told you."

The men ordered cheese-and-tomato toasted sandwiches (surprise, surprise). More passengers appeared, wide-eyed and unsteady. The men's mustaches bristled. The women gave nervous tugs on their fingerless mittens. Another flash of lightning lit the dining car and set off a chain of screams from women and men.

An old man grabbed the back string of Sibilla's apron. "Boy, what time do we arrive at next station?"

"He doesn't know, sir," Hodie called quickly. "He's just the boy."

"He's just the uvver boy." Sibilla freed herself and kept her head down.

"I have table-of-time," said a woman in a sequined hat. "It usually is very wrong." She pulled it from an enormous spangly handbag.

A third flickering blue flash lit the dining car. A gust rattled the kitchen window and it slid open. Sibilla reached to close it, but a little paw appeared and a saturated squirrel struggled in.

"Oo!" Sibilla said. "Shoo! Oh, goodness—you're cold."

*Tck-chrr.* It jumped onto the counter then to the floor where it crouched and shivered. Then it perked up, eyed something in the corner, and pounced—on the little Queen's bag. Before Hodie could stop it, the squirrel clawed the bag open. Out fell the metal bird. The squirrel sat back and looked disgusted.

A voice began to speak, buzzing and faint. "Come back …(*erk*)…Eastern Isles…Lady Beatrrrr…(*erx*)…*Royal Traveler*…(*erk-zerk*)."

The squirrel swiped at it. King Jasper's bird came apart in a pile of wires and springs. Sibilla flung a tea towel over it.

Hodie tried to stand so that he blocked the kitchen floor from view, but a tall passenger had craned over the counter.

"Mechanical parrot?" The man pushed past Hodie and reached down. "Youch!" he cried. The squirrel scurried off behind the trash, and the man dabbed blood from a squirrel-scratch.

An older man laughed. "Mechanical? It might be clever Fontanian spy parrot!"

A young man sucked his teeth in a sarcastic manner. "The Great Prowdd'on protects us from Fontanians."

"Emperor's first aim is protect Emperor Prowdd'on," said someone else. "Poor Fontania could not even take away his golden spoon—too kind and gentle, sorry for him!"

The carriage filled with waves of grown-up laughter at a grown-up sort of joke.

The tall man patted Sibilla's cap. "Little waiter-boy, take no offence. You need good clean-up, but you will grow out of very daft look. It is your royal family that is hopeless. Magic? Excellent joke. *Phoof!* Dreams in air."

Sibilla's jaw clenched as if she might let out the Royal Swear Word. But all she did was dump the tea towel and bits of metal in the trash can.

"Maybe it is Prowdd'on's bird," a stout man said. "Spying on own people. Hunting for rebels."

"Of course he hunt for rebels. They are not loyal," said the woman in the sequined hat.

"They are not loyal to Emperor, that is why they are called rebels. But they have own admirable leader whom they adore. So I heard," replied the man.

Chattering continued. People nibbled on their crusts to make them last. Hodie listened. If there was trouble in Um'Binnia—because rebels wanted to get rid of Emperor Prowdd'on—would it be easier or harder for the Queen and Murgott to travel home? They might be able to get a message to King Jasper and the *Excellent Eagle*. Or what about the King's fiancée, Lady Beatrix, and the *Royal Traveler?* At the moment, Queen Sibilla was being a very good (though grubby) boy waiter. If she kept pretending as well as this, she might eventually be reunited with her family. Hodie felt a twinge of self-pity, but he was definitely fine all by himself. He'd got over the shock about his mother. He could forget her. Some day he'd find his own home.

He whispered to the little Queen. "Maybe Murgott can use the tools on his pocketknife to fix the bird. Could you send it back to the King with your own message?"

Sibilla gave a grateful, worried smile.

~

The wind-train swerved violently. The floor tipped and for a moment became the wall. Dishes toppled. Passengers screamed. The grater flew against the oven with a musical *clang!* Sibilla grabbed one of the brass poles, hung on tight, then dived at the trash can. Good for her. Hodie braced himself between the counter and kitchen wall so that Sibilla couldn't be thrown past before she had the bird again.

The sails creaked and groaned. The engine driver's voice came through a loudspeaker. "Emergency. Emergency landing ahead at Shattered Rock."

Murgott clambered over fallen dishes toward Hodie and the Queen. "Don't worry," he muttered. "When I was at sea, the darkest moments always came before it started getting better."

Hodie felt a flare of hope. "Really?"

"I've learned not to lie," Murgott said. "So I should add that getting better never actually meant becoming good."

It was pitch black outside now. In another lurch Hodie was thrown under a table. There was a crash as the carriage behind bumped into the dining car, another crash as it bumped the one ahead. The squirrel skidded out from somewhere and slid the whole length of the dining car, chittering like mad. A bump jarred Hodie's bones. Bigger bumps followed. Murgott let out a little scream (which was surprising). There were yelps and cries from the passengers. Hodie caught a glimpse of Sibilla, hanging onto the counter now, eyes wide, face ashen.

There was another stomach-dropping swoop and one last bump—then Hodie saw lights glowing outside. The wind-train had landed.

—

# DUBIOUS PIE OR STALE MUFFIN
# IN THE CANTEEN

Hodie staggered up and peered through a window. Grit dashed against it. Across a wide platform he saw a long, low building like the Depot, though much bigger. The name on a battered notice was:...*battered Roc*... This is where he'd got himself—halfway to Um'Binnia instead of peaceful southern fields with a chuckling stream, a flock of sheep (or goats) (or even llamas), and plenty of sunshine.

A station official in a yellow storm jacket beckoned from a doorway. Passengers had begun to struggle off the wind-train and grip stout barriers of rope. Coats billowing, clutching their hats and sometimes each other, they stumbled across. The wind scooped under a little girl's cloak. She nearly took off like a bird. Her parents tugged her down and huddled her between them. She probably thought she was lucky to have parents... Hodie realized the lump in his stomach was self-pity. He gave himself a buffet on the chin.

The Queen put her head beside his at the window.

"Look," she whispered. "More wind-trains. Maybe the Emperor is here. Maybe you'll find your stuff."

He felt very much ashamed that he planned to leave her. "You must be careful," he muttered back, "especially if the telegraph's been fixed. Maybe we should swap hats."

She eyed his cap. "My hair wouldn't fit in that. But thank you…" In a small voice she added, "Hodie? I'm sorry you're mixed up in this."

He felt even worse. "I'm sorry you're mixed up in it, too…er…little brother."

She gave half a laugh and made him grin. She smiled back. He thought her quite pretty if you didn't look at the dirt and also if you knew she was a girl.

At one platform a long wind-train was tied down with hooks and hawsers. A shorter wind-train was being tethered at another platform. Through the gloom and glimmer Hodie could make out a few small wind-cars that might be like private carriages. A strut of broken wind-sail bowled along the platform followed by scraps of paper and a lost sunbonnet.

The station guard fought through the gale toward the dining car and tapped the window. Murgott pushed Hodie aside and slid it open. Sibilla stepped back, hand on her cap.

"I hear there is cook and helpers," the guard called in. "Ah, yes. Wait in canteen. Get something warm into boys. To me, little bloke looks worth not one penny."

Hodie felt Sibilla stiffen, but he elbowed her and gave an older-brother sneer. She made a little-brother toothy-face at him.

"Terrible storm. Could last for days?" asked Murgott.

"All services are stopped for storm and other reason," the guard said. "Rebels attacked wind-train of Emperor. He was not hurt. Commander Gree'sle not hurt either. But Princessa Lu'nedda? She has been kidnapped."

Murgott stood to attention, shock written on his freckly brow.

"Yes. Terrible news." The guard actually seemed to think it was rather a joke.

Murgott ran a trembling hand over his bald spot. "The poor lady!"

The guard shrugged and struggled off into the wind. Hodie felt Sibilla's finger prod his ribs. "Lu'nedda will annoy the rebels so much they'll send her back home faster than you'd drop a hot potato!" she hissed.

Hodie gave a snort of laughter. He'd never eaten a hot potato, let alone touched one, but he knew the expression. He had to admit that given the circumstances Queen Sibilla was being brave.

Murgott still looked upset but he settled his duffle bag over his shoulder and put a finger to his lips. "Now listen, *boys*. We must not let a certain royal Sibilla be discovered. Since she must not be discovered, even though we're still not at war, I am in charge. Orright?"

"I suppose so," said Sibilla.

Hodie nodded. From the canteen, there might be a chance to leave the Queen and Murgott to it. They'd be fine without him. He could stow away again on a likely wind-train to the Beaches of Summerland. From there he might manage…

"And," Murgott added, "we will keep our eyes and ears open in the canteen. Pirates learn an awful lot by listening and watching in canteens. So does the army. Orright?"

"Orright," said Sibilla.

"Orright. If you say so," muttered Hodie.

~

The canteen door swung closed behind them. Hodie had never been in a place like this. It smelled of fatty hamburgers which he could see were decorated with tiny strips of browny-green. Was it meant to be lettuce? If so, it hadn't grown in fresh air and water like the vegetables in the gardens of the Grand Palace.

Murgott cocked his head, one hand on Hodie's shoulder, the other on the Queen's. In Um'Binnian accents, customers were saying things like, "Not bad hot coffee, considering it taste remarkably like cold mud." And, "I chose tea—*urrggh*. Never again."

Scraps of other conversations floated around. "Kidnap Princessa Lu'nedda?" somebody said. "I thought rebels were clever people. Rebels are fools!"

"Quiet!" another voice shouted. "There might be government informer!"

"What is gov-ing-mint informer?"

"A spy, you idiot!"

"Should we also watch for rebel information-er?"

"Yes, indeed, because fools are dangerous."

Murgott spoke up, pretending-jolly. "Is there a table here for a thirsty traveler who was also second-in-command on the pirate ship the *Double Cross*?"

"You are far from home on very stormy night," said a thick-set Um'Binnian with a half-eaten hamburger. "Are boys part of pirate crew? Or—ha ha!—are they what you will scramble for your dinner!"

"We is on a school trip." Sibilla simpered the way people often did when they first met her. (Hodie had seen her turn away and stick a finger down her throat and Lady Helen scold her for it.) "But I'd rather be home wiv my new puppy."

A scrawny lady with a suntan smiled. She had a big blue coat on the back of her chair. "What sort of puppy, dear?"

"I don't have it yet." Sibilla wiped her nose. "But when I'm home, I'm going to whine like stink until I get one."

A man sitting next to the suntanned lady laughed and flicked at the little Queen's cap.

"Oi." Murgott showed his fist, still pretend-jolly. "These are my boys. If there's roughing up to do, I do it. Orright?"

The customers chuckled and went back to curling their lips at the coffee and tea and jumping at the bangs and pounding of the gale outside. If you asked Hodie, Sibilla had just had a lucky escape.

"Don't overdo it," he muttered.

An explosion of gravel hit the roof. Hodie started. So did the Queen.

A skinny man in a check beret grinned at them. "Don't worry. Wind hurls around bones of little boys who cheek Emperor Prowdd'on. You are Fontanian? I recognize accent?"

Murgott pushed Sibilla and Hodie to a table against the wall. "Just a pair of travel-sick kids. Why I said I'd travel with 'em, I'll never know."

The skinny man scratched under his beret. "Terrible thing, children traveling in Stones of Beyond. There is not weather report in Fontania?"

A man in a big red scarf let out a chuckle. "Fontania? Nobody governs there in any manner. They rely on two very large chickens that never lay eggs."

More laughter filled the canteen. "They think magic will save them. Tired old magic against Um'Binnian machines!" Billows of laughter and more chatter.

"Have you volunteered for army yet?"

"I will wait till Emperor makes me."

"For crying-in-your-tea, watch for government informer."

"Shut up and have sip of stone-cold *urrggh*."

Hodie heard Sibilla take a shuddery scared breath. But she turned to Murgott, blinked, and did a buck-tooth smile. "Uncle, can I please 'ave an 'ot chocolate?"

A man at the next table glanced at Hodie under his hat brim. "You are also from Fontania?"

Hodie shrugged and pushed his bangs over his eyes. Luckily, just then a waiter came around. Murgott gave an order for pies, a ginger beer, and two hot chocolates. Sibilla started to kick her chair leg, *bump-bump-bump*, just like a boy. It was excellent acting indeed and very fast it was annoying.

A canteen ogre lumbered up with their plates of pies. Hodie was starving. He snatched his pie and dropped it back. "Ow!"

"Use the cutlery!" said Murgott. "You're not a pirate."

"It's hot!" Hodie blew on his fingers. Why did people ever want hot food?

"It's not hot, only warm." Sibilla grabbed one in her fingertips and started nibbling. "*Ew*—it's stale. *Ew*—what is it? Not pork—not chicken—I don't think it's carrot…"

"Don't ask," said Murgott. "Shut up, eat up, and be grateful."

The canteen ogre clattered dirty dishes onto his tray. "What kind of father bring boys into Stones?" he muttered to Murgott. "For shame, for shame."

Sibilla's eyes were cautious but she showed her front teeth in a goofy smile. "He's not our Daddy, he's an Uncly."

The ogre scowled. "Tell Uncle to beware of riff-raff."

She looked uneasy. "What's wiff-waff?"

The ogre's face softened. "Riff-raff is bandits," he said. "Riff-raff is spies and rebels."

"Oo, all of them?" asked Sibilla. "S-spies for who?"

"The other side." The ogre winked. "No matter what side you are on, there is always other side. And rebels are against own side." He kept smiling at Sibilla.

"But there's no webels in Fontania," Sibilla said.

The ogre spoke from the corner of his mouth. "That is because Fontanians have good royal family who do not give ordinary folk a lot of bother. They are not very bright and best at laziness."

A frizzy curl sprang out the back of Sibilla's cap. Hodie kicked her. She poked the curl back and scratched her hands all over the cap. "It must be my little nits," she muttered. "Very bad itchies."

The ogre had started to lean closer but drew back. "I say no more. But some folk in Um'Binnia think democracy would be improvement." He finished loading the tray.

Sibilla kept both hands on her cap. "How would democra-what improve the Emperor?"

Hodie put his hands over his eyes. Any moment she would give herself away. They'd all be in trouble.

"Democracy," muttered the ogre, "is even better than having lazy King and little girl Queen."

Murgott drew in a sharp breath and glanced at Sibilla. The ogre continued. "Democracy is when people spend time arguing about what is best, not just say Hoorah for Emperor to his face and heaven-save-us-all-especially-ogres behind his back."

The man in the check beret leaned over too. "Democracy is also not paying taxes to buy fancy footwear for Princessa."

"Ha! Man is not wrong." The ogre staggered off with his heavy tray.

A gust of wind tossed more gravel onto the roof (unless it was bones). Hodie tested his pie and had a cautious bite. He was just deciding it wasn't too terrible when a tug at the string around his boot made him glance down. A small squirrel, ears perked, sat and watched him. Was it the one from the wind-train? Could it even be the one whose friend Prowdd'on had squeezed to death? Hodie held out a crumb. It ate from his hand. Its whiskers tickled.

"Such nice boy." It was the lady with the suntan and the big blue coat. She turned to the man in the beret. "I do not think there is much wrong about Fontanians. I do not understand why there will be war."

"Agreement with you," said the man. "We do not need

to own Beaches of Summerland. And if Fontanians believe in magic, what is the harm?"

Hodie saw Sibilla's jaw clench.

Murgott put a big hand over hers. "I've seen magic at work," he whispered to her. "One day you will find your abilities. Wait and see."

Her eyes filled with tears. She gave a little shrug and shook her head but stayed quiet, sipping her chocolate.

Hodie covered how uncomfortable he felt by holding out another crumb for the squirrel. The squirrel accepted it but stared at him, tail flouncing and eyes narrowed.

~

At a nearby table sat three rough-looking men. One had a bandage around his wrist. Another had one over his ear. The third kept crinkling his eyes shut as if he had a pain where Hodie couldn't see. The wind had died back and Hodie realized he could hear what the men were saying in their thick accents. He stayed down and pretended to retie the string around his worn-out boot.

"Ogg'ward says we have to hide out till we can return to our hideout."

"Where is our hideout from here?"

"Ogg'ward will not say. It is secret hideout."

"But we are all going to hide in it, yes? When we find it?"

"Oh yes. Ogg'ward very clever."

They glanced toward the counter. A broad-shouldered man in a tweed coat and thick black beanie was buying himself another coffee—it must be Ogg'ward. He had an enormous black mustache.

The men huddled closer. "We agree Ogg'ward would kidnap Princessa. But what did he do? No Princessa, but one of her slippers! Much easier to hide than such tall lady. Slipper is decorated with expensive jewels. We will be rich."

Hodie's heart raced. These were the rebels! These men wanted to get rid of Emperor Prowdd'on! He sat up for a better look at Ogg'ward. There was definitely something heroic about the man. Maybe Hodie could join the rebels. They might help him out of the Stones and show him a safe way of getting south.

"But where is Princessa?" said one of the rebels.

"Ah, Ogg'ward has not told us where she is, to keep it secret," said another.

"Our leader has such clever brain," agreed the third.

Ogg'ward glanced over at the men. They pretended not to know him but weren't actually terribly good actors. Ogg'ward trudged off to a corner table by himself. He sipped his coffee, spluttered, and put a hand to the mustache as if he was scared he'd cough it off. It was by far the biggest mustache Hodie had seen yet, like half a guinea pig glued under the man's nose.

After another sip of coffee, Ogg'ward stood, picked up a red bag from the chair beside him, and slung it over his shoulder. He tugged the beanie down to his eyebrows and tried to tiptoe to the door. He wore huge boots, not at all good for being sneaky, but Hodie saw that the other rebels didn't notice him clomp out. They were too busy laughing, and one of them was doodling on a paper napkin.

"Soon we can retire from being rebels by ransom of slipper!"

"Yes, covered in emeralds and fluff from chin of mountain dove. Worth many thousand of dolleros. We can buy weapon for overpowering very bad Emper…(*cough-cough*)…you-know-who. Or, yes, we could give up being rebels—run to Fontania and live as lazy as their royal family." The rebel seemed to think it a great joke.

Murgott put an arm round Sibilla's shoulders. It looked as if she was crying silent tears into her hot chocolate—by now it would be cold and salty chocolate.

The duffel bag on the back of Murgott's chair showed the bulge of the probably matching slipper he had picked up back at the Depot. Perhaps he too planned to sell it to retire on thousands of dolleros.

Someone opened the door. A thread of wind stole in and under the rebel's table napkin, and it fluttered to the floor. The three men hunched over and muttered again. They hadn't noticed the fallen napkin, but the squirrel had—it scuttled over and punctured it in its sharp claws.

"Boy, let's have a squizz at that scribble," Murgott murmured. "Never know, it could be useful."

Hodie eased the napkin from the squirrel's grubby paws and passed it over. Sibilla tried to see too, but Murgott squinted at the napkin close to his nose. He let out a trembly sigh. Sibilla tugged his arm down, and Hodie had a good view.

The rebel had sketched Lu'nedda's slipper—flat heel, pointy turned-up toe, a jeweled butterfly ornament with bird fluff for wings. He had drawn it lying on top of Ogg'ward's bag.

"I know you picked up Lu'nedda's other slipper at the Depot, Murgott," Sibilla said in an undertone. "You think I didn't notice."

The edges of Murgott's ears flared purple-red. The napkin crumpled in his fist. Sibilla took it and tried to uncrumple it. Hodie had another glance. Definitely, Lu'nedda's slipper—the emerald pair.

The door banged open. A tall Um'Binnian officer stood there, a pistol in his holster. "Attention! Important news!" he announced. "Telegraph is fixed!"

Everybody stopped mid-sip, mid-bite, mid-grumble. Hodie felt as if something knocked into his chest. He should have paid more attention—he had noticed the wind had dropped, but he hadn't thought about the telegraph.

"War with Fontania!" the officer shouted. "Hoo-rah for Emperor Prowdd'on! Give me big Hoo! Give me big Rah! War is declared!"

"Hoo-rah!" cried half the crowd in a scattery way. "Hoo-hoo. Rah!"

Sibilla was still holding the napkin flat and staring at the officer. Hodie glanced at the sketch again—the pencil lines had blurred and were beginning to show something inside the bag the rebel had drawn. Then Sibilla screwed the napkin up and popped it in her empty chocolate mug.

"Stop…" Hodie grabbed the napkin out. It was soggy with dregs. Bits stuck to his fingers. Sibilla stared at him as if he'd gone mad. So did Murgott.

Hodie thought he had definitely gone mad. For a moment he'd thought he'd seen, stuffed into the red bag in the sketch, a bag like the one stolen from his lean-to. He must have imagined it. Anyway, now the napkin was shredded and torn.

The squirrel leaped onto Hodie's lap. Wind pounded the roof.

"I'll distract the officer," Hodie muttered to Sibilla. "Get behind Murgott. I'm off on my own." Then he stood up so fast the squirrel screeched. "Thanks for the chocolate, Corporal."

"Oi!" said Murgott.

"Boy!" shouted the officer. "Come here and take your cap off!"

Hodie kept his hands on his cap, ran for the door, ducked under the officer's arm, and darted out into the wind.

He had a last glimpse of Sibilla and Murgott and the scrawny lady with the suntan jumping up in front of them.

⌣

# NOT PLENTY OF CHOICE
# OUTSIDE EITHER

The gale slapped Hodie from every direction, and he pressed himself against the station wall to get his bearings. The officer ran out after him but didn't see him and kept running down to search the platform. The wind pushed the man into a nook behind some machinery.

Wind-trains and wind-cars bucked and jerked in their tethers. A small, sleek wind-car was still being lashed down by soldiers. It bore the sunburst sign of Emperor Prowdd'on. Muzzles of guns poked out its sides. Another military wind-car buffeted into the station and landed behind it.

Now how could Hodie get away?

There was Ogg'ward in his beanie on a side platform. Hodie took a step in that direction and the gale nearly made him fall over. He had to go down on one knee and close his eyes. Again he saw the picture on the napkin changing under the Queen's fingers. No—he was so tired his mind had played tricks. Ogg'ward had nothing to do with his mother's stuff. All Hodie wanted was a way south out of the Stones. The little Queen had Murgott—two people had more chance of hiding than three. And Hodie deserved the chance of a good life.

He pulled his collar up, held his cap on with one hand, and with the other held tight to a rope barrier. But he couldn't stop himself from taking one last look back at the canteen door.

The door flung open again, shouts sounded inside, and the rebels came tumbling out. They hauled themselves along the ropes, bullied past Hodie, and reached Ogg'ward.

All of them seemed to be gesturing to the military wind-cars. One of them pointed to a small battered wind-car, urging them all to pile in and get away (Hodie could tell from the way the rebel's arms waved). Ogg'ward slipped the red bag from his shoulder and opened it to let them peer in. The gale snatched at the bag. Ogg'ward kept it tight in his fist, but the wind scooped out a newspaper, a glittering green slipper, and half a pie. The slipper flew toward Hodie. His hand went out automatically. He gripped the slipper—help, the jewels made it heavy! The four rebels turned, but the wind swallowed whatever they shouted.

"Hey!" a voice yelled behind him. "That boy!" Hodie glanced round. It was the Um'Binnian officer, fighting toward him. "Boy, take your hat off!"

Hodie flung his cap into the wind and it scudded away.

Behind the officer, a man and a fat lady in a big blue coat tottered out of the canteen. It was Murgott—but who was he with? Where was the Queen? The storm howled and scattered grit. The officer had to put both hands over his eyes.

Staggering on the spot, Hodie still held the slipper. Ogg'ward shouted and beckoned to him. The wind strengthened every moment—it tugged a piece of roofing and hurled it away like a broken bird. The fat lady was holding her long coat over her belly, and Murgott steadied her.

"Clear platform!" roared a voice through a loudspeaker. "Force Ten gale! Take cover! Risk of severe damage! Everyone inside very fast! That means army too! I am in charge here!"

Hodie would have said the wind was actually in charge. But his insides clenched. Where was she—where was Sibilla?

"Clear platform!" roared the loudspeaker. "Clear platform! Even those rebels!"

The three rebels from the canteen began running for the small, battered wind-bus. Soldiers struggled after them in the gale. Lights along the station began to pop and go out. Another piece of roof tugged free and soared away.

Ogg'ward avoided the soldiers and came right at Hodie. Hodie expected him to grab the slipper, but it was his arm that Ogg'ward was after. He yanked Hodie over to a smaller, even more battered wind-bus.

"Inside!" Ogg'ward ordered. "Keep head down!" He thrust Hodie in and hauled himself toward the tethers at the front of the wind-bus. Through the window Hodie saw the man's hands in thick black fingerless mittens loosening the hooks.

Hodie fell into a seat, still with the slipper. He was getting away! At last! He squeezed his eyes shut for a moment.

The wind swirled in through the door. *But the Queen*, he thought, *there's room for her and Murgott too!*

He took in a huge fresh breath then scrambled to the back window and waved the slipper to catch Murgott's eye. "Where is she?" he shouted. "Over here! Quick!"

Murgott waved back. He gave the fat lady a kiss on the cheek, the fat lady flung open her coat, and now Hodie saw it was actually the scrawny lady. The fatness had been Sibilla (still with her cap on) in excellent hiding.

The loudspeaker was going crazy. Guards and more Um'Binnian soldiers began pouring out of the canteen. Hodie heard Murgott's voice, and Sibilla tumbled into the wind-bus, flat onto the floor.

"Stay out of sight!" Murgott yelled. He stayed in the open doorway, hanging on.

The wind-bus bucked. Any second it would jerk up into the gale. There was no need for pulleys here—the wild wind of the Stones would do the job.

Ogg'ward barreled into the wind-bus and shoved Murgott back onto the platform. The wind-bus rose into the air, its door still open. Ogg'ward grabbed the slipper from Hodie and slung the red bag under the driver's seat, slipper on top. Then he flung himself at the controls.

"Murgott?" Sibilla clambered up into a seat. "Where's Murgott!"

The wings of the wind-bus gripped the storm. The Um'Binnian officer drew his pistol and fired, fired again—

But the wind-bus was high in the night, a glow from the engine, a glimmer of moonlight and stars. The few lights of Shattered Rock were no more than a glittering patch in the canyon below.

"Murgott!" screamed Sibilla. "We've lost Murgott!"

There was a yell right underneath. Murgott's hairy hand appeared over the step. Sibilla sprawled on the floor again and grabbed his wrist. Hodie sprawled too and grabbed Murgott's sleeve. With struggling and various curses, Murgott squirmed into the wind-bus. The ugly squirrel was clamped to his left leg.

~

Ogg'ward kept hold of the controls, let out curses of his own, and clapped a hand to his mustache. How awful if the chief rebel got air-sick. Hodie shuffled away a safe distance.

Murgott lay on a bench seat, eyes closed, mopping his forehead and neck. The wind had scuffed up the little squirrel so that its fur looked stuck on backwards. It sent a disgusted look at Hodie then leaped into the luggage rack. Hodie actually did feel a bit ashamed that he'd been thinking he might run off, but he had saved Sibilla in the end. He scowled at the squirrel.

Sibilla ducked down behind a seat, took her cap off, and combed her fingers through her hair. She crammed the cap on again and mouthed something to Hodie—*Did Ogg'ward notice?* Hodie didn't think so. She sat up properly again.

The wind-bus flew on over the darkness of the Stones.

Nobody ever wanted Hodie's opinion, but still, the chief rebel had helped out.

"Er…thank you," he called to Ogg'ward.

"What for?" the rebel growled.

"Um…for saving us?" Hodie said.

"Oh!" Sibilla sat up straighter. "Of course. Thank you."

Hodie knotted his eyebrows. "Disguise," he muttered.

She did her little-boy buck-teeth at once. "I was scared as any-fink, mister! Fank you a lot!"

Ogg'ward locked a lever into place then jerked his head at Hodie. "Him, I save. You other two were big mistake." His voice was muffled by that mustache and the creaking of the wind-sails. He peered into the darkness behind the wind-bus. "We are low on fuel for such heavy passengers. Wind carries us up, but once we get to edge of the Stones we need Toad Oil to stay up. Also need engine to land without crashing." His eyes glittered beneath the black beanie. "Tell me if we are followed. It is very important I am not followed."

He wiped sweat from the back of his neck. One hand worked on the levers while he held the other to his mustache again. Air-sick for sure.

Hodie eased over to whisper to Murgott. "Where's he taking us?"

"If I knew that," Murgott rumbled, "I'd have an answer."

"Just ask him," said Sibilla.

"Wait," Murgott muttered. "I'm not in uniform."

"So?" Sibilla asked.

"Listen, if Um'Binnia realizes who I am, I could be shot for spying." Murgott shone with sweat again. "Even though I'm not a spy."

"I thought things couldn't get worse," Sibilla breathed.

"My rule is never say that," Murgott said. "It's tempting fate."

"Surely we're sort of safe," said Hodie. "Ogg'ward's a rebel."

Murgott grumbled. "We're safe from the rebels, maybe. But who's after them?"

A bright light flared behind the wind-car. Ogg'ward glanced back. "Military wind-car! Keep heads down!"

"That's my point," Murgott growled.

The wind-bus soared up with a scream from the sail struts. An arm's-length on either side, in a glimmer of starlight, Hodie saw the rocks of a narrow canyon. A swerve, another swoop, and they coasted just above the tops of the Stones. He had no idea in which direction they were flying, but the lights of the military wind-car were left far behind.

The wings of the wind-bus creaked with effort. There were squeaks as well, very worrying till Hodie realized the squirrel was snoring.

At last Sibilla spoke in her little-boy voice. "Excuse me…Mr. Ogg'ward, I don't understand. You're a webel, yes? Why did you save Hodie? Why didn't you save the uvver webels?"

Ogg'ward's teeth showed underneath that thick mustache. "Any answer is too difficult for tiny-boy mind." He bent down and shoved Lu'nedda's slipper into his bag.

Sibilla's face was furious, scared, and frustrated. Hodie tried to laugh like an older brother would. She scowled at him.

"Don't argue, boys," said Murgott. "Uncle says."

"That is right. Or I drop little one in Great Salt Moat," snarled Ogg'ward.

Sibilla was silent for a moment…"What's the Great Salt Moat?"

"Dumbo," Hodie said (it was all right to be rude to a Queen if she was pretending to be your little brother). "It's the sea around the Mountain of Um'Binnia. That's what Um'Binnia is—a mountain. The Um'Binnian capital city is there."

"On the mountain?" Sibilla asked.

"Actually," he began, then realized—Ogg'ward must be flying to Um'Binnia. It felt as if his heart and stomach plunged together into the canyon.

Murgott sat up. "All right, man! Where are you heading? Where's your secret hideout?"

"My secret hideout?" Ogg'ward laughed. "Yes, I have secret. But I do not exactly have hideout."

No hideout in Um'Binnia? Hodie wanted to lie under a seat and simply die.

Ogg'ward was still talking. "We will be over Great Salt Moat when sun rises in forty-five minutes. Boys must shut up." He gripped the controls. "One boy I want. Squitty little boy and uncle, I do not wish for! I must concentrate on old-model wind-bus. If we are not on target first time, we have to ditch into dangerous sea."

"No!" Murgott looked exactly like a terrified soldier in disguise. "Not into the Moat!"

Ogg'ward nodded. "Just when Ocean Toads are seeking breakfast."

It was not reassuring for Hodie to see Murgott break out into a new sweat on top of all those old ones.

~

In the blue glow from the engine, Murgott breathed heavily. His bristly eyebrows drew together. He whispered to the little Queen and Hodie. "Boy, if you betray the little Queen I'll make you eat your own head, garnished with parsley. Now, the pair of you, listen hard. An old pirate's trick: step one, be nice till you've quelled suspicion. Step two: grab the helm yourself."

"Do you know how to fly a wind-bus?" Hodie whispered back.

Murgott's face was sickly gray. "No. But it's got sails and I know sails. It's the first step that is hardest—being nice." He cleared his throat, gave Hodie his darkest look yet, and stumbled down the bus to sit near Ogg'ward.

Sibilla grabbed Hodie's sleeve. "What else do you know about Um'Binnia?"

He felt so afraid and sick he lost his temper. "I couldn't listen to all your lessons! I had to fix faucets and oil hinges and sweep horse droppings!"

"Keep your voice down," she hissed.

He couldn't stop. "You were too lazy to learn things that a Queen needs to know. But you had plenty of time for your tantrums."

Her eyes brightened with anger. "Watch out or I'll punch you!"

"Shut up or I throw out two boys!" Ogg'ward yelled.

"Don't you lay a finger on the…er…squitty one!" shouted Murgott.

"All shut up!" bellowed Ogg'ward. "Sit down now!"

Murgott grumbled to himself. Hodie huddled in the back corner. His head ached with the noise of the wind, the creaking wings, the sputters from the oil-chamber.

Sibilla looked furious and scared. If the Um'Binnians discovered who she was, she'd have no escape. Hodie felt sick again but in a different way. He should tell her about the way he thought the sketch had changed beneath her fingers. It had simply been a trick of his eyes, but it might make her feel more hopeful, and that might help her go on. If she believed him. If she would even listen to him now.

He slid over anyway. "In the canteen…" Sibilla turned away, but he kept going—the possible small flash, the first hint that maybe she had come into her magical abilities after all. But his voice was wobbly and flat, the way it always was when he didn't really believe in something. She'd gone all wooden—so she too didn't think that magic could be real.

"It's what everyone expects." He tried to be more convincing. "You know—that you'll be like your brother, that you'll have a special link with the Dragon-eagles, that there is magic." He actually felt a bit sick when he said this, because it would be really wonderful if only it were true.

She turned and stared at him, just for a moment. "I can't stand it. Please, go away."

He'd tried at least. The sky had turned the same shade Hodie felt from lack of sleep, a sickly gray-yellow. Below, in the sour dawn, the craters and canyons of the Stones of Beyond were a grayish yellow too.

"But why?" It exploded from Hodie and he jumped up from his seat. "Ogg'ward, I'm nobody. Why did you help me?"

Ogg'ward gave a bitter chuckle. "Who is this nobody boy? Somebody's son."

His father? Did Ogg'ward mean it was something to do with his father?

Sibilla sat up and spoke without her little-boy lisp. "Dardy's alive?"

"Dardy? Ha, yes, alive in Um'Binnia." Ogg'ward gave an odd laugh. "So is boy's mother."

The words circled around Hodie's head but didn't go in.

"Hodie said he didn't have a mother," Sibilla said.

"His mother," replied Ogg'ward in a gruff voice, "is best friend of Princessa Lu'nedda."

Hodie tried to say that must be nonsense, but all that came out was a failing squeak.

"Now shut up again. All stay shut!" Ogg'ward cried. "I must concentrate completely or we ditch in Great Salt Moat!"

—

# FAT CHANCE OF
# ANY CHOICE RIGHT NOW

The wind-bus hurtled on. Hodie's father was alive? It was difficult to learn this and know any minute he might drown in the Great Salt Moat. And he still had a mother! But... best friend of the Princessa? That would be why she hadn't bothered about her baby son and sent him away. The best thing might be for Hodie to drown.

The squirrel scrambled along the luggage rack and chittered like mad above Hodie's head.

"Hold on!" Ogg'ward cried.

The sky grew lighter each moment. The wind-bus passed a line of cliffs with wreckage littered on a wild shore then soared out over churning gray sea. Wind leaped from every direction. The wind-bus tossed and tilted. A huge gust knocked it down toward the waves. Ogg'ward yanked on the controls, and the engine fired with a grinding roar. The sails screamed. Hodie gripped a safety rail. Sibilla's cap bounced and wriggled but at least stayed on her head.

"Grab oil-can!" Ogg'ward yelled to Murgott. "Squeeze

last drop of Toad Oil into hole under controls!" The Corporal staggered up. You could tell he was used to taking orders in windy conditions.

In front of the wind-bus, a mountain, its head wreathed in mud-colored clouds, reared from the waves. The wind-bus sped on, thrown this way and that. Hodie felt sicker every minute, sick in stomach, heart, and soul. A few huge industrial pipes jutted into the sea. He saw no other sign of a city on the mountain, nor even a town. There was only cliff piled on cliff, on top of more cliffs scarred by gullies choked with rock falls. As they flew closer, he glimpsed small terraces and patches of golden waving stuff like corn. Tiny houses dotted valleys far below...

The wind-bus swerved closer, closer to the mountainside. Hodie saw moss on the rocks, the puff of a rabbit's tail vanishing into a burrow. The wind-bus hovered for a moment and the engine rose to a high pitch. Hodie waited to crash.

Then a flock of birds spiraled past, riding the wind...

*I haven't had enough of this world yet*, Hodie thought. *I want to see every last moment. I am going to face my death with my eyes open.*

He expected a smash then utter darkness. He caught a last sight of cliff lilies, a trace of scent so sweet it was like somebody saying they loved you. A true mother's voice might be as sweet... He wasn't usually as soppy as this. It was probably because he was going to die.

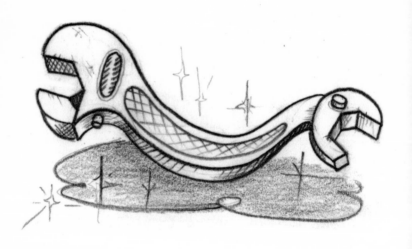

PART FOUR OF HODIE'S JOURNEY

# MANY SHOCKS AND MANY TEMPTATIONS

THE QUEEN AND THE NOBODY BOY

# MUSTACHE

Hodie gripped the seat in front of him so hard his hands cramped. Then under the whine of the engine, he heard a deep groan that sounded like the rocks themselves—and actually, it was. The cliff in front of them moved open like a great door sliding—and actually (again), it was a door.

The engine sputtered, and Ogg'ward eased a lever. Jerking to and fro, the wind-bus flew inside the mountain and landed in a parking space in an enormous cavern. With another groan, the stone door began to roll shut. There was a *screel* and a clank of machinery. The slab was stuck. A crack of morning sky showed down the side. In light from fittings on the cavern walls, figures in overalls milled about, dropping oilcans and screwdrivers, scratching their heads (and sometimes armpits).

Ogg'ward swore again in a high voice. It meant he hadn't thought they'd make it, and he quaked with relief. The squirrel said *chit!* and stayed in the luggage rack. Hodie stayed where he was too, so shaken he didn't trust his legs. Sibilla looked pale as milk (but dirtier).

Murgott struggled to his feet and peered through the back window. "No chance of getting out again that way, I'd bet my parrot."

"You haven't got one," Sibilla said in a thready voice.

"Not anymore. Green and yellow. Sat on my shoulder, dropped seeds in my ear. Got rid of it." Murgott called to Ogg'ward. "What's the best way out of here?"

"Unimportant hanger-on, we must not draw attention." Ogg'ward turned up his coat collar and tugged the beanie down to his eyebrows. "Be quiet and trust me."

In half a second Murgott had out his pocketknife. "I'll trust you at the end of this!"

"You've opened the little pliers," Hodie said. "Are you going to pluck his mustache?" He still felt wobbly, otherwise he would never have dared sass Murgott. Sibilla's laugh sounded more like a frightened chirp.

Murgott folded the pliers away. "You're funny, boy," he growled at Hodie. "But I don't trust Ogg'ward. And I'm not sure I can trust you. I'll be honest, boy, and admit there have been days when I've looked in a mirror and I wouldn't even trust myself."

The cave entrance shut at last with an echoing bump and ragged jubilation from the workers. A soldier hurried across. Sibilla put on her toothy-boy smile. Ogg'ward swore again under his breath. He rolled open the door of the wind-bus and popped out his head (mostly beanie).

The soldier touched a finger to his cap in a sloppy salute. "Very good parking. Do you carry uncertified baggage? Please, hurry up."

Ogg'ward pressed a hand over his mustache and shook his head.

The soldier peered into the wind-bus and under the seats. "No animal? No bird? No animal or bird allowed today. By order. Biggest order, by Emperor." He peered up at the luggage rack. "What is that?"

"A...beret for my muvver," said Sibilla. "Made of cat fur."

"Looks more like dead squirrel," the soldier said. "And let us hope mother suits gray. Ah, more thing—Princessa Lu'nedda has been kidnapped. Did you see strange behavior over Stones of Beyond?"

A gleam showed in Ogg'ward's eyes. The mustache twitched. "Prowdd'on is terribly upset? There is reward?"

"Prowdd'on upset! Ha, not at all. Very good joke. There is no reward, either." The soldier turned on his heel.

Ogg'ward's chin trembled.

The soldier swung back. "Ah—extra thing again. Smallish bag went missing with Princessa Lu'nedda. Emperor is furious. Big reward for finding that."

A buzzer sounded. The soldier touched a finger to his cap and sprinted off to join some of the Um'Binnians looking extremely busy at the cavern entrance. A few others were clearing a space in the center of the garage.

Ogg'ward muttered dark things and pressed two fists to his huge mustache.

Sibilla looked worried for him. "Cheer up," she said. "You don't have the Princessa, but you have her expensive slipper..."

Hodie kicked her ankle to make her shut up.

She scowled and made her lower lip tremble. "Big bruvvers ought not kick uvver bruvvers."

"He knows you're not my brother," muttered Hodie.

Ogg'ward hadn't taken any notice, which was lucky. The rebel leader was peeling off his fingerless mittens. He shoved them in his pocket and clenched his hands into big fists—not hairy like Murgott's, but most men's weren't. "I am calm now," Ogg'ward said. "All follow me and say nothing."

There was a chitter from the luggage rack. The furry beret raised its tail and was again a dusty squirrel.

"The ugly thing must not stay here," said Ogg'ward. "Emperor's orders."

Sibilla hoisted her bag over her shoulder and scooped up the squirrel. It wiped its grimy face on hers. Murgott took it from her and popped it inside his jacket.

Ogg'ward poked his beanie out the door and looked about. "I must get us all to my apartment without fuss."

The rebel leader had his own apartment? Hodie was impressed.

"I must clean self up." Ogg'ward continued. "Then we discuss how to get rid of you two tagalongs and hideous animal." He stepped down to the wind-garage floor.

That didn't sound exactly friendly. Perhaps Hodie was very wrong to be impressed.

Sibilla jumped down after Ogg'ward, wiped her nose with her wrist, and sniffed loudly like a boy with no manners.

"Um...'scuse me, Mr. Rebel?" Her voice shook.

Ogg'ward looked as if he'd like to squash her with his foot. "A lady said the Emperor wanted his scientists to examine...um...Fontanian children. Um...do you know why?"

"You are safe, runny-nose boy." Ogg'ward clutched the red bag to his chest. "Scientists want to examine little Queen at age of twelve. Not ordinary child, not rag-tag oik such as you."

Sibilla paled and Hodie's heart jolted. With one bad choice after another, he had brought the little Queen into terrible danger.

"We must go quickly before we draw attention." Ogg'ward frowned down at Hodie. "Also, I warn you. Soon you meet your mother. I have no way to tell her you are coming." He strode off toward a big inner door. His boots echoed on the cavern floor.

Hodie stumbled after him. Behind them the buzzing and activity at the cavern door had grown louder. A mechanical groan made Hodie turn around. He was already so shaken that his eyes could hardly focus. Light through the opening door dazzled him too—but maybe he and Sibilla should dash toward it and try to escape...

The thought dwindled as a huge wind-truck covered in canvas entered slowly as if it carried precious cargo. He heard Sibilla give a little gasp. Hands to her heart, she stared at the truck as if she sensed what was inside.

The truck settled on the floor in the center of the garage. Officers and soldiers edged forward with rifles, pikes, swords at the ready. At an order from an officer, workers began to fold the canvas off the top and sides of the wind-truck. There, through stout iron bars, Hodie saw something moving, something alive, something that glowed like silver. He heard the softest chime, as if the wind breathed through silver leaves. It was—it had to be—a Dragon-eagle.

Hodie saw Sibilla take a step toward the truck, but her knees gave way. Corporal Murgott gathered her up. She was as floppy as a squirrel that had been squeezed.

# BAD CHOICE, BAD CHOICE,
# AND BAD CHOICE LEADS TO ...

Murgott, the little Queen in his arms (and the squirrel peering out up by his collar), kneed Hodie on after Ogg'ward, through the inner exit of the wind-garage. Dizzy, heart racing, Hodie realized he stood on a landing inside the cavern city. This was Um'Binnia.

Ogg'ward grabbed his arm and yanked him down a flight of steps. After two more flights they reached the street—how strange it was with the cave roof high overhead. Murgott set Sibilla on her feet, straightened her cap, and let her lean on his soldierly bulk.

Shops and houses were stacked against the cavern walls, and street stalls sold ice cream, second-hand clothes, and pickled cabbage. It was all chatter, clatter, rowdiness, the whirr of work and business, the clang of carriage bells. Some people strode about importantly in their best clothes. Various untidy ones loitered, picking on their friends and picking their (own) noses.

"We walk," Ogg'ward said. "Very long way."

"The boys can't walk, they're all worn out," growled Murgott. "Where is your heart?"

Ogg'ward thumped a fist onto his chest as if he had a sudden ache. "Do not question my heart, tagalong man. It is in right place and very big."

An open carriage pulled by an ogre was rattling past. Ogg'ward glared at Murgott and beckoned it to stop. He hustled Hodie up and into the front-facing seat. Murgott and Sibilla (and the squirrel) climbed in the other seat (which faced backwards).

"Take us to Imperial Palace." Ogg'ward had a hand on his mustache again. "At once. Be quiet. No fuss."

To the Palace? Hodie tried to pull away, but his arm was in Ogg'ward's tight grip.

The ogre adjusted the harness over his chest and set off. Here and there trolls carried packages, washed windows, or pasted up signs. A pair of dwarfs were digging a little trench next to a roadway. A smallish ogre sold pies at a street stall.

"So noble of you to travel in humble taxi-carriage." The ogre talked over his shoulder, not even puffing. "You are travelers? Big news. Yesterday the Great Prowdd'on return in triumph. We have not had bigger procession in Um'Binnia since last time!"

"But his daughter has been kidnapped." Ogg'ward sat up and clenched his fists. "The Emperor in good temper? You must be wrong."

"Oh, not in good temper," the ogre said. "In terrible rage. But still in triumph. War is declared. Why should we share Stones of Beyond? Why should we not own Beaches of Summerland? Soon pretty little Fontania will be under foot of Great Prowdd'on."

"His very big foot," muttered Hodie. He saw how pale Sibilla was. She must be terrified someone would see through her disguise. Murgott obviously thought so too because he gave the little Queen one of those shakes that is really a comforting hug. But Murgott himself looked gray and drawn. Hodie wished he had a way to help the Queen, but she was hardly an odd job where all he needed was a hammer, an oilcan, or a wrench. Besides round about now he would have rather liked a hug himself.

They rode through interlocking caverns. Ogg'ward kept his tweedy collar up, the beanie down. Several people looked curiously at Hodie and Sibilla. Most people stared at Murgott then quickly away. He was very off-putting—a balding ex-pirate who hadn't shaved and who looked as if he'd punch anyone who even blinked at the grimy blue-eyed boy on the seat beside him.

How long till they reached the Palace? It was hard for Hodie to breathe and only partly because of the stuffiness of the mountain city. He felt Murgott's boot give his a nudge. The Corporal's expression was as grim as ever but this time it included a wink.

"Brace yourself." He gave Hodie's knee a gentle pat—well, Murgott might have meant it to be a pat, but it was more like a huge dry animal falling on Hodie's leg. Actually, the pat jarred the wound on Hodie's calf—the one from the spikes on the Bridge of Teeth. Actually, his entire leg felt sore now.

The ogre had begun to puff and pant. "Nearly there," he said. "Almost at Imperial Palace…" There was a clunk, a pop, and his harness broke. "Oh, sorry. You must walk last steps to Supreme Door of Imperial Palace."

"Then no payment for ride that is too short." In one stride Ogg'ward was out of the carriage, dragging Hodie behind him. Hodie stumbled. Murgott helped Sibilla out and settled her cap again. The squirrel shook its fur and stretched its hind legs.

"Pay for nearly there?" the ogre said. "Be fair to ogres?"

"I could report you to Emperor," muttered Ogg'ward. "But all right—I give half dollero."

The ogre trudged off as quietly as anyone can when they're trundling a carriage.

"Ha," said Ogg'ward, "we are not going in Supreme Door anyway. We use small private door right here." He rummaged in a pocket and brought out a key.

How did the chief rebel come to have a key to the Supreme Palace? Hodie exchanged a worried look with Murgott. The Corporal's eyes had narrowed. Yet what choice did they have but to follow Ogg'ward?

Inside, there was just room for them all in a tiny foyer. Ogg'ward shut the door again and locked it from the inside. Then he shrugged off his heavy overcoat and hung it on a fancy hook. He pulled off his beanie and shook out his hair—it turned out to be black and ringletty like the Princessa's (though the ringlets were very much flattened). He undid a few buttons around his waistband, shook his trouser legs, and they billowed out to become a long skirt with straps and frills. Then he peeled off the furry mustache and cried, "Ouch!"

Ogg'ward, chief rebel, was Princessa Lu'nedda.

⁓

# CHOOSING HOW TO SAY HELLO

Hodie blinked several times, but the rebel really was Lu'nedda. Murgott let out a long quiet whistle. It looked as if Sibilla nearly curtsied, as she'd been taught when greeting another royal person. Luckily she turned it into a sniff and wiped her nose on the arm of her jacket. Luckily, too, the Princessa still didn't seem to have recognized Sibilla or the Corporal. Hodie blinked again and muttered to himself, *Please let it stay all right.*

The Princessa looked at the false mustache in her hand as if she didn't know what to do with it. Then she stuffed it deep in the red bag and began striding up the stairway.

Hodie's heart thudded. This might be when he met his mother. She might be at the top. He had no idea what he was going to say or what to expect. If she was Fontanian, she was a traitor. And his Um'Binnian father must be a spy. Why should this happen to him, to Hodie?

He trudged up more stairs. Well, he supposed one thing was that nobody could choose their parents—their mother or their father. If they turned out to be a spy, a traitor, or just a really bad parent, nobody could unchoose them either. But even if Hodie himself was safe with the mother he hadn't even known he had, would she and the Princessa toss Murgott and Sibilla into prison just because they were Fontanian?

Up another flight of stairs they hurried, along a narrow corridor, then up another flight of stairs. The bag bumped on Lu'nedda's back. Hodie still didn't know for sure if his mother's bag (or any other bag) was inside that bag, and (if it was) whether it would still hold the old cup, the long thin wrench, and the beads or pebbles (could they be jewels for hats or slippers?), or Murgott's notebook.

The little squirrel hoisted itself up step after step till Hodie lifted it and carried it in his arms. The wound on Hodie's leg beat like a drum. On a landing with an open window he stopped for air. There was no breeze at all, of course, just a whiff like last week's cooking and unwashed Um'Binnians (they smelled exactly as if they were unwashed Fontanians).

The stairs seemed to rise forever. The higher they climbed, the hotter it grew. Everything natural was crushed in this place. There was nothing to lift Hodie's heart and tug his mouth into a grin. He climbed and huffed and tried to catch glimpses into the work chambers as they passed. Absolutely everyone there, whether Um'Binnian, dwarf, ogre, or whatever else, looked frazzled and sweaty.

When Hodie glanced back he also saw drops of sweat among the freckles on Murgott's bald patch. The Corporal was helping Sibilla and carrying his duffel bag, which included that slipper he'd found back at the Depot. Would he hand it over to Lu'nedda? No—Murgott probably did plan to sell it or at least sell the emeralds and the mountain dove's chin-fluff.

Hodie was pleased that by now he was not thinking about his mother. Not at all. He wouldn't recognize her anyway. She would definitely not know him because she hadn't seen him since he was two or three. She hadn't wanted him. She'd sent him and his father away. Why should he want or need a mother now? Anyway, he wasn't thinking about her. He was just climbing, lugging a squirrel.

At last Lu'nedda's boots stopped clomping. She opened a door.

Murgott's big hand (sort of gently) shoved Hodie in.

~

It was a large chamber with a long couch under a window where pale light flickered from the street far below. There was a table and chairs and another soft couch. Hodie looked at everything—the cupboards and shelves, the yellow and blue rug on the floor, the lamps around the walls, anywhere except at the woman who stood up from a work table when they entered. At the same time, he could have described every detail about her from the tiny moment he saw her before he turned to everything else like the lamps and the table, the rug, the cupboards and shelves.

His mother was older than Lu'nedda, about the same age as Lady Helen. She was short. Her hair was curly and light brown. Her pleated green dress had a lacy collar and a bright green belt. She wore lacy half-mittens. Her stockings were green with yellow flowers, and her yellow shoes had tiny green heels. She wasn't smiling, but Hodie knew that when she did the smile went crooked as if she had so much to tell you that the words crowded on her tongue to be first out. Her gray eyes stared at him. She hadn't glanced once at Sibilla or Murgott. Hodie knew that even though his mother hadn't seen him since he was so small his head kept bumping the corner of the table, she knew exactly who he was.

At last he made himself look at her properly. She had her head a little to one side. Her lips had parted. One hand still held a pot of glue, the other a hat with jeweled butterflies clustering around the brim. The squirrel clambered on the bench beside her and pawed a knife. She glanced away from Hodie as if it hurt her eyes to do so and held the squirrel steady. Just like a mother with a squirming child. She looked back at Hodie.

"Lu'nedda?" said his mother in a husky voice. "Who… who is this boy?"

The Princessa slung her coat and red bag over a chair and wriggled a hand as if she had a sticky insect on her fingers. "Good morning, Allana. I promised to bring news of your boy. Maybe this is better—maybe not. Instead of news, I bring your boy himself."

Allana—Hodie's mother—steadied herself against the table then took a step toward him. Her hands came up, her arms started to reach out. Hodie stepped back and kept his arms tight at his sides.

Silence. But he could tell that everyone had a hundred things they'd like to say.

The Princessa sat down, thrust her hands into her black ringlets, and gave them a tug. They didn't come off so they weren't false like the mustache. Sibilla was leaning on Murgott again. The Corporal eased her onto a chair beside the one where Lu'nedda had slung the bag. Sibilla brushed her eyes with a hand and gave a shiver.

Lu'nedda spoke into the silence. "I recognize your boy on last day in Fontania. He has lived like lowest servant."

His mother had started trembling. The silence continued. Maybe it was up to Hodie. He gave a little nod at his mother. He cleared his throat.

"Hello." (The first word had to be something.) "I hope you are well." (The first sentence had to be something too.) "I didn't think I remembered you at all."

"But you do remember," said the woman—Allana—his mother. She was still trembling. Hodie had expected he would shake too, but not even his voice had wobbled when he spoke. He wasn't going to say anything else, though. Not a word. Not till his mother explained why she'd sent him and Dardy away for so many years, and they'd had to wear ragged clothes and live in a lean-to while in the Imperial Palace of Um'Binnia she wore pretty yellow shoes and lacy mittens. And he wasn't going to ask where Dardy was.

There was another silence except for Murgott shuffling his boots and a *tck-tck* from the squirrel.

"Well!" Sibilla gave a wavery smile, which was pretty funny with her face so grubby underneath that boy's cap—if you had time for a chuckle and, very strangely, Hodie felt one bump into his throat. She stood up and crossed her legs.

"Please, do you 'ave a bathroom? It's been hours."

"Good idea." The Princessa pointed to a door.

"Fank you." Sibilla went in and closed it. Murgott gave a polite cough and sort of propped himself against the wall near the bathroom with his eyes closed.

Hodie's mother fumbled for the chair behind her and sat down as if her yellow shoes would not do the job of holding her steady any longer. "My boy," she whispered, still staring at him.

"They call him Hodie." Lu'nedda's voice was gruff and choked. "When I recognize him, I am not exactly sure that I am right. I find where he sleep to have good look at him. I tuck him in tight. Then your boy turn up again in huge gale at Shattered Rock. What else can I do but bring him to you?"

Hodie's mother didn't move. It looked as if she was trying hard to work out what Lu'nedda had said. "He was at the Grand Palace? A servant?"

Lu'nedda continued. "Indeed. Gree'sle followed me to your boy's hut. That hut is only place in whole Grand Palace where skinny Gree'sle and his officers had not thought to search. It take one minute to look at everything the boy has—he does not have much. Gree'sle grab old bag off hook and sneak it away. When we are starting to hurry home, he show bag to my father, and my father is very pleased with him indeed. So when I pretend to be kidnapped, I decide to sneak bag away myself. It will show my father that Gree'sle is not so clever after all. Allana, look inside. What do you think?" Lu'nedda reached out and patted the red bag.

Hodie's mother gave the squirrel's neck a last rub—Hodie could tell it was in love with her by now—and walked over to the bag. She pulled out the slipper the rebels had argued about and set it on the floor. She reached in again and pulled out the drawstring bag (the false mustache was sort of hitched up on the string, most likely because of its glue). Her shoulders seemed to slump the least little bit.

"It is right one?" Lu'nedda asked.

Allana—Hodie's mother—straightened her shoulders. She eased the top of the old bag open, peered in, and seemed puzzled. "I don't remember a book…but it's been a long time." Fingers shaking, she tightened the drawstring again, and Hodie saw the mustache end up caught inside. "I have to get over one shock before I can begin to think about another."

"Best friends should not lie to each other," said the Princessa.

Hodie's mother rested the bag on her work table. She sat down, folded her hands, and spoke in a soft but firm voice. "Years ago, Lu'nedda, you were a child and I was a young woman new to Um'Binnia. You needed a friend very badly. But you always knew my wish was to return to Fontania one day. When I had my little boy, you knew I still hoped to return home. I never lied to you. I just kept a promise and a secret for another very dear friend." She glanced up. "Lu'nedda, this very minute I cannot swear that the bag holds what your father—and other people—have been searching for."

Lu'nedda clapped her hands together. "Anyway, I have

no time for chatter about trinkets. I have had a big adventure. My father thinks I am in great danger. He must be very worried. Yes?"

"Oh…yes, he must," said Hodie's mother. But Hodie heard her tone really say, *Good grief, poor silly girl, do you really expect him to have changed?*

Lu'nedda's ringlets quivered. "My father will be very pleased to see me, especially when I take stolen bag to him. He will not suspect that I myself have become chief rebel."

Murgott's eyes were still closed, but Hodie thought his ears were working overtime. Hodie knew the feeling—his own were working double-overtime.

Allana didn't look at Hodie, though he could see she almost did. "What made Gree'sle so sure this is the bag?"

"First, why else is it in hut with your boy?" Lu'nedda said. "Answer, because Dardy always obeyed your orders and waited for you. Second, I look inside and signs say to me, maybe this is right bag, but only maybe. Third, I will give bag to my father, which will make him pleased with me and angry with Gree'sle, so I do not care if it is right bag or not. But my father will order scientists to work hard. They will examine bag and say if The Ties of Fontania are here. If they are, very good. If they are not, Gree'sle will be in big trouble and I will not have to keep promise to marry him."

Hodie felt as if something hit him several times under the chin. The Ties of Fontania. The missing Ties, in that shabby old bag? Under his bed for years, gathering cobwebs? Why would his mother ever have had The Ties?

His mother must be a spy too—but what sort of spies could his parents be (besides obviously not being very good ones)?

"Please, Lu'nedda." Allana's voice was huskier now. "Don't tell your father yet. Wait till I can think, look again, and try to remember."

The Princessa shrugged and pressed a button on the wall. The apartment door opened. Two ogres lumbered in.

Lu'nedda pointed at Murgott. "Handcuffs for that one."

"Oi!" said Murgott, but an ogre clamped a hand over his big mouth. The second ogre grabbed Murgott's wrists and manacled them behind his back.

"We should have clapped earmuffs on him too!" Lu'nedda said.

Murgott wrested his head away from the ogre's hand. "I heard every word, ma'am. But I understood none."

If Hodie believed that, he would also believe that the White Squirrel slipped half a dollero in your shoe each time you lost one of your teeth.

Allana looked very tense. One of her hands, hidden from Lu'nedda, gestured to Hodie: *Wait, please wait.* He didn't want to do anything she asked, but there wasn't much choice. At least she'd got over wanting to hug him.

Lu'nedda clicked her fingers. The ogres saluted. "Find out where my father is. Tell him I am safely home. He will want happy reunion in Great Throne Room."

One of the ogres bowed and left the apartment. Murgott growled but the huge hand of the other ogre muffled him again.

"One more yell and you are in prison," Lu'nedda said.

The ogre slowly took his hand away. Murgott twisted his head and rubbed his mouth on the shoulder of his jacket. "Princessa, you don't need to cuff me. I used to be a pirate. Such men are usually bought easily."

"If that is true or not, why should I trust you?" snapped the Princessa. "No more than I would trust deserter from Fontanian Army! Yes, I recognize you all along, Corporal Murgott. You desert your army and travel with such ragamuffin boys."

Murgott looked pleased and aghast all at once. It was a comical expression, though Hodie didn't dare laugh. He had to think fast. Lu'nedda still hadn't recognized Sibilla— the little Queen must escape from Um'Binnia as soon she could.

"Princessa, you can trust Murgott," Hodie said. "Um... he's admired you since he first saw you. He wrote a poem the third day you were at the Grand Palace. I sneaked a look."

A blush spread over Lu'nedda's face. She seemed really pretty for a moment. Murgott blushed too and even he looked rather sweet, though upset that Hodie should have read his notebook.

"Besides, pirates always side with the winner, and you've definitely won," Hodie continued.

Lu'nedda nodded at the ogre. There was a click as the manacles came off the Corporal.

Hodie's leg was hurting—not much, but it still made a good excuse. He needed to say something only Murgott would hear. He let himself slide sort of sideways and leaned on Murgott. His mother was watching, but he avoided her gaze. "My leg's sore," he said quietly to the Corporal. "But I really want to say, I trust you." It was actually true.

"I haven't been the nicest of men to you, boy." Something like kindness showed in Murgott's eyes.

Hodie's own eyes hadn't worked properly for hours, not since he'd seen the sketch on the napkin in the canteen. But the sketch was right—the drawstring bag had been in Ogg'ward's bag. Now it lay on his mother's table within Hodie's reach and was supposed to hold The Ties.

Allana stood up as if she was going to come and see if Hodie was all right.

"And we're the only ones who can save the Queen," he whispered quickly to Murgott. "And maybe save magic. If magic exists. Of course it doesn't, and the Queen doesn't think so either."

"I've seen it at work, boy. The Queen is on the brink of it. I'll believe in it for you as well as me. Now," Murgott said. "Think tactics. Tactics is a recipe for success. I want you to faint."

Hodie kept his head turned away from his mother. "My leg got sliced on the Bridge of Teeth."

"Good," muttered Murgott, "if you understand me. It will mean the ladies don't take too much notice of you-know-who still in the bathroom. And it will take the ladies' minds right off that bag."

All of a sudden he grabbed Hodie's shoulders. "Shiver me timbers! The boy's collapsing."

So, tactics at work. Hodie let himself slide out of Murgott's hands and down to the floor. His mother rushed to his side.

"Good lad," he heard Murgott mutter.

# CHOOSING A SUITABLE
# REAR END

Murgott lugged Hodie to the sofa and laid him flat. "What's this? Look at the boy's leg! Disinfectant! Bandages!"

Eyes shut, Hodie heard Allana knock on the bathroom door.

"I haven't finished yet!" shouted Sibilla like a cross little boy.

Allana ordered an ogre to fetch a medical kit.

"He should'a told me earlier about this cut," grumbled the Corporal, mopping gently at Hodie's calf. "But I've seen worse things by far at sea. I've seen worse things in a kitchen too."

Hodie felt someone with slim fingers—his mother—take his boots off and make angry exclamations about how full of holes they were. Well, whose fault was that?

"Listen," hissed Murgott in his ear. "What you heard about The Ties—do not mention it to the Queen unless you're absolutely sure not a soul can overhear. She might do something reckless. I'd make bets on it. Orright?"

Hodie nodded. He heard the bathroom door at last and opened his eyes. His mother, looking ferocious, was hovering about with a bandage. Sibilla—cleaner in the face and with her cap on tight—peered down at his leg.

"Yucky! Blood!" she said with a small boy's relish.

Hodie's mother and Murgott finished bandaging his leg. He did feel better after lying down. He refused to meet his mother's eyes, though, and eventually she sat back at her work table, hand on her forehead. Murgott went and spoke quietly with her. She'd be trying to tell Murgott she wasn't a spy. Lu'nedda went for her turn in the bathroom, probably scrubbing off the remains of glue from the false mustache.

Sibilla took her own bag into a corner and rummaged out the bits of Jasper's bird. She fitted part of it together, frowned, and showed Hodie.

"Borrow Murgott's pocketknife," he whispered.

With the little screwdriver and pliers, he and Sibilla worked out where to put a tiny metal coil, and the bird's head fitted like…no, that didn't work. The squirrel crept over. It nudged a silver coil with a paw, then a silver screw, a golden nut, a tiny bolt, three small shards of dark red stone—jasper, like the King's name—that went where a real bird would have its heart. Whenever Sibilla touched the bird, the metal felt almost alive in Hodie's grasp. It was just her warm hands, of course. Nothing magic.

He still refused to even look in Allana's direction. She hugged her arms around herself, and stood out on a little balcony, her back to the room.

At last Sibilla held the bird up, back together except for

tail feathers. "It can't fly without some," she murmured.

The squirrel *tck-tcked* then turned its back and fluffed its tail.

"Good idea," said Hodie.

With a pair of Allana's scissors, Sibilla snipped three of the least ragged strands from the squirrel's tail and held them to the metal bird's rear end. A lot less than perfect. But with a dab of Allana's glue the strands held firm. Sibilla ferreted through the bits and pieces on the work table and found three small green feathers to add to the rear attachment.

Allana came back in when Lu'nedda returned from the bathroom, ringlets bouncing. "Children playing so nicely," Lu'nedda said. "It is good for child to have friend. I never had friend till I was ten." She smiled at Allana, who smiled back as if it was something of a strain.

Sibilla crept behind the sofa and Hodie heard her whisper to the bird. "Jasper, Prowdd'on has the Dragon-eagle. I saw it. I think that's why he left Fontania so fast. I'm in Um'Binnia…" Her head popped up near Hodie's. "How will the bird get out of here?" she whispered.

"Keep it hidden till we find a way," he whispered back.

Murgott's eye was on him and Hodie remembered he had promised not to tell the Queen about The Ties. But, if he had a chance, he could whisper to the bird himself. King Jasper ought to know.

The Princessa was saying something to his mother. "Your boy must have new boots. Fine leather boots."

Hodie grabbed his battered ones and shoved his feet in.

"I've got these!" He stood up but the string around the soles fell apart at his first step.

"We can argue later," his mother said to him. "We both need time." She sounded very much like Lady Helen talking to her children. Maybe all mothers sounded like that. "The children need food. Lu'nedda, you too. Lunch time."

There was no point in a Queen not eating. No point in Hodie starving, either. Lunch was a small choice but a good one to make right now.

—

# WHAT TO SAY OR NOT
# ABOUT THAT MUSTACHE

Hodie sat at the table in his holey socks, a plate of scrambled eggs steaming in front of him. He screwed up his nose. Allana took his fork—did she want to feed him? He grabbed it back, tested the eggs, and decided that once you got used to it, warm food was fairly nice. The others were eating scrambled eggs as well. Murgott pushed his about as if he would have done a better job of cooking them.

What was going to happen next? Where was his father? And, at the right moment, Hodie or Murgott had to tell Sibilla what the Um'Binnians thought was in the bag. Not now because his mother watched him across the table. She'd been worried about his leg—it had felt strange to see that, actually, and Hodie wasn't sure if he liked it or not. Anyway, she was still a traitor. And a spy. But how nice it would be to have a moment with a normal mother and say, "Have you heard from Dad lately? How is he doing?" or, "I finally figured out how to use a hacksaw," and other normal things that Hodie had heard families (even royal ones) chat about.

Lu'nedda finished her lunch and rushed into another room where there was plenty of rustling. Hodie saw a red high-heeled boot roll across the floor, several hats, an orange net petticoat with layers of ribbons.

From where Hodie sat he could also see the old bag, still on the work table. The missing Ties? What a laugh. A battered cup, moldy old beads, and a useful wrench.

As he stared at it, frowning, the bag twitched. Hodie blinked. Then, through the closed drawstring, something black and whiskery appeared. It was the fake mustache! Hodie blinked again. It crept out like a slow, medium-sized guinea pig then crawled down the table leg and away under a cupboard. Hodie put a hand over his eyes—he must be suffering from travel weariness and too many shocks.

He looked up again at the sound of more rustling. Lu'nedda appeared in a very big blue and pink Um'Binnian frock. She wore a top hat made of pink net stuff and pink fingerless mittens. Her blue boots had sparkly laces (maybe with sapphires), and her stockings had a sequin stripe. Hodie heard Murgott take in a breath as if he was about to sneeze (though more likely it was another poem coming on).

Lu'nedda looked determined and excited. She clapped her hands once. An ogre entered. "I am ready for reunion with my father, Great Prowdd'on. My father knows I am back and safe and well? My father wait for his daughter, Princessa Lu'nedda?"

The ogre looked as if he braved a sudden stomach pain. "Princessa, I try before lunch to tell him you are here. Gree'sle say Emperor is not to be bother."

"Hmmm." Lu'nedda gave a tight smile. "The Emperor has great city to control and war to fight. He is supremely busy."

The ogre bowed. "Princessa, Emperor has gone to Great Zoo. To open magnificent new cage. Biggest cage yet."

The Princessa looked pleased and even more determined. "I will go there unexpectedly and overjoy him in front of crowd. I will announce what I have brought for him. He will be excited and in great expectation. He will think I risk my life to get dear father what heart desires."

Hodie's mother didn't look as if she agreed, but Lu'nedda smoothed her fingers in the lacy pink mittens. "Now, my only friend must come with me. And her son, who now lives with us. Get boy ready, Allana, and yourself." She looked at Murgott and Sibilla (in her cap) and made a face. "Bother. How to keep eye on tagalongs? They must come too. But little boy must take cap off when he sees Prowdd'on."

"Y'know what kids are like, ma'am." Murgott touched his forehead in a little salute. "Lay a finger on that cap and he throws a first-rate tantrum."

Sibilla looked slightly shocked then very pleased.

"In that case, keep nasty little boy well under thumb and out of sight." Lu'nedda rearranged the flounces on her skirt and admired her own boots.

Hodie's mother came to help him off the chair. He didn't need help. He didn't want her to touch him. Her hands were gentle, her scent warm as he remembered, like a flower. He shrugged her away. His leg only hurt a little bit. So he should be able to get away to help Murgott get Sibilla out of Um'Binnia.

"We might be wise to dress both boys as Um'Binnian, Lu'nedda," said Hodie's mother. "And there is a chance that Gree'sle could recognize Murgott."

"Gree'sle—*ugh!*" Lu'nedda said. "Disguise. Useful idea."

Allana considered Sibilla. "We could disguise you as a girl. Now your face is cleaner, it could work well."

"Yuck! A girl!" Sibilla made a strangling sound as if she was going to throw up.

Murgott's face had gone sweaty again. Hodie had gone sweaty too. "Tantrum," Murgott said. "That's just the first stage."

Lu'nedda tossed a narrow-brimmed Um'Binnian hat at Murgott and gave him a brown cloak. She gave Hodie a cap and cloaks to Sibilla and Hodie, dark green ones that came halfway down Hodie's calves but reached Sibilla's ankles.

An ogre fetched Hodie new socks and a pair of brown boots with studs and ankle straps. Far better than Murgott's best ones. Hodie found himself stroking the leather and wiggling his toes to settle them in. Then he noticed Murgott noticing and he stopped.

Lu'nedda threw a dark blue cape around her shoulders and buttoned it over her bright dress. "I am in disguise too, till I am revealed. Now come," said the Princessa. "Allana, put cape on, and off we go to Great Zoo."

"No," Hodie said, sweating like mad. "I have to leave the city now. This other boy and Murgott must come too. Thank you for the boots. And cloaks. Thank you for lunch," he added.

"Leave…" Hodie's mother took a step toward him,

then stopped with her hands in a double fist. "Leave the city?" She exchanged a glance with the Princessa. "Oh, Hodie—even if you could get out, there is only the mountain and the Great Salt Moat. Nobody can swim the Great Salt Moat."

"I'm not frightened of the ocean." Hodie looked right at his mother. Deep in her eyes he saw a flicker of something that surprised him and made him feel warm—a flicker that meant she was proud of him. This was a good moment about his mother. It would probably be the only one.

"But the Toads," Murgott said, "the Ocean Toads…"

"Shut up." Lu'nedda glared at Hodie, threw the apartment door open, then marched back to the work table. "I must make sure Gree'sle cannot sneak and notice this." She slung the drawstring bag into a small cabinet, turned a tiny key on it, and dropped the key in her handbag. She marched to the door again and waited, blue boot tapping.

The others crowded to the door. Hodie tested a few paces in his boots then caught up with Sibilla. She carried her bag with the bird in it. "How are your blisters?" he whispered.

"They've all popped," she muttered. "Very gooey."

It didn't take as long going down as it had coming up, but stairs were like that. The squirrel hopped between them like a mangy gray ghost. Why had it adopted them? Or had they adopted it? Some questions, Hodie knew, just couldn't be answered.

‿

# HOW TO TRAVEL
# TO THE ZOO

Hodie expected them to hire another ogre carriage. Instead Lu'nedda waved a hand and two low-slung cycle-chairs rolled up, pedaled by dwarfs.

"Keep heads down," said Lu'nedda. "And cloak collar up as if we do not like bad city-smell."

"I certainly don't," muttered Sibilla.

Lu'nedda frowned. "Do not attract attention. Surprise, that is what I am after. Happy surprise for Great Prowdd'on and bad surprise for Gree'sle. Allana—take a happy-family moment with your boy."

She hauled Sibilla with her into a cycle-chair. Sibilla gave Hodie and Murgott a horrified glance and clamped a hand tight to her cap. Hodie's mother hesitated. Murgott eyed her then Hodie and scooped the squirrel with him into the Princessa's cycle-chair. Sibilla blinked with relief. But it left Hodie and his mother on their own.

~

Hodie pretended he was too busy looking at the city to

look at Allana. He leaned out, cloak over his nose. The bad smells were ripe. The cycle-chair rolled past stalls that sold handbags, scarves, and cheap toys that would break as soon as the shopkeeper had your dolleros. If you had any dolleros in the first place. Hodie didn't and never had, which was in large part because of his mother. He didn't count those dolleros from Murgott because he'd only had them for minutes before they fell down the pulley tower along with the pie, lemon cordial, and whiffy blanket.

The cycle-chair with Sibilla trundled ahead. Hodie gave a small wave, but she didn't see. Bag on her lap, she was peering up each flight of stairs. Seeking a way out for the bird, of course. She'd better not let it go in public—it would definitely draw attention.

Hodie sat back. That meant his shoulder touched his mother's. It felt as if a current rippled through him. He made himself as narrow as he could.

His mother stirred and cleared her throat. "Your name isn't really Hodie," she said. "It's Ro'lan…"

"My name is Hodie. Only Hodie."

"I know you're angry. Of course you are. I understand." His mother clasped her hands tight on her lap.

"More probably you don't." He sounded like any ordinary boy grumbling at any mother, but it was hardly another good moment.

"There were many reasons why you and I could not be together."

"Dardy and I lived like nobodies," Hodie said. "But you lived with a Princessa. I'm not sorry for myself—well, sometimes I am, but I try to get over it. I'm sorry for you. And sorry for my father. He might be a spy too, but he wasn't happy very often."

"A spy?" His mother cleared her throat again. "Hodie, you have every right to be furious with me. But why with your father? And—a spy! No, Hodie…"

He made the first sound of an angry sentence, then stopped. "I didn't say I was furious. I said I was sorry. And I don't understand why you're a spy."

His mother's voice shook. "I'm not a… Hodie, I don't have much time to explain. Listen, please. When Lady Gall began ruling Fontania, Lady Helen was very worried. She knew how wicked, how selfish Lady Gall was, and she decided it was best to hide all the royal treasures so that Lady Gall couldn't get her hands on them—she would have tried to use them wrongly or even destroyed them. I promised Lady Helen that I would take The Ties and…"

"But…" Hodie began.

"Hush." His mother glanced at the cycle-chair dwarf. "Excuse me," she called, "could you entertain us by singing the latest hit?"

The dwarf groaned but broke into a hum. Allana talked under cover of the tune. "Without The Ties, the Dragon-eagles won't survive…"

"I know that's what people think," whispered Hodie. "But even if they are so important, why did you have to do anything? Why were you the one who had to hide them? You should have said no."

"I was Lady Helen's Chief Attendant…"

"She ordered you to do it?"

"Shush—I was at school with her. She's my dear friend ..." His mother looked into Hodie's eyes. In her eyes he saw feelings jostling to fly out. "I had to help for the sake of magic. For the sake of Lady Helen's little son. I didn't have a child of my own then, nor a husband. I just had a loving friend, Lady Helen, who needed help."

The dwarf sang. *The Emperor's arms are very wi-iide, Stretching from the imperial si-iide...*

The cycle-chair jolted up a ramp to the next street. Like any mother, Allana reached out to stop Hodie knocking his head. He pulled away.

His mother whispered urgently. "Hodie, I decided on my own to bring The Ties to Um'Binnia. It seemed the most unlikely place. Such a bad choice! But I met the Princessa. What a sad child she was—no mother, everyone too afraid to be her friend. I also met your father—we married and had you—and still I kept The Ties safely hidden. Your father..." Her hands folded together as if she held something precious like a memory. "I could have told him about The Ties, but I kept my promise to Lady Helen."

Hodie still didn't understand. His mother's hand came over his.

"Your father was the first inventor of wind-travel. He was brave, kind, and clever. I miss him still."

Why didn't she just say where Dardy was? Mothers were maddening.

She choked back a sigh and spoke more quickly. "When Fontania was saved from Lady Gall, I was free to go back home. But it had to be in secret. I had said so often how much I loved living in Um'Binnia—well, I had to say that. So people would have asked very awkward questions. And everyone, everywhere, was wondering what had happened to the Fontanian treasures. If Prowdd'on had ever realized I had The Ties, he'd have taken them—he'd been wanting them for years out of sheer greed." She glanced again at the dwarf then continued. "My mistake was going at the last minute to say goodbye to Lu'nedda—she was still only sixteen and very upset. Gree'sle overheard. He suspected I might have The Ties and stopped me from leaving with Dardy and you."

The dwarf sang loudly... *teeth are glittering and bi-iig, All his own hair but looks magnificent in wi-iig...*

Allana whispered. "Dardy, in his turn, overheard Gree'sle calling the guards—I broke away for just a moment and cried out to Dardy to escape with you and not give the bag to anyone—to wait for me to join him. Then I was trapped. I didn't know how to send Dardy a message, and I didn't hear from him at all. I knew Fontania did not have The Ties, and I thought he and you had died—on the Moat or in the Stones."

His mother's face was too full of sorrow for Hodie to look at. She was still whispering and sounded exhausted. "I'll examine the bag again when Lu'nedda isn't watching. If it is the right one, I must find a way to send it to King Jasper. Perhaps Corporal Murgott could do it."

So many thoughts jangled in Hodie's brain. "There must be a mistake. The stuff in the bag looks like old junk.

Why didn't my father just show someone who could explain?"

Allana's head jerked up. "Your father! No, Hodie—how do I tell you? Dardy isn't your father. Dardy is Fontanian. He was my servant."

The awful thing was that Hodie knew at once this was the truth.

The dwarf sang on. *Great Prowdd'on's smiles are very ki-iind, When he punish you, you mustn't mi-iind...*

Allana kept her voice low. "If only I'd told Dardy to give the bag to Lady Helen—he had no way of knowing it contained the royal treasures. I only learned a few months ago that he was alive. Gree'sle's men discovered him and had him dragged back to Um'Binnia. Poor Dardy—now he's forced to tend the Ocean Toads. Their poison will kill him. He must realize by now about The Ties, but I don't think he has told the Emperor. I have not been not allowed to speak to him. Gree'sle watches me all the time..." She brushed a hand over her eyes. "But I was telling you about your father. Your father was Lord Fer'nan of Um'Binnia— so brave, so clever. Oh, my son, you look very like him. He died in a wind-travel experiment two years after you were born—before Lady Gall was defeated."

Hodie bowed his head into his hands. All he could think was that his father the lord might have been brave, but he definitely could not have been all that clever.

"My darling..." His mother stopped as if she wanted to taste that word. "Hodie," she continued, "I have missed you every day with all my heart."

He had to look up. Her face was so strained, her eyes

full of distress. All this was because of the bag that had been lying under his bed for about nine years? He didn't want to have been that close to anything magic. But no— even if magic was real, surely it would seep away, just as water evaporated and biscuits grew stale. Then he remembered Lu'nedda's false mustache, in the bag for only an hour. Could magic seep into things nearby? Perhaps the mustache really had transformed into a rodent. Hodie's heart juddered.

His mother put a soft hand on his again. "If you see Dardy at the Zoo, please do not speak to him. But Hodie, whatever happens, wherever The Ties are, they must go to King Jasper and his sister the little Queen. The Ties, and what they mean to magic, are more important than—" her voice choked—"than my son…" She hunched over as if an overwhelming pain had stricken her.

The cycle-chair bumped to a stop. *Prow-wow wow!* sang the dwarf. "End of journey. Extra charge for having to sing hit tune."

Ahead was the entrance to a cavern where a notice said: *Grand Zoological Park of the Great Prowdd'on. Creatures large and small. Praise and admire.*

Underneath was a notice saying: *Magnificent New Attraction Opening Now.*

—

## WHERE AND HOW TO HIDE
## IN THE GRAND ZOO

Hodie's brain juddered just like his heart. His mother was tangled up in huge secrets about Fontania and magic, and that was why his family had been torn apart. How could she! And Dardy was not his father? How dare Dardy fool him about that!

"Come on," said his mother (the dwarf was looking very pleased with what she'd paid him). "Climb out. Look normal. Blend in."

Allana sounded very much like a normal mother. But Hodie doubted he could pretend to be normal when he had so much to think about. Though, actually, he was the son of the best friend of the Princessa. Actually again, when you wore such excellent boots you should try a swagger. He experimented but found it hard to walk at all as well as think.

"Act normally, I said!" his mother hissed. She'd got over her terrible grief, although perhaps she was simply a good actor.

The Zoo had notices at every corner as well as between

them. *Thanks to Great Prowdd'on for imperial generosity in providing very large facility and huge public garden to people of Um'Binnia. Praise and admire.* All of them had the sign of a sunburst and a purple crown.

"That's stupid. There's no sun inside this city," muttered Hodie.

"It's the sign of the Emperor," said his mother in a flat tone. "He thought it up himself. It shows how wonderful he is, how regal and dazzling." The side of her mouth twitched, as if she would laugh if she were allowed.

Maybe he could quite like her, if things were different. Maybe most mothers could be difficult to figure out.

Hodie tried another small swagger. Allana frowned. She stayed close by him as they walked on into the Zoo behind Lu'nedda, Murgott (squirrel peering through the buttons of his cloak), and Sibilla, who kicked at things like a very normal boy. She was certainly a good actor. Hodie decided not to kick things in case it ruined his new brown boots.

Knots of people dressed in hats and gloves, tight trousers and pointy toe shoes (men), or long tight skirts and frilly dresses (women) lingered near the sunburst notices. When anyone passed, they said loudly how impressed they were by Emperor Prowdd'on and how they were looking forward to the great unveiling. More quietly, they mumbled about how tough times were, how hard it had become to make a dollero. They didn't seem at all interested in the few potted plants dotted about, yellow and limp (these were the great public gardens?). They didn't seem the least interested in the nearby cages of striped lions and spotted bears.

The animals seemed well treated, if being in a cage at all was any good. Which sometimes it might be, if the animal would be hurt out in the open or needed treatment of some sort. Hodie remembered the elephant at the Grand Palace. His father—he meant Dardy—used to coax it to lie down to have its teeth cleaned. Dardy had explained that in an elephant new teeth grew at the back then moved gradually along till they reached the front. By then they were all worn down and fell out. It seemed a sensible idea. The elephant had loved Dardy. The chickens had liked him too. So had the horses, the dogs, the Grand Palace cats, the pair of squirrels... A homesick sob leaped into Hodie's throat, but he made it sound like a normal cough.

He was very conscious of the bag back in that cupboard. If he simply told the Emperor about it, would Prowdd'on set his mother and Sibilla—and Dardy—free? No—when Prowdd'on saw the rubbish in the bag, they'd be in worse trouble. It looked to Hodie as if Dardy might be the only one to know where the real Ties were hidden. After all, in a single glance his mother would have seen that the bag didn't hold any ropes or Dragon-eagle harness. But what if the actual Ties were not gold ropes or harnesses? The rubbish in the bag might really be The Ties.

An awful thought made Hodie stop walking. He had been closest to the stuff for nearly ten years. He'd traveled with it across the Stones of Beyond when he was little, then the bag had been kept under his bed. If magic seeped out... No. It was only royal children who were supposed to develop magical ability. Hodie didn't believe in magic anyway. All he had to worry about was finding out exactly what the stuff was. Perhaps The Ties were in the bag but invisible—but that would mean magic was real—but then, that mustache…

It was far too tricky to think about right now.

Hodie walked on in the new brown boots. It couldn't hurt to have another day or so being the son of the best friend of the Princessa—son of Lady Allana and the inventor of wind-travel, Lord Fer'nan of Um'Binnia.

~

Back at the main gate a halfhearted cheer rose up. A group of school children, with teachers and parent helpers, had lined up either side of the big entrance. They didn't look at all excited. They didn't even stare about like children usually did (Fontanian children at any rate). They just waited, glum, holding folded purple and gold flags in their hands.

They cheered again, quarterhearted. Lu'nedda tugged her collar over her chin. Allana pulled Hodie into shadow along with Murgott and Sibilla. By now the squirrel was half hidden beneath Sibilla's cloak—she looked like a boy with a fake tatty tail.

A trumpet sounded a long echoing note that hurt Hodie's ears. A troop of soldiers marched in, bayonets on their rifles. Why? Because the Emperor thought he was in danger? From the rebels? Clearly the Emperor didn't know his own daughter was the chief rebel—though was that mostly to make her father upset that she'd been kidnapped? Honestly, thought Hodie, why try to please a dad like Prowdd'on?

The lights became a blinding dazzle. In rolled a mechanical carriage. A driver and Commander Gree'sle sat in the front. In a high back seat like a throne sat the Great Prowdd'on. Today his mustache was waxed into three twirly circles on each side. He wore a purple hat and waved big purple gloves in a gracious manner. The teachers prodded the children. The children unfolded their flags, dangled them, and began a ragged sort of chant: "Thank you, Great Prowdd'on! Thanks for this exciting public facility."

The chant didn't sound at all excited, and some of the children found it hard to say facility (not to mention it being awfully spitty). But Prowdd'on waved and smiled wider. The trumpet played a phrase from the latest hit, *Prow-wow-wow.*

The Princessa clenched her jaw and scowled at Gree'sle.

"Drive on!" cried the Great Prowdd'on. The carriage motored into the Zoo. Everyone trailed along in the dreadful smell from its back end. Hodie gave a long real cough. The children's flags and banners drooped to the ground. The teachers scolded them. Some held the banners higher for a moment (but not many).

Allana touched the Princessa's arm, stood on tiptoe, and murmured, "This is a bad idea, Lu'nedda. Your father's busy."

"You would think he had more concern for missing daughter." Lu'nedda sounded just like Ogg'ward. "Maybe he pretends while his heart breaks." She found a handkerchief and blew her nose (*a-hriiiiiff, a-hriiiiff*).

Hodie didn't let on that he'd heard what she said or the angry nose-blowing. The little Queen scooped up the squirrel, gave it to Murgott, and took a step after the school children.

"Stay here," rumbled Murgott.

Sibilla shook her head. "Murgott, please stay out of sight." Her voice trembled but something steely came into it as she continued. "The Commander might recognize you. I want to see this for myself. I think I know what it must be. Hodie…" She grabbed his hand. "Please behave like a big brother for another few minutes."

He didn't want to, but what could he do? Sibilla's hand was sweaty. His probably was too.

They hurried along in as many shadows as they could find. One of the children's flags had dropped off its stick. Hodie picked it up. If someone realized there were two extra boys, it might help their disguise.

Almost running now, Hodie and the Queen entered a cavern with cages full of small ugly animals (dark blue part-bald rats and a miniature rhinoceros with horns on its shoulders as well as its nose) and a cavern with large ugly animals (hippo-geese, too awful to look at. How could anyone find words to describe their horny orange webbed feet as big as drain covers and their beaks with yellowy teeth like cracked tent pegs?).

Hodie stopped and held Sibilla's hand tight so she had to stop too. At the far end of this cavern waited the carriage. Prowdd'on was standing up in it. Behind him a heavy purple curtain draped from the cave ceiling to the floor. In front of him waited the school children and all the men and women in fancy best clothes. Commander Gree'sle held a little mirror for the Emperor. Prowdd'on patted his circly mustache.

At last Prowdd'on turned to the crowd. His voice boomed out. "I have taken most precious creature of Fontania. Today, in this cage—" trumpets sounded long and loud—"huge Dragon-eagle!" He tipped his head, smiling, and folded his hands on his purple waistcoat.

Beside Hodie, Sibilla gave a shivering sigh. Her cap began to lift on her royal hair.

Commander Gree'sle cheered and clapped. The men and women cheered too, checking sideways to make sure everyone saw them.

"Oh, yay," said the children, dull and plodding. "Yay, yay." They flicked their flags a little bit.

The teachers yelled loudly. "Wonderful Prowdd'on of Um'Binnia! Great Emperor!"

Prowdd'on held up his hands for silence. His smile looked more self-satisfied each moment. "Very expensive cage. Soon you will see. Biggest bars. Biggest lock on door. Golden drinking bowl. I have done this for Um'Binnia. I have captured Dragon-eagle!"

"He hardly did it himself," muttered Hodie. "I bet he made his soldiers do it." He kept an eye on Sibilla's cap.

Prowdd'on reached and tugged a golden cord. The curtains opened on a cage that rose to the cavern roof. The Emperor's sun signs glinted at the top and bottom of every bar. One fake tree glimmered like gold. There was a drinking bowl, also obviously fake gold.

Huddled on the floor behind the tree was a curve of

something silver, a dull green glow, the slow breathing of something huge and beautiful, something in pain and despair.

"The young Dragon-eagle!" Prowdd'on cried. "Department of Science will search out its secrets. I have done this for all children of Um'Binnia."

The school children actually looked worried, as if they'd rather go and lie down in a quiet room.

Hodie was afraid that Sibilla might faint again like she had in the wind-garage. But for a moment she seemed taller—regal and determined. What if she came into her magic right now? With mingled excitement and fear for a shred of a moment Hodie believed it was possible… Then she pressed her hand on her cap and was just a scared girl disguised as a boy who didn't know what on earth she ought to do. Hodie had never seen her look so ordinary. He couldn't bear to keep looking either at the Queen or the Dragon-eagle. He wanted to cry.

He turned aside to brush his eyes and caught a movement at the back of the crowd. An ogre had just come from behind another cage and was holding a chain around the waist of a man in overalls and workman's cap. A Zoo-worker in chains? The ogre and the man watched Prowdd'on for a moment. Then the ogre grunted, gave the chain a little tug, and they turned to shuffle back into the shadows. For one moment, the man's face was in the light. Hodie's heart jolted. It was Dardy.

~

Hodie hugged himself beneath his cloak and stepped back from the little Queen's side. She was still staring at the

Dragon-eagle and didn't notice. Hodie ducked after Dardy and the ogre.

He expected there to be a narrow stinky space with doors into the cages for easy feeding of the animals. He expected to trip over a broom and a shovel, a sack of toad pellets, that sort of thing. For seven leaps and seven strides, it was exactly as he expected. Then the narrow way split into two.

There was no breeze to help him, but a thread of air sifted past and Hodie pelted down the darkest way. A glimmer of moisture on the tunnel wall, a faint spark of glow-worm, another thread of air so faint it might have been silk spun by a spider—now he was in total darkness. He skidded to a stop, slowly tipped his head this way and that— even the skin of his face waiting for a thread, a sign, a scent.

The smell of ogre was bitter. So was the reek of captured creatures. The air moved the slightest amount, and he knew someone turned a head in his direction. In Hodie's heart a wind began to blow as if it hurled chimney pots around in scuds of excitement. He didn't move. He waited for the air in the cavern to shift again. And though Dardy moved so silently that there was not the faintest sound, Hodie reached out his arms and Dardy's arms reached out too and folded him tight.

They pulled apart a little. "I hate you!" Hodie breathed. "You should have told me you weren't my father."

"I didn't want to see you here," Dardy whispered.

"Actually it's so dark we can't see anything." Hodie gripped Dardy's arms tight.

"True," Dardy said, "but I know it's you. Hodie, Um'Binnian spies grabbed me at the market. I'd sworn never to leave you. But I wish you hadn't come here. This is no place for you, my boy."

"I've done everything wrong, haven't I?" Hodie's voice shuddered. "My mother said I mustn't talk to you."

Dardy folded him into another hug. "She's right. You shouldn't talk to me at all. Oh, Hodie, what a terrible mess. The number of times I nearly told Lady Helen and the King what had happened to Lady Allana... But if I had spoken, Gree'sle and Prowdd'on would have learned sooner or later. It would have put Lady Allana in terrible danger. So I waited. And waited. I obeyed her last cry to me—'Do not give the bag to anyone! Look after my child!' I knew the bag held something precious but had no idea what or how those bits and pieces could be important. If only I'd realized the bag held The Ties, I would have—at least, I should have—gone to Lady Helen in a flash." Dardy smothered a cough.

Something moved. There was a chink of metal and the bitter scent of ogre in the gloom. "Dardy," said the ogre, low as the wind far off beyond the mountain. "Move on. Too risky to hang about."

"Wait," said Hodie. "What would happen if...if I had that bag you left behind?"

Dardy gave a sharp intake of breath then coughed again. For a moment there was silence. "Now that I know what the bag contains, all I can say is that it must be put into the hands of Lady Helen or King Jasper very quickly."

"What about the little Queen's hands?" Hodie asked.

"Oh, no. Not unless she has definitely come into her magic," Dardy said. "If she failed, it would be the end of magic. That is too big a load for a child to bear. It would be terrible for her and everyone in every country. All this pain would be for nothing."

Dardy gave Hodie another quick hug, gripped his arms for a moment, then stepped back and disappeared into the dark.

—

# WHAT NOT TO BLOW
# YOUR NOSE ON

Hodie felt his way back through the narrow tunnel. He tripped over the sacks of animal feed, but a breeze of joy still ran through his heart. Dardy—the man who had been his father for so long—was alive. Hodie had also met his mother and found she hadn't left him (well, she sort of had but it was very complicated) and that she loved him.

At the same time he felt worse than before. Dardy was a prisoner who had to tend the Toads and was led about on a chain by an ogre. He didn't seem well. And Hodie's mother was the friend of the Princessa. Both Dardy and his mother believed everything depended on The Ties and King Jasper and Queen Sibilla. They believed magic was so important that to save it you should tear families apart.

He sidled out between the cages to the main part of Zoo where lamps burned on the walls. He was a bit lost. An Ocean Toad as big as a cart hopped to the front of a cage of thick glass. Slime dribbled from the corner of its mouth and, even through the glass, there came a stench like rotten onion. Hodie edged by, keeping in shadow, and found the cavern where the crowd stared in silence at the Dragon-eagle and Prowdd'on stood proudly.

Hodie's leg ached. His eyes could do with a wipe. His nose needed blowing. He sat down on a ledge and fished in his pocket. He pulled out a silky crumple—oh, right, the purple flag. Hodie put it to his nose and had a good honk.

~

Commander Gree'sle's voice roared out. "What's that noise—what's that boy doing? How dare he blow his nose on royal flag! Bring that boy here!"

A soldier dragged Hodie to the front of the crowd, threw him to his knees, and shoved his head down. The ground smelled damp. Ugly animals, big and small, shrieked and squealed as if they applauded. Commander Gree'sle's Um'Binnian military boots stood right in front of him. Behind them Hodie saw the metal wheels of Prowdd'on's carriage.

"Show me his face!" shouted Gree'sle.

Hodie was yanked up again by military hands. The children clustered behind the carriage. Some looked pleased to see someone else in trouble. Others looked worried. One boy did a secret thumbs-up to show he was delighted to see someone brave enough to wipe snot on the Emperor's flag.

Also there was his mother, eyes wide with shock. Lu'nedda had a grip on Allana's arm. And there was Murgott, and there Sibilla—thank goodness, still with her cap on. The squirrel's tail stuck out under her cloak.

A Zoo official had begun to close the curtains of the Dragon-eagle's cage.

Prowdd'on stood in the carriage and glowered at Hodie. "How dare…" He reared back and roared with laughter. "Boy from backyard of little Grand Palace! Boy who had nerve to say Emperor had done wrong! Did you come after bag of tricks, boy? You won't find bag here. It was stolen from me."

Hodie clenched his teeth to stop from shouting, *You can't have something stolen from you when you stole it from somebody else in the first place!*

Prowdd'on smiled at the school children. "How should I punish half-Fontanian brat?"

The children looked scared.

"I haven't done anything," Hodie said. "I came here by accident."

"No excuse!" Gree'sle declared.

"Sir!" Hodie looked Prowdd'on right in the eye. "A good leader finds out every side of a situation before he decides what's right and wrong."

The children blinked in surprise. The boy who'd done the thumbs-up did another with both hands.

Gree'sle's thin mustache quirked up. "Emperor has biggest heart and mind in all Um'Binnia. He knows what is right and wrong."

The Emperor smiled. "It is right or wrong if I say so. I say boy will join crew who tend Ocean Toads."

There were gasps, screams, and urgent shush-shushings. Over by the dark alley, Hodie saw Dardy and the ogre.

Dardy started to cry out, but the ogre slung an arm round Dardy's neck, hand over his mouth, and tried to haul him out of sight. Dardy struggled free and Gree'sle turned.

"Sire, look!" Gree'sle shouted. "Wretched servant is still alive!"

For a moment everything was quiet.

Then Prowdd'on roared and gestured. Soldiers dragged Dardy in front of the carriage. The Emperor smiled down at him and the circles of the mustache crawled nearer his ears.

"I was just talking about poisonous Toads. And here we have forgotten servant of Lady Allana, not already poisoned by my Toads and very long dead. Highly interesting. Gree'sle, move gathering to Imperial Hall. Bring me biggest audience in all Um'Binnia."

# HOW TO BEHAVE WELL (OR BADLY) IN THE GRAND IMPERIAL HALL OF THE GREAT MOUNTAIN CITY OF THE WONDERFUL COUNTRY OF UM'BINNIA, IN FRONT OF THE GREATEST EMPEROR THE WORLD HAS EVER KNOWN, AND NOT THROW UP

Hodie had no way of talking to Dardy. There was a lot of being marched through the city streets with people staring. There was a lot of being shoved about in the Imperial Palace and into a room beside the Grand Hall. The guards laughed about putting handcuffs on a boy—what harm could a skinny boy do the soldiers of Um'Binnia? They put cuffs on Dardy, though.

Between two muscular guards with pistols, Hodie managed to peer though a half-open door into the Hall. Hundreds of Um'Binnians crowded in, important ones with solemn mustaches or imposing handbags. Imperial

Um'Binnian guards stood around the walls, some with pikes as if they were going to barbecue something huge. Some had swords as if they expected to carve the barbecue. They all had holsters on their belts with pistols (and a dagger or two).

The guard nearest the throne banged his pike on the floor. At the far end of the huge hall, an enormous double door swung open. The crowd had to bunch up to make room because in straggled the school children, teachers, and parent helpers. In crowded an even bigger crowd of city folk. Some were very old. One of the parent helpers looked as if she was going to have a baby any day, but there were no chairs for anyone except the Emperor. The Imperial Throne was the biggest chair for one person Hodie had ever seen. The high back was twirls of gold. So were the arms. The purple cushion looked comfortable though.

Four troll guards led Hodie and Dardy in to face the Throne. The stale air here seemed bitter, like winds that had been caged for many years.

The trumpet sounded again, higher and longer, to show someone very grand was coming in. No need to guess who.

Prowdd'on had changed into another purple hat, a soft one with a brim like a gold coronet. He wore a purple shirt, purple trousers, gold boots, and a golden waistcoat. Did he have purple and gold underwear? Hodie guessed yes. The imperial mustache had been waxed again, into spikes, and gilded, probably to look like a sunburst. It looked more like a self-conscious yellow sea anemone.

To reach the throne Prowdd'on had to walk up three golden steps. He smiled that crawly smile beneath the spikes of his mustache, sat down, and sighed.

"Exhausting work," Hodie muttered to Dardy. Dardy started to grin and muffled a chuckle.

Commander Gree'sle offered Prowdd'on a golden flask. Prowdd'on admired himself in the mirror on its side and took a sip. Gree'sle slid the flask back into his pocket.

Prowdd'on didn't welcome anyone. He just began talking.

"Reporters are present from all magazines and daily paper? Good. I work enormously hard for many years. I am tireless, night and day. I make Um'Binnia greatest city, greatest country, to have all biggest and best things from entire world." He folded his hands and waited as if he expected to hear something.

"Thank you, Great Emperor Prowdd'on!" chorused the people.

There was a flurry from a side door. Princessa Lu'nedda strode in, stood before her father (in front of Hodie, actually—she had a row of square blue buttons all down her back), and spread her arms. "Papa! I am safely returned!"

"Not now," the Emperor said.

"Papa, I save myself from rebel kidnappers! And also, for you, hidden safely in…"

"If you want to stay, be quiet," Prowdd'on said.

Gree'sle narrowed his eyes.

The Princessa lowered her arms and walked to stand near the throne. She'd turned red, a red you should be careful of, if you asked Hodie—you could probably call it rebel red. Allana trailed from the side room too and stood near Lu'nedda, eyes down as if it was hard not to glance at Hodie. And there, behind Allana, were Murgott and Sibilla.

Murgott eyed Hodie, a warning not to give the little Queen away. Sibilla gaped at the throne with her best pesty-boy expression. As an actor she was excellent, that was for sure.

"Now," said Prowdd'on. "I have one Dragon-eagle. I must have Fontanian treasures too. Dardy, Fontanian servant, now Toad-keeper—you had two years to tell me about Ties, but you said nothing. Finally I found them. Then they were stolen. Where are they now?"

Dardy stared dead ahead and said nothing.

Hodie glanced at Sibilla, who looked truly confused. Her own father and grandfather had been hunting The Ties for years. The King's fiancée, Lady Beatrix, had joined the hunt too. Hodie felt sick—if Sibilla realized Prowdd'on was talking about the bag of stuff from Hodie's lean-to, she might give herself away.

The Emperor turned to Hodie. "Boy?"

Hodie used a voice he knew would be annoying. "Don't know about treasure. I only ever had ten dolleros and I lost 'em."

Prowdd'on rolled his eyes. "Treasures of Fontania. Missing Ties. You had them in unpleasant little hut. Then I had them. Then thief stole Ties from me. I will have Ties again."

Sibilla had stiffened. Murgott put a hand on her shoulder. Hodie blinked at the Emperor, trying to look young and useless.

Prowdd'on spoke again. "There is also map that shows Dragon-eagle nest. It is map of fine silver. Where is that?"

Hodie shifted his weight to the other foot, still playing stupid, but in fact he'd never heard about this treasure. "You don't need a map. The Dragon-eagles live in the Eastern Isle."

Prowdd'on's smile hardened. "Don't tell me what Prowdd'on need! The map shows where Dragon-eagle lays egg—great golden egg out of which hatches new Dragon-eagle."

Sibilla wrinkled her nose as if the Emperor talked utter nonsense. Hodie shrugged and ducked his head.

"Don't shrug at Emperor!" Gree'sle roared. "You are Um'Binnian! The Great Prowdd'on is your Emperor!"

Hodie's head came up. "I'm half-Um'Binnian," he said. "So he's partial Emperor." He ducked his head again.

The Emperor gripped the arms of the golden throne. "Odd-job boy, do you know who stole Ties from me!"

Hodie didn't feel like giving Lu'nedda away. He blinked at her to let her know he wouldn't and tried to look more puzzled, more and more stupid. And actually it was all pretty stupid. If magic was real, it should be able to defend itself. So, if it was real, it wasn't much good. If Hodie had the chance to choose between ten dolleros or a pouch of old pebbles and a bashed-up cup, he'd take the dolleros and run.

Sibilla took a step forward, clutching the bag that held Jasper's bird. Murgott put both hands on her shoulders and drew her back.

Prowdd'on had turned his attention from Hodie now and was glaring at Dardy. "You and that woman!" he roared. "Ties were right under my nose in this great city. Lady Allana, you let your servant smuggle them away. It is time for punishment."

The important Um'Binnians gave a smattering of applause.

Hodie glanced at Dardy and saw his breathing falter. But Allana stepped out and bowed a little to the Emperor.

"The Ties were not mine to give to you then, and I don't have them now. I do know that without them the Dragon-eagles cannot live. Your city runs on science, but hearts need magic. Without The Ties, there will be no more children who grow up and discover they have a link with magic and all things of the natural world."

Allana's face was fiery, as if she longed to punch Prowdd'on. "While there is still a chance that my boy, and all children, will live in a better world than this one of yours, I will not even tell you how to tie your shoe."

Hodie's little mother also threw a defiant glance at the Princessa. Lu'nedda shifted and seemed uncomfortable. Queen Sibilla's cap looked very unsteady, but she was gazing at Allana now as if she realized *Of course, she's that Lady Allana! Oh, I understand it all now!*

"One last time," said Prowdd'on. "Lady Allana, Allana's brat—speak up."

Hodie's heart thrummed in his throat. Sibilla's hands gripped her bag, pulling around the shape of the bird inside.

"Speak!" repeated Prowdd'on. "Or you and your brat shall both go to Ocean Toads and lingering death."

A little cry escaped Allana, another from Dardy. A curl burst out from beneath Sibilla's cap. Murgott had his hands tight on her shoulders.

"In that case, good riddance to bad rubbish." The Emperor signaled. "Take them to Industrial Toad Ponds!"

"No!" cried Allana.

Princessa Lu'nedda put an arm around her. "Father, wait!"

"No more from you, daughter," Prowdd'on roared. "Guards, escort Princessa to her apartment!"

Guards began to hustle toward the Princessa. All Lu'nedda had to do was say she had the bag, and it would be over. Hodie had to get in first to try and delay.

"Let Hodie go!" Dardy cried. "He's just a boy! He's nobody!"

"I am someone!" yelled Hodie. "I know where to find the bag!"

The Grand Imperial Hall filled with gasps and cries from the crowd.

"Shut up!" roared Gree'sle.

The noise stopped. Lu'nedda looked very like Ogg'ward again and strangely interested (though very wary) about what Hodie would say next. He heard Prowdd'on breathing—it sounded as if he ought to say excuse me and use his hanky.

"What was that?" Prowdd'on asked Hodie.

Hodie stood as straight as his mother had done. "I know where the bag is."

"No!" his mother said.

Hodie raised his chin and looked at Prowdd'on. "I will tell you. But first, promise to let my mother and her servant Dardy leave Um'Binnia…"

He glanced at Sibilla. Her eyes glimmered with tears. He hoped she understood he was trying to help her escape. He gave the Queen and his mother a tiny smile and looked back at the Emperor. "Let them leave the city with the two people who came here with me, especially the other boy." He glanced briefly again at Sibilla and Murgott.

Commander Gree'sle spoke. "You ask the Great Emperor to make you, a boy, an imperial promise?"

"Yes. He has to promise!" Hodie shouted. The corners of the great hall echoed *Promise!*

"Promise!" Hodie yelled, and the hall echoed again.

"Promise and keep the promise!" Hodie shouted a third time. The echo built until it sounded like a gale that shook the walls and the ground beneath his feet. *Keep the promise, promise promise…!*

Prowdd'on spread his hands to show he couldn't believe that Hodie thought he had to ask. "Boy—what can I say?"

"Just make the promise," Hodie said.

"I hear you," said Prowdd'on.

He gestured to the guards. One took the handcuffs off Dardy, who rubbed his wrists, trembling. Prowdd'on gestured again, and Allana moved to stand beside Hodie. She was trembling too.

"Now," said Prowdd'on to Hodie. "Where is missing bag?"

Hodie saw a smile crawling under the gilded spikes of

Prowdd'on's mustache. A boy in the crowd let out a cry. The teachers hushed him. Hodie opened his mouth.

"Stop!" cried out Sibilla. "Wait a moment!"

She ducked out of Murgott's grip and raced to Hodie. Hand on his shoulder, she whispered quickly. "Prowdd'on didn't make the promise. He weaseled out of it."

Hodie felt an utter fool. She whispered on. "He'll punish you and never let you go. I'm a useless Queen and I'll never have magic, but I can do this for you and Lady Allana and for Fontania. Send the bird to Jasper the minute you can! Tell Jasper where The Ties are. You must not let Prowdd'on get the bag. Do *you* promise?"

She stared into his eyes until he nodded. Hodie definitely wanted to throw up now. "But…"

"Another foreign brat with no manners!" Gree'sle cried. "Stop wasting time! Lock him away!"

Sibilla glanced at Hodie's hands then turned toward Prowdd'on. She was holding the bird behind her back. She pressed it into Hodie's grasp. The bird felt warm again, alive.

Then Sibilla lifted her chin, faced the Emperor like a Queen, and took her cap off. Her hair sprang up as if the strongest wind rushed through it. Prowdd'on's mouth dropped open. Gasps and murmurs filled the Hall.

Queen Sibilla bowed as she'd been taught.

"Greetings, Emperor Prowdd'on," Sibilla said. "I, Queen Sibilla of Fontania, find myself on an unexpected visit to your city."

~

## PROBLEMS WITH CHOOSING
## THE GOOD THINGS

Um'Binnian soldiers tromped all over the Hall, Sibilla was surrounded, and Hodie couldn't see what had happened to her.

"No!" Hodie yelled. He kept on yelling but it was not a scrap of good. As soon as Dardy was freed from the handcuffs, he grabbed Hodie in a headlock to stop him from trying to reach Sibilla. Hodie kicked and struggled, but it was difficult when he had to keep the metal bird well out of sight.

At one point there was a bellow from Prowdd'on. "Something bit me! A rodent! How dare it! Find it! Kill it!"

Dardy, Allana, and Murgott dragged Hodie out of the Grand Hall and hurried to catch up with the Princessa. Lu'nedda led them up flights of stairs, along corridors, back to her apartment. A split second before the Princessa slammed and locked her door, in dashed the squirrel. It crouched under the work table, tail lashing, wiping its mouth and spitting. *Ptha! Ptha! Ppppthah-ah-ah!*

Hodie tried to unlock the door and beat upon it. Murgott came over and held his wrists. "I hate you," Hodie shouted. "I hate you all!"

"D'you think I plan to leave the little Queen to Prowdd'on's mercy?" the Corporal muttered. "Tactics, boy. We're only helpless till we figure out what to do. I'll get her out of this stinkin' cave city, but it needs thought. Half your brain must be Fontanian, so blasted well use it." He rubbed his hands over his freckly forehead. His eyes welled with tears.

The Princessa sat down and steepled her fingers. "Interesting twist," she muttered. "Thank you, boy, for not giving me away. I am not sure what to do next. A good idea is always wait and see if good idea comes."

Dardy had collapsed into an armchair. The squirrel, asking questions to itself, circled him, decided it knew him, and sprang on his lap to soothe him with chitters.

Hodie found a chair to huddle in. He was still wearing his cloak to hide Jasper's present. He hadn't had a chance to send the bird off to find the King. The chance might never come at all! He thought with as much brain as he could manage. He realized it wouldn't take long before Prowdd'on remembered Hodie had said he knew where that wretched bag was and found a way to weasel around his empty promise.

Allana wiped her eyes. "Hodie, you should take your cloak off when you're inside."

Hodie ignored her and pretended to mope like a normal boy. For safety, for now, he buckled the bird into his satchel.

He'd simply have to find some way to send it away before Prowdd'on's scientists examined Sibilla. Oh no…that awful Professor Glimp and the Madame-Professor—Hodie bet that when they learned Sibilla had been captured, they'd be rushing home to Um'Binnia as fast as possible.

Hodie had made so many mistakes—mainly because he hadn't known how important everyone thought that tatty bag was with its wrench and the blackened cup (and Murgott's notebook). The only good thing was that Prowdd'on still didn't have the bag. If only Hodie could examine it himself. If only he could know for sure whether it held any Ties.

His mother and Murgott were talking quietly with Dardy now, an earnest chat. Lu'nedda paced about and finally stopped beside Hodie's chair.

"Boy," she said, "I knew you when you were a baby."

"Don't bother to say I was cute," Hodie said.

"You shrieked like rat," said Lu'nedda. "You threw up three times each day."

"I'm glad you hated me." He didn't bother to say he hated her too. It must be obvious.

"But you didn't betray me to Father," said the Princessa. "And you are son of my best friend…"

*You're her worst enemy*, he thought.

Lu'nedda's eyebrows rose as if she knew what he was thinking. "Your mother saw how much I am alone without real friend." Her mouth twisted. "Who can be true friend for girl and then woman whose father is Prowdd'on?"

"My mother felt sorry for you," Hodie muttered. "And you

made a fuss when she should have escaped. You caused all this."

"I was still young. Why should I explain myself to another child now? Listen, if you can understand." The Princessa's eyes were angry and worried. "When Gree'sle realized your mother had sent Ties out of his grasp, I had to protect her. If he promise to keep her out of prison and not tell my Father she harbored The Ties, I promise to marry him when I am twenty-five. Twenty-five is when Um'Binnian princes and princessas have to marry, and twenty-five is coming fast for me. I like to keep promises if possible, but I do not like sneaky Gree'sle. My plan is to show my father that Gree'sle is greedy fool. I do not need husband of any kind, especially not greedy fool."

"What about Sibilla?" Hodie asked.

"What about, indeed?" The Princessa glanced at Allana and Murgott. "I think tonight there is no choice but to make best of it. We have chance to be all friends together— your mother and Dardy, me and you. Mr. Murgott—I should say, *Mister* Murgott to protect him—will have dinner with us too."

She clapped her hands. Two servants ran in. They set the table with silver knives and forks and spoons and vast lacy napkins for wiping your fingers and chin. Lu'nedda made everyone wash their hands, and Allana told Lu'nedda to wash hers too. Then the Princessa sat at one end of the table in the best chair and gestured to Hodie.

"You are son of famous wind-train hero Lord Fer'nan and beautiful foreigner Lady Allana. You are important person now, not Nobody Odd-job. Time to rest, to eat, be comfortable." Lu'nedda gave him a rather sweet smile, which made his heart hurt. "Please, sit opposite me in the other best chair."

His mother was looking at him, too. A best chair. Son of a lord. Son of a hero. Son of a lady, and she'd been brave too. He realized his mother was still being extremely brave. Hodie folded his cloak over his satchel (with the bird inside) and set it under the chair. Although he didn't want to, he sat down.

With a large match, Lu'nedda lit the candle in the middle of the table. Servants carried in dish after huge dish. Big baked potatoes stuffed with cheese. Slices of fish in golden batter. Chicken drumsticks dripping with savory sauce. Hodie couldn't stop himself from staring at the food or his mouth from watering. But he did make himself look through the candle flame at the Princessa and speak up.

"What will Queen Sibilla have for dinner?"

Lu'nedda's mouth stretched at the corners in a smile that meant the smiler was not happy. "Queen Sibilla will be treated as Queen."

"Until she's no more use to the Emperor," muttered Murgott.

Hodie risked nudging the Corporal with his new boots. He felt a return nudge. It was both nice and worrying that his only friend was someone who a few days ago had threatened to starve him. Murgott's dark grin showed he had not forgotten his pirate past or his duty to the little Queen. He might not be bright, but he was bright enough and he'd learned to be steadfast. He might be gruff, but his first thought was always for Queen Sibilla. Hodie was glad the Corporal was on his side.

"Good food," said Murgott loudly. "Very suitable for the son of a lord and lady. Just think, for years he's been eatin' scraps on the back doorstep of the Grand Palace."

"It must be comfort that your son was looked after by brave man such as Mr. Murgott on journey over Stones," said Lu'nedda to Hodie's mother.

"My first duty is to the Queen," said Murgott loudly.

Lu'nedda nodded. "And tomorrow, we discuss our every duty. More potatoes? More fish? Another drumstick?"

"You have very ordinary-sized chickens in Um'Binnia," Hodie said.

Lu'nedda's mouth twitched. "And only two drumsticks on each one. Now, Um'Binnian Cabbage Pudding," she said. "Spicy and sweet."

Hodie refused it. So did Murgott though he chatted with Lu'nedda about the recipe and suggested that grated apple might improve it. Dardy simply pushed his food around the plate. He didn't seem to have an appetite at all.

"Now, boy will sleep in small room," said Lu'nedda. "Mr. Murgott and Dardy will sleep in even smaller room. You will find beds very comfortable, made with soft expensive silk-wool. Not like dirty lumpy mattress in hut behind very small Grand Palace."

Hodie caught Murgott's eye. The Corporal winked then pretended his eye was watering from candle smoke.

"A good night's sleep will make us all feel better," said Lady Allana, though she didn't look as if she believed it.

A servant bowed to Hodie. "I will show young lord to his room."

Lord Hodie. Well, he was actually Lord Ro'lan, but Hodie liked Hodie better.

Murgott's eyes were on him. So were Dardy's. Dardy seemed weary to death, his skin gray.

Hodie bowed to Lu'nedda and his mother, followed the servant, and closed the door quietly but firmly so Allana wouldn't think she could come and tuck him in. He put himself to bed in new blue pajamas.

For the first time since he was two years old, he was in the same place as his mother. He had eaten two excellent meals in one day, with silver cutlery. He'd sat in one of the best chairs. Now he lay on a soft mattress and pillow. Yet, in a dim glow that came from the ceiling he felt more alone than ever in his life.

Something scratched at his door. It opened and Murgott spoke. "Company for you."

The squirrel pattered in and climbed on the end of Hodie's bed. Murgott closed the door again. After some tiny sounds like squirrel-weeping and teeth-gnashing, the squirrel fell asleep under the tattered blanket of its own tail.

—

## IS IT THIEVERY OR NOT?

Hodie lay on the soft mattress in the dim night light. Pictures flickered in his head. If he liked, he could stay in Um'Binnia. Fine clothes. Good food every day, hot or cold, however he wanted, whenever he wanted. His mother and Dardy, together with him. His mother could still be Lu'nedda's friend.

The squirrel let out a chitter as if it scented something on a breeze in a rodent dream. Other pictures slowly moved though Hodie's thoughts. Hardly ever being allowed to see the sun, never feeling a gust of wind call him to run to the wharves and see steamships head into harbor or sailboats billow over the waves. Never hunting in rock pools for crabs and anemones, never steering a trolley down a hill.

Through all the other pictures in Hodie's mind floated one of a twelve-year-old girl and others of the possible first signs of newest magic. How terrible if magic were true and starting to show in Sibilla and she never had the chance to let it grow stronger. But it didn't matter if magic was true or not—the little Queen should still be allowed to return home to be with her parents.

He waited till he heard Lu'nedda and the others turn down the lamps and go to bed. In the handsome blue pajamas he creaked his door open and crept into the main room of the apartment. Among his mother's tools on the work table was a small metal hook. The cabinet that held the drawstring bag had a gimcrack lock. Any odd-job boy could have it open in less than a second. Listening for the slightest movement from the other rooms, Hodie picked the lock. The bag almost flew into his hands. He fiddled the metal hook till the cabinet locked again.

The squirrel raised its head and watched him smuggle the bag back into the little bedroom. Hodie sat on the bed. Somebody might wake and come in, so he arranged the cloak so that he could throw it at once over the bag if he needed to. He loosened the drawstring.

The first thing his hand touched was Murgott's notebook. He flicked it open in the shadows of the room. It hadn't been transformed by being in the bag. The same poems, not very good ones. Hodie supposed that if you wrote poetry just for yourself it didn't have to be much good, just be heartfelt. There were poems to Murgott's mother about wishing he had been a better son. There were several about being a pirate and a few about the Fontanian Army—very stirring. One was to a baby girl who held the promise of the whole world in her tiny hands. The last one was about a majestic princess who was far above a lowly corporal...actually, Hodie had seen this one before. It was very private. He didn't want to chuckle at it. Well, really he wanted to roll on the bed and scream with laughter, but the general circumstances of the night were far too solemn. He stuffed the book into the bottom of the bag because if Murgott saw him with it now the circumstances could become far worse than horrible.

Next Hodie pulled out the metal cup. It looked as it had always done, as if something heavy had trodden on it. Around the rim was faint curly carving, hard to see in the poor light. When he traced it with his fingers, black dust came off. It was impossible that the old cup could be a treasure. Hodie stuffed it back beside the book of heartfelt poems and wiped his hands on his pajama shirt.

He knew the wrench so well that he left it where it was. It was a wrench any workman would like in his toolbox. Anything he'd used it on had stayed truly fixed so in that sense it was a treasure. But how could it help anyone ride a Dragon-eagle?

Last of all he pulled out the pouch of roundish things, the beads or pebbles. The pouch had faint curly markings on it too. The round things smelled of dust. They weren't at all pretty. Could they be polished? There were enough to make a bracelet or to decorate a hat. He spilled them from hand to hand then tipped them back into the pouch. One fell onto the coverlet. The squirrel sat up. *Tck-tck!*

Could it be a nut? Hodie offered it to the squirrel. The squirrel stared, gave a whispery *chrrr*, backed away, and curled right down beneath its tail. So, not a nut. Hodie began to put it back with the others, but a door opened somewhere in the apartment. It was probably just someone going to the bathroom, but Hodie shoved the bag under the cloak. He thrust the last round thing under his pillow and lay down as if he was asleep.

—

# THE MOST DELICIOUS OF
# ALL BREAKFASTS

It turned out to be a real sleep, a very deep one. An ogre tapped on Hodie's door. "Breakfast, Lord Hodie, is ready at once."

He hurried to dress. His leg didn't hurt at all. He had fresh socks. Fresh undershirt and underpants. New clean trousers, new shirt (dark blue) with button-down pockets. He shoved his feet in those excellent boots.

Breakfast looked as delicious as a princessa's breakfast in a story. Hot toast. Large eggs. Strips of hot bacon. Marmalade and raspberry jam in lordly dishes. Orange juice so cold the jug was wet on the outside (as well as in).

Allana watched Hodie as if she was starved, though it wasn't for food. Lu'nedda eyed him as well. Dardy just picked at a slice of toast.

Murgott concentrated on four slices of toast and three eggs. "Tuck in, boy," he muttered. "An army marches on its stomach. So does a boy. Orright? Are you still with me?"

"Orright," Hodie muttered back. "You still with me?"

Murgott gave a dark chuckle. "Some people's tactics is to wait years and years for the right chance. Other people's tactics is to have a good night's sleep. Then your brain can suss out the situation, then you can start pushin'. Orright. I'm at the sussin' stage." With a little cough he looked at Lu'nedda. "Very good bacon. Excellent eggs. Most grateful, ma'am. Yes, I would appreciate the ogre pourin' more coffee, thanks very much. Now, ma'am, can you tell me how this wonderful city is ventilated?"

"I have other things to think about," said Lu'nedda.

Hodie tried to smile at his mother and the Princessa. "Can I sit outside—that is, on the balcony?" he asked.

"We need to talk…" began Allana but after another look at Hodie, she nodded. "Brush your teeth. Then put on your cloak."

~

An obedient son would certainly put on a cloak. But first, in his bedroom, Hodie whispered to the bird. "King Jasper, this is Hodie. I'm in Um'Binnia. I might have The Ties— well, it's a cup and some other old junk. The Queen is captured. Murgott and I will try to get her out. I can't promise. That's all. Bye."

He stuffed the bag into his satchel, slung the satchel over his shoulder, then fastened the cloak over the lot with the bird under an arm.

An ogre came in to make the bed. It whisked up the pillow and thumped it with both fists. The last little nugget lay on the sheet—Hodie scooped it up and managed to pop it under the cloak into his top shirt pocket, which he buttoned safely.

He'd have expected a princessa's balcony to be perfect. Bits of rock were crumbling off and scaly gray lichen grew in patches on the railing. There was no point in sitting here to get fresh air. He tried to feel the least little breath from outside the mountain city, wishing a breeze could whisk the place clean. Where was a chink through which the bird might fly out and find the sky? If the bird was magic, it should be able to pass through the rock wall. Or even to send messages through rock walls. Well, if anyone asked Hodie, he'd say a magic bird wouldn't be made with screws and wires like this one, even though it sometimes felt warm and its chest swelled occasionally as if it breathed. It was just the mechanism. The bird simply had to do its job and find King Jasper.

"Hey," said a quiet voice nearby. Hodie glanced to the side, then down a little. Someone else leaned on the balcony of another apartment—the boy from the Zoo, the thumbs-up boy. He carried a sketch pad and pencil and grinned from ear to ear—they had huge teeth in Um'Binnia.

Hodie eased to the side of the balcony. "What?"

"Are you really from Fontania?" mouthed the boy.

Hodie nodded.

The boy leaned over his balcony as far as possible and whispered. "Are you going to live here now?"

Hodie wrinkled his forehead and shrugged.

The boy wrinkled his forehead too as if he didn't think it would be a great choice. "My name is O'sel."

The squirrel jumped on the rail and rubbed its face against Hodie's sleeve.

"Is that yours?" whispered O'sel.

Hodie shook his head. "It belongs to itself. Like people should."

O'sel took one long breath, gave one short nod. "Is Allana your mother?"

Hodie gave a very short nod.

"She tells us stories. She's not supposed to…" O'sel glanced over his shoulder, then whispered again. "Stories about *outside!*" He breathed the word as if it were pure magic.

"How often do you get out of the mountain?" whispered Hodie.

O'sel held his thumb and forefinger in a small pinch. "I visited farm once. I went nearly to edge of Great Salt Moat."

"Where's the best way out?" Hodie held his breath.

O'sel shook his head and took a step back. Hodie held up the bird—the metal glowed softly—and asked again with a silent shrug, an open palm.

With one slow nod, O'sel pointed up and to the side—a narrow stair.

The lamp near the stair flickered as if a thread of the sour city air stirred there. Hodie stroked the tiny metal feathers shaped by King Jasper. The bird's fat little body was warm again because Hodie had been holding it, of course. He stroked the wings that hid the key that turned the mechanism and made the metal wings begin to whirr.

He held the metal bird up again in both hands. It trembled, and for a moment Hodie let himself imagine that he, an ordinary boy, had been granted a moment of magic. He breathed so close to the bird that the metal misted.

"Find King Jasper. Tell him where to find his sister and the missing Dragon-eagle. Tell him he must hurry here and save them both or they will die."

~

The bird rose from Hodie's hands into the cavern. It lurched then headed for the stairs where O'sel had pointed. A bit of squirrel fluff dropped off its tail, then the bird was gone.

Hodie nodded thank you to the boy. Wide-eyed, O'sel stared at him. Then with a sudden grin he gestured, *Hurry, be secret, come down*, and disappeared back into his apartment.

Hodie peered over the railing. In the square below, teachers were gathering a group of children. Hodie watched as O'sel ran out and joined them. He knew exactly what to do.

Still at the breakfast table, Allana and Dardy murmured to each other, frowning. Lu'nedda blinked angrily at her reflection in a spoon. Hodie slipped past the table and winked at Murgott. The Corporal winked back. The squirrel hopped on Murgott's knee.

Hodie crept down and out the side door of the palace. Not a soul spoke to him. Not even the teachers noticed one extra boy arrive.

The huddle of children made room and drew him in. "We bet you can escape," they whispered, soft and sharp. "Watch O'sel. Then be quick!"

O'sel winked at the others and dropped his pencil case. Pens rolled everywhere. The children pretended to gather them, kicking, scrambling, rolling them further. The teachers jumped out of the way and called instructions.

In the scuffling and noise, O'sel took Hodie aside and drew a quick sketch in a notebook. Hodie realized it was a map of the mountain city, how the tunnels and caverns linked up.

As the sketch grew beneath his pencil, O'sel whispered, "Do not believe Emperor. You are not safe. Gree'sle will make sure of that. Get away, soon as you can, with Lady Allana." He drew arrows that led to three exits and marked the lowest one with an asterisk. "This way is best—busy but nearest. Highest one is for royal wind-car—dangerous—guards at door."

Hodie pointed to the middle exit, but O'sel shook his head.

"Very many guards. Secret wind-cars. Rumors say they are military wind-ships. If that is true, there are many weapons. Do not go to it. Yes?"

Hodie nodded thank you and gripped O'sel's arm. "Where are the laboratories? Where is Queen Sibilla?"

O'sel glanced across the square at a large door. "Do not dare. You cannot help. Nobody wins against Prowdd'on. If you and Lady Allana escape, it is miracle. I do not know how you will survive when you are outside. But when you were baby, Dardy carried you and treasures Prowdd'on wants, on foot, over Stones of Beyond. A servant hero— that is precious and rare. You must have been saved for good reason."

O'sel ripped the map from his notebook and squashed it into Hodie's hand. The other children gathered up the last pencils and then lined up for the teachers as neatly and silently as dolls.

~

Hodie slipped back into Lu'nedda's apartment. Good—his mother and Lu'nedda looked as if they hadn't moved. Allana gave him half a smile, but Lu'nedda didn't even notice. Murgott, still at the table, crumbled leftover toast for the squirrel. Dardy was back in the very small room, lying down. Hodie glanced in—his skin was gray, his breathing labored. He'd had to tend the Ocean Toads for nearly two years—Toad poison was terrible stuff.

Sometimes if Hodie made his outside look calm and confident, his inside felt confident too. It didn't work this time. But he winked at Murgott, who tapped the side of his nose and gave a slight nod. Then Hodie bowed to Lu'nedda, exactly the way Sibilla bowed.

"Many thanks for the magnificent breakfast, Princessa Lu'nedda."

Lu'nedda sat up and dropped the spoon. "Oh, thank you for saying thank you."

Hodie bowed to his mother. "Perhaps Dardy needs some air? Murgott could help him along."

Lu'nedda threw her hands up. "You must lie low, for many reasons."

But Hodie's mother gave a small nod. "A gentle walk, maybe."

"For goodness sake," Lu'nedda said, "do what you like. I am going to see Father and see if he will keep promise." She smiled with a smile that made her look as tough as Ogg'ward (even without the beanie). "I will say nothing about mysterious bag that rebels stole from under Gree'sle's nose.

If my father knows I have it now, it will be awkward." She shook her ringlets. "Skinny Gree'sle is bad influence. He encourage my father to spend money on war and very bad experiments." She thumped a fist into the other hand. "Money should go to schools, I think. Money should not go to bother neighboring country. It should definitely not go to torment little girl. But I am not Empress yet. I must take care not to make Father so angry that he shut me away for all time in beautiful apartment."

Murgott glanced up. "Many beautiful ladies would be happy in such a beautiful apartment." By the time he'd finished, his color was as red as a rose.

"Then many beautiful ladies need development of brain!" Lu'nedda strode into her room to get herself ready. "Allana? Mr. Murgott? Do not try to get out of city," she called though the half-open door. There was more tossing across the room of petticoats, hats, handbags, a ringlet brush.

Dardy came out of the very small room as slowly as an old man.

Hodie's mother pulled Lu'nedda's door closed. "Mr. Murgott, I am guessing there is a plan? It will be safer to talk while we move about the city. But I do not wish to leave Lu'nedda in danger."

A wisp of the stale air brushed Hodie's hand. It felt like sorrow now, still threaded through with bitter rage. He knew it came from levels far below. From the laboratory, he bet. They had to hurry.

He muttered to Murgott. "Bring your duffel bag." Hodie still had his satchel with the drawstring bag in it, under his cloak. "We have to move before somebody stops us."

Murgott's ex-pirate's eyes bored into Hodie's. "Let's hope your brain's figured out a better idea than mine, boy."

"What's your idea?" asked Hodie.

"None." Murgott clapped his Um'Binnian hat on and took Dardy's arm. "One two, one two," he counted. "That's the way, one foot in front of the other, then switch 'em around. We call it walking. I bet you'd like a cold Fontanian ginger beer back on the veranda of the barracks. Smarten up, old friend, smarten up."

As they started down the stairs, Dardy began to seem better with Murgott's urging. The squirrel rode on Allana's shoulder. They reached the street.

"Go that way." Hodie pointed to a little alleyway. According to O'sel's map, it joined the stairs to the main wind-garage without having to go the way they'd come through the main streets. "Wait for me on the second landing."

"Where are you..." began his mother.

"Didn't you know boys need to burn off energy? I'm going a steeper way." Hodie raced around a corner to the square.

He hadn't lied. He simply hadn't said the steeper way was down to the Department of Science—if only he could get through the door O'sel had glanced at.

If even one of the things in the bag was some kind of treasure, Sibilla should have it. She'd told him not to let Prowdd'on have the bag, and Hodie wouldn't. Dardy had said the little Queen might fail, and so she might. But whether she was a Queen or an ordinary girl, Hodie was going to try to get her out.

He looked around the square. It was empty. In the far corner, he found the door. A notice on it said *Authorized Personnel only* and showed the sign of a knife. It looked like a scalpel.

—

# WHY ALL UM'BINNIAN MAGAZINES
# ARE SO VERY BORING

Hodie opened the door enough to slip through and started down a stairwell. Heat from the lower levels rose to meet him, a skein of smells, chemicals and animals, and what seemed to be ginger biscuits. Halfway down the first flight, footsteps pattered behind him...a squirrel that looked like a gathering of dust and sweepings. And soft footfalls... Murgott in his Um'Binnian disguise, looking very determined and trying to tiptoe. Hodie grinned a serious grin, and Murgott grinned back.

Two flights down, the smell of animals and ginger had grown stronger. Hodie eased open the landing door and heard echoey voices in one room. There was the chink of cups and coffee break talk.

"Have you seen latest *Emperor Daily News*? We will vanquish Fontania in days."

"*Prow-wow-wow,*" sang a lady's voice.

"Do shut up," said somebody else.

"What do you think of Emperor's latest hats? Do you

know each one cost three hundred dollero?"

"Yes, and we are stuck with cheapest biscuits."

The scientists. It sounded as if they hadn't started work seriously yet. Maybe they had to wait for that until Madame-Professor Winterbee and Master-Professor Glimp arrived back. But Hodie bet that after the last lick of coffee from their scientific lips, these ones would at least be trying to look in the little Queen's ears and up her nose.

Another scientist spoke now. "Already I count her toes. Five on each foot. Not very unusual. I expect her to be regal and kick me. And she did. Then she say sorry."

"She is young and frightened girl, not Queen with magic. But we keep examining."

"And we examine extremely hard this afternoon when Winterbee and Glimp come back and take charge!"

Hodie and Murgott gripped each other's arms. Even if there was such a thing as magical ability, it would not be something that scientists could scrape off a tongue or find inside like a lump of liver. Probably Prowdd'on would punish them for not finding anything. Maybe they'd make up false results so they wouldn't have to tend the Ocean Toads.

There was the trickle of more tea and coffee being poured, and the scientists began testing each other on their equations. The footsteps of Murgott behind him, Hodie crept along the corridor past stacks of animal crates, past rooms full of even more cages. Something gave a soft *quack*. A softer *yip* and *purr* replied as if the rabbits and birds and mice were giving signals.

The squirrel skittered ahead, peered in a room, and flicked its tail. Hodie darted up and stopped in the doorway.

Sibilla lay on a big chair tilted back like a bed, her hands on the arms of the chair, and her hair a frizzy cloud. She wore pink-and-white striped pajamas and a pink hospital dressing gown. She still had her pendant, but her feet were bare. On her lap was a pile of magazines. Dozens of others lay scattered on the floor. Every open page showed a picture of the Emperor.

She looked up and saw Hodie. For a moment hope flashed across her eyes, then she looked horrified. "What are you doing? Please, leave the city." Her voice cracked. Her arms didn't move, but her fingers trembled. She half sat up and another magazine slid *splat* to hit the floor.

Hodie kept an ear cocked in the direction of the staff room. "If Prowdd'on can wangle promises into lies, you shouldn't have to keep any promise to him. He isn't going to let us go! We have to escape." He beckoned Murgott hard, then hissed at Sibilla. "Come on! You're brave, but this is stupid."

"Mind your manners to Her Majesty," growled Murgott in Hodie's ear. "Your Majesty, hurry."

A tear rolled down her cheek, but still only her fingers moved.

"We're risking our lives for you. This is the only chance. I've sent the bird out, but…" Hodie rested a hand over the satchel beneath his cloak. "I have something else, in here. You know what it is. The drawstring bag that Prow'ddon's after."

The little Queen's face changed at once. "With The Ties," she whispered. "The Ties."

Murgott gasped. "You've stolen them back? Good lad!"

"If you won't come," Hodie hissed to the Queen, "Prowdd'on might get hold of them."

"Hodie, I'm strapped to the chair!"

He dashed to her side. "You should have said at once you couldn't move!"

"I would expect a clever boy to notice." Her voice cracked again.

Hodie wrestled at the buckles around her wrists, but Murgott strode in, opened his pocketknife, slipped it under the straps, and simply slashed them.

# ONE CHOICE LEADS TO SOME LUCK BUT ...

The little Queen rubbed her face and eased her arms after the hours sitting tied up.

"Quick," Hodie whispered.

"Hurry quietly," Murgott added. He held a pair of small pink slippers in his hand and the little Queen's bag.

From the staff room, Hodie heard the clattering of cups into a sink and grumbles about whose turn it was to rinse the dishes.

But Sibilla tipped her head as if she was listening to something else, and a new look came into her eyes. She stepped to the door and across the corridor. She put her hands on a strong iron door, drew a breath, and rolled it open. Hodie ran to see. Murgott was behind him, keeping guard.

The room was nearly all cage. Inside was the huddle of silver, the curve of a great beak, the movement of shallow breathing from a great feather-scaled chest. It was the Dragon-eagle, brought down from the Zoo.

The creature raised its head and looked at Sibilla. Something began to ring in Hodie's ears.

~ *Your Majesty* ~ a silver whisper said ~ *Please go* ~

Sibilla stretched a hand toward it.

~ *My companion is dying* ~ came the chime of silver ~ *Find my companion. Only then can you and the King rescue me* ~ The creature's coronet of feathers was a dim flicker of silver and green ~ *My wing is broken* ~

"How…what shall I do?" Sibilla whispered.

~ *Courage first* ~ said the Dragon-eagle ~ *Magic later* ~ The great eye looked right at Hodie ~ *Release the wind* ~ The eye closed and the great head lowered.

Hodie's ears rang with a silvery echo. His whole being seemed to shiver.

Murgott pulled him and the Queen back into the corridor and rolled the door shut. Ears still ringing, Hodie hauled Sibilla into a gap between stacks of cages. She fumbled into the pink slippers. Murgott wriggled under his cloak to shuck off his jacket. He helped the little Queen into it over her dressing gown—it was masses too big, but he rolled the cuffs up, stuffed her hair down into the jacket collar, and fastened the buttons at her neck. "Hope to blazes that'll hold it," he muttered and slung her bag over her shoulder.

They sidled for the stairwell. In another room Hodie saw the scruffy squirrel patting the locks of cage after cage. The doors fell open. A guinea pig scuttled out and off down to the staff room. A rabbit followed.

There was a yell. The bustle of scientists rushed about.

Dishes smashed and there were scientific curses. The guinea pig hurtled out and disappeared along the corridor. A scientist chased after it and bumped into Murgott.

Murgott pointed to an open door across the hall. "It went that way!"

The scientist ran in. Murgott slammed the door and turned a lock. Scientists came scrambling from the staff room on hands and knees after rabbits, frogs, mice, pink salamanders.

Hodie, the Queen, and Murgott started to run. Whiffs of heat filled the corridor. But Hodie knew that now there was a chance they might escape. *Release the wind*, the silver voice had said. Of course. Hodie knew about wind. But they'd have to climb as high as possible. They must jam open all the doors between the levels of the cavern city.

They made it to the door into the square without being stopped. Hodie would have to loosen a nut so the door would jam open. He thrust a hand into his satchel and into the bag. The spindly wrench fit into his palm.

They rushed up to the next level and the next. With the wrench Hodie managed to jam the doors open each time. Heat from the lower levels rose and rose behind them, almost unbearable. Up they climbed from the square, up three more levels. Everywhere the people they passed were puffing and fanning themselves. Most of the women and girls wore silly shoes, and nobody questioned the little Queen's pink slippers. The effort of climbing turned Murgott's face purple. Sibilla's face was patchy red. Hodie's lungs hurt. The heat pushed and shoved behind them.

At last they saw Allana and Dardy waiting outside the door to the main wind-garage.

"Is that the…?" Allana immediately gritted her teeth as if she was a mother with a sulky daughter, then she hugged Queen Sibilla to her side and threw her own light cloak over Sibilla's head. Sibilla stuck her chin out and slumped her shoulders. Any passersby quickly looked in another direction because sulkiness is extremely unattractive.

Hodie used the wrench on the bolts of the wind-garage door so it couldn't be opened without tools from either side. "Now up," he gasped. "Further up." His idea—the Dragon-eagle's idea—might not work, but Hodie trusted the map O'sel had drawn.

"There's a faster way," Allana gasped. "The Emperor has a special elevator pulled by ogres…"

"We have to do it this way," Hodie puffed back.

Up they climbed, up. Dardy stumbled, pale as paper. Murgott half-carried him. The stairs narrowed. Sirens began to shriek, along with an announcement from loudspeakers: "Fontanians on loose! Catch all Fontanians!"

Luckily they were above the crowds by now. They kept climbing in the rising heat—squirrel too—and finally came to the top level. No sirens blared here, so that was more luck. Hodie slipped the wrench back into the bag safe within his satchel.

There were two doors. One, marked with a small sunburst, was for the Emperor's elevator. The other showed a huge sunburst. In front of it sat two guards at a little table. One hummed the latest hit. The other was cleaning his thumbnail with his bayonet. Hodie's heart began to fall.

Panting with exertion, Sibilla nodded to the guards. "Thank you," she said, though the guards had done nothing. "Let us in, by royal command."

The guards scrambled to their feet, slightly puzzled.

"Fontanians?" said the one with half-clean fingernails.

"Of course not, we're Um'binnian," said Lady Allana. "You can tell. Look at our footwear."

"School trip with best friend of Princessa." Murgott wiped his forehead on his sleeve. "Boy—girl—writin' essay. School. Silly children, project nearly overdue, you know how it is."

The guards chuckled, opened the door, and let them through.

Inside there was only one wind-car. Though it was small (a real surprise!), its roof was adorned with twirls of gold. And there, directly opposite where Hodie stood, was the exit to the outside, a closed slab of marble.

Hodie shut the door back into the stairwell as swiftly as possible. He grabbed a pair of pliers from a handy rack (there was always such a rack in any garage) and placed them near the door so he could wedge it open at the right time.

The squirrel wheezed to show how difficult and long the climb had been. Hodie's mother crouched to gain her breath. Dardy looked especially faint.

"Into the wind-car," Hodie gasped.

Dardy's chest heaved, but he staggered with Sibilla into the wind-car. Allana stumbled after them. Hodie and Murgott clambered in too. The seats were gold and twirly, one brighter and more twirly than the others (no prize for guessing whose). Little cabinets with gold doors lined the rear. The wind-car's walls glittered with mirrors, reflections of purple and gold.

"Dardy, do you know how to start the engine?" Hodie asked.

Dardy shook his head.

Hodie turned to Murgott. "You watched Lu'nedda with the sails, when she was Ogg'ward. Show Dardy, quick."

The Corporal chewed his lip and shook his head.

Hodie had got them this far and they wanted to give up! He'd had one night—just one night—living like a lord, and now everything was for nothing. Self-pity and frustration began to choke in Hodie's chest. Of course there was no such thing as marvelous magic! If there were, it would be here to help the Queen! The squirrel gave an angry chitter and nipped his boot.

"All right." Hodie jabbed Dardy with a finger. "You taught me all I know about how things work—these controls can't be difficult. The engine would probably have helped, but I hope we don't need it. Now listen. When the slab to the outside is fully open, I'm going to jam open the door into the stairwell. Air will rush up from inside the mountain—it should lift the wind-car up and send it well out. All we have to do is get enough height to glide over the Moat."

With a little more color in his face, Dardy examined the controls.

"Your Majesty and my mother," Hodie continued. "Just sit and hang on tight."

Allana grabbed Sibilla by the hand. Hodie felt a flicker of jealousy, but the plan was moving on.

Sibilla's eyes shone. "What about you?"

"When Murgott and I have got the slab open, Murgott leaps in and helps Dardy. Then I jam open the door and hope the guards don't catch me. I'll jump in at the last moment."

Hodie checked the satchel was firm on his back, nodded just like a soldier to Murgott, and Murgott signaled back (just like a Corporal). Then the two of them raced over to the marble slab. The Corporal heaved a lever. Slowly the slab began to roll…there was the dazzle of sky…

A yell rang out behind the inner door, and it was flung wide open. Hot air from deep inside Um'Binnia began to rush into the cavern much too soon.

"What's going on? Close exit at once!" It was Commander Gree'sle, pistol drawn, Prowdd'on behind him, and Princessa Lu'nedda in a bright pink dress with matching handbag and slippers with rubies. She clutched a hand over her mouth.

"Dardy! Steady the wind-car!" Hodie yelled.

"Stop criminal Fontanian!" roared Prowdd'on.

The guards rushed in behind the Emperor.

Warning bells began to ring, but the slab continued to roll open. Murgott wedged his Um'Binnian hat behind the lever to hold it down, ran to the wind-car, and dived in.

Gree'sle sprinted and caught Hodie's wrist. Hodie tugged to free himself, but the Commander's skinny hand was strong as iron.

"Hodie!" Dardy plunged out of the wind-car and staggered down onto his knees.

Gree'sle's pistol aimed at Dardy. Hodie kicked and spoiled the shot. The Commander wrestled Hodie along the floor, but Hodie managed to steer him toward the pliers. He scooped them up and whacked the back of Gree'sle's knee. The Commander buckled. Dardy recovered his footing and helped Hodie pull free. They leaped past the guards, back into the wind-car.

Murgott was struggling with the controls. "Dardy," he cried, "give me a hand!"

"Hurry!" cried Hodie. The hot blast would only last another moment.

The wind-car bucked, lifted, and bounced on the cavern floor. Hodie glanced up through the window—its sails were spread.

But a guard was scrambling in. Murgott raised a boot and pushed him out. The wind-car rose then dropped again.

"We're too heavy!" Murgott cried. "Ditch the ballast!"

Dardy looked at Lady Allana and the Queen. He let go the controls, gave Lady Allana a salute, and jumped from the wind-car. A guard was on him at once with the flash of a sword. Dardy was flung down like an old cloak.

'No!' screamed Allana.

She leaned too close to the door. The second guard reached in and dragged her out in the jangling of the warning bells.

The wind-car quivered on the brink. It must still be too heavy…

"Take the controls, Hodie!" Murgott cried. "Save the Queen!"

Murgott leaped out.

Only Hodie and Sibilla were left in the wind-car. Which lever would save her? This one? That? The wind-car still teetered.

"Hodie!" cried his mother's voice. "Go! Now!"

A fresh group of guards rushed in and ran for the wind-car. Somebody thrust between them, landed in the aisle, and slammed the door. It was Lu'nedda. She grabbed the controls and the engine roared. With a jerk, the royal wind-car soared into the air…

The engine spluttered. Lu'nedda cursed. The wind-car began falling. Hodie tumbled, tumbled again. He saw his reflection in many mirrors—a hundred Hodies, a hundred royal wind-cars, falling, falling.

—

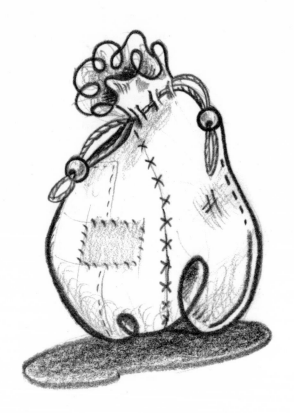

# WHAT TO DO WHEN YOU'VE ESCAPED BUT ONLY SO FAR

# CHOOSE ANY WAY YOU LIKE
## AS LONG AS IT'S DOWN

The wind-car bumped against the cliff, bumped again and rested, rocking, swaying. Hodie was jammed under a seat. Toward the rear the little Queen was on the floor too, white knuckles gripping the base of the golden throne. He couldn't see the Princessa from where he was. Had she tried to save them? Did she know by now the bag was gone from her apartment? Maybe she thought she'd captured them.

Lu'nedda let out a low groan, up at the controls. "No Toad Oil. I ruin engine."

The wind-car lurched. Hodie felt the wind swirl and catch the sails. He saw a flash of rock, then sky—*This is luck*, he thought, *we don't need magic…*

But the moment of limping flight turned into a spinning plummet, another terrible long fall.

The bottom of the wind-car thumped again—branches scraped past, cracking and tearing in the rustle of a million leaves. More bumps—more tearing and scraping—a branch smashed through one window and speared through another on the opposite side. The wind-car hung, suspended. Hodie and the Queen were still flat under the seats. But Hodie could see a way out.

The branch wasn't thick and wouldn't hold for long. With great care he edged backwards, avoiding broken glass as best as he could. His Um'Binnian cloak was some protection. Each time the wind-car moved, he caught his breath. He reached Sibilla. A lot of curls had escaped from the Corporal's jacket collar.

"Can you move?" he asked. She blinked as if she didn't know the answer. "Follow me, slowly."

He slid toward to the door. Lu'nedda was slumped at the controls. Was she hurt? Well... To Hodie, managing one royal female at a time seemed a practical plan for the next steps.

The wind-car wobbled. With a groan, Lu'nedda raised her head, reflected in all the shattered mirrors. The sight of so many Princessas all at once hurt Hodie's brain.

He reached up, fiddled the catch, and the door half-opened. When he peered out, he wanted to throw up.

"We're just a...a bit above the ground." Sometimes a lie was all right, if it would do a necessary job. "The little Queen should climb out first. Princessa, when the wind-car steadies again, it's your turn."

The whole tree creaked. The wind-car shuddered and tilted backwards. The squirrel appeared from somewhere, scampered over Hodie's head (claws in his ear!), and disappeared out into the tree. Lu'nedda was sitting up now, eyes squeezed tight—it looked more with fury than being afraid.

Hodie clung to the door jamb. "Hurry. Or we just wait till we slide off and crash. Sibilla, climb over me and out."

She slid up beside him. "Follow me at once. I won't budge until you promise."

He nodded to make her shut up. "As soon as you're down, run. Run for your life."

"We're much higher than you said! But here goes…" She set a knee into his back (much worse than a paw in his ear). Then she gripped the branch and eased along. He saw her hand stretch for the trunk. There was a splitting noise—the branch held—she managed to scramble down two more branches. She thumped to the ground and started running.

"Get away!" he yelled.

"Hodie, come on!" Sibilla cried.

He turned to urge Lu'nedda, but the satchel under his arm hitched him up. As he freed it, a gust of wind blew, and the branch jerked and tipped him out. He lunged at the trunk, slithered past several branches and somehow landed on his knees below the wind-car, still with the satchel.

"Run!" screamed Sibilla.

The tree creaked again. Hodie dashed to where the little Queen crouched beside a tree stump. The branch stuck through the wind-car cracked and split a little more.

"Princessa!" yelled Sibilla. "Slide out now!"

Lu'nedda appeared, handbag slung over a wrist, a slipper clenched in her teeth. She flailed round and grabbed the branch.

"Get both hands on it," Hodie called. "Now swing your

feet to the branch just below… Right! Work your way to the trunk…now just climb. Down," he added. "Climb down. Down further. Down a lot more."

Lu'nedda landed on the ground and staggered. The branch began a long creak. The Princessa screamed, the slipper dropped, she rushed toward Hodie and Sibilla, and fell into a hollow behind the stump. There was an almighty thud and the ground rocked.

The royal wind-car lay flat on its belly beneath the tree. Glass tinkled again inside for several moments. The twirly gold bits had become spikes full of birds' nests and twigs. The wings were smashed. The only sign of Lu'nedda's slipper was a toe sticking out from under the wind-car.

The Princessa crawled out of the hollow. "You helped me." Her eyes seemed funny, as if she stared at something far away. "You saved me. Both of you."

"You tried to save us first. At least, I think you did," Sibilla said. "So don't go on about it. Sit quietly and recover. Hodie has to decide what we do next."

Hodie actually thought that saving Lu'nedda was an enormous complication. He didn't have a clue what to do now. There the Princessa was, one foot in a ruby slipper, the other in a royal sock. A breeze carried her muttering to him. "Allana…so brave. Dardy…so faithful. And Murgott. How brave. How loyal and brave, and once he used to be a pirate. So loyal. Steadfast. Brave."

Sibilla dragged him away from Lu'nedda's hearing. "What's your plan?"

He closed his eyes. Every plan he'd tried had failed.

This was all because of a load of rubbish that didn't belong to his mother or to him. He slipped the satchel off his shoulder and held it out.

"The stuff's in here. It's yours—you'd better take it." All he wanted was to be left alone. He was obviously hopeless at having parents. He'd found his mother—only by accident—and lost her again almost at once. His real father was dead. Now Dardy was really dead too.

The Queen stepped back. More hair sprang out around her shoulders. "You can't give up now, Hodie. Did you send the bird to Jasper?"

"Well, I sent it away," he said.

"Thank goodness," she said.

"But what use is that?"

Again, she looked as if she'd like to punch him.

He pressed a hand to his chest to help him speak—he owed her that much. "The bird means your brother the King is a clever inventor. But how far can it fly? Does it know where King Jasper is? Can we be sure it flew out of the mountain? It might be stuck in a shopkeeper's wardrobe."

Sibilla looked totally furious as well as ridiculous in Murgott's jacket over pajamas and dressing gown and with the pink slippers. "But Hodie, you held the bird. Did you begin to feel it might be alive?"

He nearly said yes, but shook his head.

"I thought—but maybe it wasn't…" She blinked away tears. "But something else—you knew the hot wind trapped inside the mountain would escape and help the wind-car into the air."

Yes, and he had nearly killed them. He tried again to walk away.

She hurried after him. "We're not even hurt!"

Had she read his thoughts? "Dardy's dead," he managed to say. "My mother's a prisoner. Murgott's dead or captured too. And it's my fault."

For a moment the Queen looked scared again, lost. "Hodie, I'm trying to let you see. We can't give up. I'll never come into my magic, but I must take The Ties to the Dragon-eagle before it dies…" She straightened her shoulders. "Please help me."

"Even if they are The Ties… Look." He took a deep breath. "I'm not your servant. I just want to go south. I don't actually believe that the Dragon-eagles…" The words started to go slippery.

Her hands flew up to hold her lucky charm. "But in the laboratory, the Dragon-eagle spoke to you as well as me. It's relying on me… And it's relying on you too."

Hodie felt a spark inside him, but just for a moment. How could he rescue her any more than he'd already done? How could he save a Dragon-eagle? He limped away and leaned against a tree. He would have liked to weep—for Dardy, his mother, Murgott, and himself—but he had no energy.

A chittering sounded above him. The squirrel, on a branch, cocked its head as if it listened. There were bird calls and a sort of rushing in Hodie's ears, but it wasn't the breeze. Through the trees he saw the gray and white churning of the Great Salt Moat. Salt water meant the sea.

The Moat had to have an opening to Old Ocean.

He stared up at the shattered wings of the royal wind-car. A breeze rattled through them. What you needed, so Dardy had taught Hodie, was common sense and a way with a hammer. What you needed, so Murgott had taught him, were tactics. The best tactic now was a way off the shore and onto the sea. This was something that an odd-job boy could do!

Of course the sea around here was said to be infested by Ocean Toads. He just had to hope like blazes it was the Toads' day off.

—

## SENSIBLE SHOES

Hodie walked around the wind-car and tapped the panels of its sides. They seemed sound, though they might be damaged underneath. Anyway, his spark of energy was back.

The squirrel chittered again, high in the tree. Hodie glanced up the mountain. Broken trees showed the path the wind-car had tumbled. Something glinted high up. If it was Um'Binnian soldiers climbing down to find them, with luck they'd stuff their boots in rabbit holes and trip.

There was rustling in the bushes and a shout. The soldiers! Hodie spun round, but the man who stumbled into the clearing was Corporal Murgott with his duffel bag and a coil of rope over his shoulders. He was bruised, tattered, scratched (and bare-headed, of course). His eyes were fierce. Sibilla looked as if she only just stopped herself running over to kiss him hello. (Hodie would have liked to hug him too but didn't let on, though he couldn't stop grinning.)

Lu'nedda glanced at Murgott, went very red, and turned

her royal nose away. After the fuss she'd been making, Hodie would have expected her to welcome the Corporal with a kind word or royal nod.

Murgott staggered to Hodie and dropped a heavy hand on his shoulder. "Boy, I'd like to say don't worry, but that's for a young man to decide for himself. What I can say is an hour ago your mother was alive, but Prowdd'on had her. As for Dardy—I'm sorry, boy. A loyal servant. A hero. He was as good a father to you as he knew how. He had faith in you, boy."

Hodie didn't trust his voice to stay steady, but he nodded and patted his hand on top of Murgott's.

The Corporal turned to salute Sibilla. She made a queenly gesture for him to sit, and he sank down at once. He blinked at Lu'nedda's one slipper, drew in a breath, and thrust a hand in his duffel bag. "Princessa," he mumbled. "For your use."

Hodie expected him to bring out the emerald slipper from the Depot (though it might have been for the wrong foot). But Murgott offered the Princessa his best boots, restored to the highest gloss.

Lu'nedda's eyebrows pulled together as if they needed to lean on each other for some support. "Oh," she said. "Oh." (Which made one *oh* for each boot.) She blushed right down her neck, accepted the boots, and tried them on. They looked surprisingly good with her pink dress. "Good workmanship. Perfect fit." She took a few steps. "Thank you, Corporal Murgott."

"Happy to be of service, ma'am." Murgott tried to

stand and salute again but collapsed to the ground. "That's record time for scalin' down a mountain. I have never been so wrecked in all my days."

Birds flew shrieking across the clearing.

"We can't sit about," Sibilla said. "Hodie's had a good idea."

How did she know? He hadn't said anything. "I know that look of yours," she said. (Again, Hodie hadn't said a word.)

He cleared his throat. "First, Corporal, do you know anything about the waters in these parts? I mean, is there a channel to the open sea?"

Murgott gave a cautious nod. Hodie felt a stronger huff of energy.

"Then, Princessa, we put the wind-car in the Moat," he said. "It was windtight, so it might be watertight. There are no holes that I can see after the crash, except for the windows. I think it will float. Anyway, it's the only idea I've had."

"My father's royal wind-car! In salt water!" The Princessa stood stock still in the clean polished boots. "Brilliant idea."

"Sweaty work," Murgott said. "But I'm up for it."

"It also rather depends on the Princessa," Hodie muttered. "She could be waiting for the moment to signal the Emperor."

"Ask me why I fling myself into wind-car at last moment," said Lu'nedda. "Ask me why I try to save your life and Queen Sibilla."

"Let's just get working." Hodie began pulling down vines to lash the broken wings together to make stout sails.

"I tell you anyway," said Lu'nedda. "I have three wishes.

One wish is to have no war. Second wish is to save life of my best friend's son. Third wish is not to have husband." She tipped her head a little and frowned. "Correction—not to have stupid husband."

"But you also want your father the Emperor to be proud of you," said Hodie.

"Parents make things complicated," Lu'nedda answered. "I will be Empress of Um'Binnia one day. Until then I must mostly be daughter—when I am not secretly being chief rebel."

"Lu'nedda," said Sibilla, "whether you want war or not, at the moment you are actually an official enemy. You don't have to help." The little Queen began to coil the vines that Hodie tore down.

Lu'nedda strode over and reached higher up the tree for some good tough creepers. Sibilla bowed. "Thank you, Princessa."

"You are welcome." Lu'nedda bowed back then yanked another length of vine.

It was sweaty work indeed. The squirrel slunk down a branch to watch. Gnats and other nibbly flying things didn't seem to bite Sibilla much but thoroughly bothered Hodie. Murgott came out with some interesting words for flying pests, and they'd be very hard to spell.

Murgott and Hodie hopped onto the top of the wind-car. They began piecing the broken wings together, lashing them with the vines and Murgott's rope.

Hodie peered up the mountain. Was that glint the soldiers of Um'Binnia coming closer?

"Sibilla, remember that you and I are sisters in royalty." Lu'nedda spoke with a piece of creeper between her teeth (which meant rather a lot of saliva). "But my father is sure to arrive soon. He will make me explain why I help you escape this far. I think up probable answers."

"We could say we captured you." Sibilla mopped her forehead and took off Murgott's jacket. A label across the back of her dressing gown read, *Property of Biggest Research Institute of Um'Binnia.*

"Of course, I love my father." Lu'nedda's voice wobbled as if she'd choked on a crust of emotion. "But that does not mean I approve of all he does. I do not approve of selfish royalty, though I am sure he started out with good intention." She tied a very tight knot and glanced at Murgott. He was gazing with unmistakable admiration. "I am not saying I would be better ruler than my father. But I would have people around me to say their honest opinion." She cleared more emotion from her throat. "I would begin by listening to other people. Disloyal people like rebels, who just want their voices heard. Honest and brave people, like various I have met in last few days."

The Princessa brushed her hands on the bright pink skirt and looked at the smashed toe of her ruby slipper, buried under the wind-car. She strode over to the other slipper, picked it up and tossed it in the bushes. Then she stood up straight.

"Now, how to shift vehicle down to the beach?"

Hodie felt a little sorry for her and also impressed. But it wasn't his business to say anything. He just got on with the job. They picked broken glass out of the wind-car very carefully, then used muscle (Murgott and the Princessa), loud and cross exclamation (all four of them), and lots of sweat (ditto). They tripped over many tree roots. They nearly tripped over the squirrel. Hodie felt the wind sneak under the belly of the wind-car to lighten the load with shoves and nudges. Birds called from the forest, the sky, and the shore.

In light that shivered through the leaves of the last few trees, the wind-car slid over bumpy tufts of grass, then crunched the pebbles of the beach and nosed the waves.

Sibilla turned to the Princessa. "Thank you. I hope you'll be all right till your father arrives."

"You think I am staying?" cried the Princessa. "I am in trouble whatever I do now. This adventure delays probable punishment of being stuck in beautiful apartment till my father dies." She tucked up her skirt and helped Sibilla scramble in the wind-car with the squirrel (*tck-tck!*), which meant she got Murgott's best boots thoroughly soaked.

Hodie's first new boots ever were soaked too. Cold water splashed to his waist. He bunched his cloak around the satchel to help keep it dry and hoisted it on his shoulder.

Faint shouts floated down the mountain.

"One last heave, boy, then hop in." Murgott set his back to the wind-car.

Waves tumbled over the pebbles and helped the wind-car—now a wind-ship—push further from shore. In the breeze, Hodie thought he heard the swish of a (proper) wind-car. Without question, the Great Emperor was on the hunt.

—

# LIFE-BOTTLES

Murgott's previous life as a pirate was a blessing. Now that water was under the wind-ship's belly he gained confidence about using the controls to tilt the sails and catch the wind. He also roared orders.

"Hodie, keep that blasted squirrel off my head. Princessa, keep your blasted weight in the middle of the vessel, pardon me, Princessa. Excuse me, Your Majesty, but shut the blasted windows tight."

"Most of them are broken," said Sibilla. "But I will if you like."

In a luggage rack, again the squirrel shivered and ground its teeth.

"Do you wish you'd had a chance to bite Prowdd'on harder?" Hodie murmured.

Its tail lashed.

"Right." Murgott grabbed Hodie by the scruff and set him at the controls. "Keep it steady."

Hodie's stomach was a pit of fright, but he felt his face split with a grin. He stood with the waves beneath, the wind above—this was as good a magic as a boy could wish for.

"Safety gear. Catch, Your Majesty!" Murgott threw seat cushions to the little Queen. "See if you can turn them into life-jackets."

What? Cushions would fill with water and drown them all at once—

"They'd be death-jackets!" Sibilla cried as if again she'd heard what Hodie thought.

"Blast," said Murgott.

"An easy mistake to make," murmured Lu'nedda. She was definitely sweet on Corporal Murgott, but still Hodie did not entirely trust her. He had thought her more reliable when she was Ogg'ward behind that mustache.

The wind-ship had sped out from shore, but now Murgott grabbed back the controls. "I'm heading no further till the little Queen has a life-jacket!" he shouted. "Do any of you own a brain that thinks?"

Lu'nedda flung open a gold cupboard, rummaged, and started hauling out bottles—*Um'Binnian Roar-juice*. "It is best that dolleros can buy." She popped a cork—there was a strong smell of cabbage and something so sweet and minty that it was horrible.

"Ugh! Wormwood!" cried Lu'nedda, and tipped the contents through a window.

"Oi!" said Murgott.

"Life-jackets," said Lu'nedda. "Empty them out, cork them tight and tie them round our waists."

"We'll float and clink." Sibilla gave the first smile Hodie

had seen from her in ages. "It would be musical."

"We can use cords from the window blinds to lash them together," Hodie said. He was trying to be helpful, though he could see that if he put on a life-jacket, he'd have to hoist the satchel higher on his shoulder.

Sibilla was at a window already. "Murgott, could you please start sailing while we're working?"

The Corporal grumbled at the Queen's polite request, but he set the wind-ship off toward the east. The squirrel clambered down to sniff an emptied bottle of Roar-juice. It licked the top. Its round black eyes looked everywhere at once. *Koff! Ptha! Ptha-ah!*

There was a splintering sound from the controls. Murgott held up a broken lever and said something that small children should never hear. Small metal nuts had rattled to the floor. Hodie fished in his satchel, into the drawstring bag, pulled out the wrench and fixed the lever tight in half a minute. He thrust the wrench back in the bag. Sibilla gave it a puzzled look but she said nothing.

The wind-ship caught the breeze and raced along. By now the Princessa was knotting cords around the bottles. Sibilla began to figure aloud how many it would take to support each person. "Eight for Murgott. Four for Hodie or maybe six…?"

Overhead was a long swishing sound. A small sleek wind-car zoomed in front of them and circled back. "Military wind-car!" cried Lu'nedda.

"Stop in name of Emperor!" boomed a voice through a megaphone. The wind-car zoomed off and back again.

Guns pointed out along its sides. "Stop! By order of Great Prowdd'on!"

"There is no need for fright." Lu'nedda didn't look as if she believed her own words. "Wind-vehicles cannot hover so they cannot aim."

Well… Fontanian soldiers would only need a moment to aim and shoot. Hodie was pretty sure Um'Binnians would be the same.

*Boom!* The wind-ship jerked. Something shattered up top.

"Just one thing," Murgott said through gritted teeth. "We don't have an anchor."

"Don't worry about anchors now!" Sibilla cried.

"Just one other thing," Murgott replied, "we need a steady wind."

Sibilla turned to Hodie, eyes hopeful. The squirrel darted to the rear of the vessel and chittered like mad.

Then Hodie found himself at the back window too, gazing high into the sky. There were strands of cloud behind the mountain. A Force Six wind, Strong Breeze, would do the job—his thought was clear and determined.

Within a second, the gusts were boisterous. Sibilla looked extremely pleased. Hodie felt afraid and very excited—this must be what it was like to have a link with magic. Was the little Queen doing this through him—calling the wind just as the Dragon-eagle said? He was not at all sure that he liked it, but the squirrel *tck-tcked!*

Gusts pushed the wind-ship on. Upper currents of wind buffeted the Um'Binnians back and forth, but the military wind-car zoomed overhead again.

Lu'nedda leaned out a window. "Stop at once! I am Princessa!"

Scraps of megaphone voice came on the wind. "It is orders... Great Prowdd'on!"

There was a flash, another *boom!* The wind-ship jolted.

"They're aiming at the sails," said Murgott. "Clever blokes, that's what I'd do."

If the sails ripped and splintered, waves would drive the wind-ship back to the rocks and stony beaches of Um'Binnia. Murgott tacked to catch the wind. The wind-car approached time and again, firing its guns, but the wind-ship's sails still held.

Though the military wind-car swooped past very close, the soldiers must have used up all their bullets. They waved in a jeering way, then the wind-car lifted and headed back toward the mountain.

Hodie studied the sky ahead, the wisps of cloud, the flight of birds—to the east he glimpsed dark jagged shapes that might be headlands.

"Is the tide coming in or going out?" he called. "Will it take us through the channel?"

"No idea!" called Murgott. "I never dared be a pirate in these parts."

"Because my father is so powerful," said Lu'nedda.

*Don't mention the Toads*, Hodie thought, *don't mention...* Murgott touched a finger to his cap. "No, ma'am. I never dared because of the Toads."

Lu'nedda screamed and banged the window shut. (Not much use. By now it was the only one not broken.) The

Corporal wrestled with the controls and kept glancing at the waves of the Great Salt Moat.

"Toads," Murgott repeated, "spit poison. With that poison, they blind you. If it gets you in the ear, it deafens you. And if it gets you on your tongue, it's a big goodnight."

"Believe him." Lu'nedda's ringlets were in tatters. "When I was little, my father told me bedtime stories about Ocean Toads. I never slept well."

"Y'poor little brat!" Murgott exclaimed then looked abashed.

"No, no." The Princessa shook her tangled ringlets. "It is what Emperor should do, tell scary stories to teach daughter to be brave. That is why I am brave now. It means I will be strong Empress when my time comes."

She yanked another cork from another bottle and stood as far from a broken window as she could while pouring out Roar-juice.

~

Waves billowed. So did the clouds. Murgott taught Hodie a bit about how to judge waves and manage sails, and he even patted Hodie's back instead of pounding it when he got something right. So the next half hour was rather less painful.

The squirrel looked more green than gray, probably due to its lick of Roar-juice. In a cupboard by the royal chair, Hodie found a can labeled "Big & Best Peanuts" which he offered the squirrel. It turned its face to the wall with a pitiful squeak. He tried one himself—stale, small, only just better than nothing—and shared the rest out.

Sibilla and Lu'nedda finished four life-jackets (eight

bottles each for Lu'nedda and Murgott, four for Hodie, two for Sibilla, and two miniature ones for the squirrel). Lu'nedda joined Murgott at the controls, where they seemed to get on shyly.

Sibilla began to help Hodie into his life-jacket. "You're fatter than I thought. I measured wrong."

He looked down. He did seem plumper on one side, under the cloak. Somehow the satchel seemed heavier. He put a hand to it, and it was definitely bigger. Something was happening in the bag, inside the satchel.

"Come on," he whispered. "You should have a look."

They climbed on the seat behind the golden throne where there was a little privacy. Hodie slipped the satchel off. Nerves fluttering, he eased out the drawstring bag and opened it just a bit.

Inside was a mass of pale fronds, hiding the wrench and notebook. They felt silky, like a caress.

"It's seedlings," Sibilla murmured. "One corner of the satchel's damp—it must have happened when you launched the wind-ship."

The beads or pebbles were really seeds? Hodie examined more closely. The pouch of brown things had burst open. Most of them still lay inside like little stones. But three others had tiny shoots. The tangle they made was pulsing as if it tried to reach the light and it was already tinged with green.

"What about the other stuff?" he whispered.

Sibilla held her pendant tight and shook her head. "Close the bag. Buckle it away again. Please, keep it hidden!"

She looked worried, said nothing more, and took Lu'nedda's and Murgott's jackets over to them.

Hodie felt helpless. Whether The Ties were magical or rubbish, it couldn't be his job to carry them. But he didn't object in case Lu'nedda overheard. He began to push the bag back in the satchel then noticed that part of the bag's lining had come away. He hadn't even known it had a lining.

Carefully, so the fronds didn't bruise, he eased his fingers through the frayed stitching—a piece of paper? He couldn't stop himself from looking further.

There, in the lining of the bag, was a secret pocket and the corner of a sheet of softest silver. The pocket folded down easily, as if it wanted to show what it had protected for so many years. Prickles of fear traced Hodie's spine.

He didn't dare touch the sheet of silver. But the warmth from his hand was like a breeze that brought the sheet to life. The silver shimmered, curving lines appeared... words...tiny etched symbols. A map—the one Prow'ddon asked about in the Grand Imperial Hall. Yes, it must be.

The silver map, with its faint glow, was so beautiful that all he wanted to do was gaze... There was the Eastern Isle where the Dragon-eagles dwelt for most of each year, the islands of Old Ocean, the City of Spires. There, behind the City, were the Stones of Beyond. There was the Great Salt Moat around the Mountain of Um'Binnia. At the top of the map were more mountains, so rugged that Hodie felt exhausted at how hard they'd be to climb.

This might be magic, or it could be just science— *Whatever it is, it shouldn't be happening to me*, he thought.

*This should be seen only by the King or Queen. I'm nobody—this is not right.*

The wind-ship tilted. Swiftly Hodie folded the pocket back up over the map, tightened the drawstring, and tucked the bag into the satchel against his side. He closed his eyes. It seemed that the wind chimed with the anxious sound of silver feathers as if a great creature shifted while it hoped for the arrival of a Queen who would know how to save it.

# HOW TO PLEASE AN
# OCEAN TOAD

The wind-ship tipped back and forth so much that Hodie was sure he would throw up. Salt spray blew in the windows, out the other side, then in again.

Murgott let out a roar. "Breakers ahead! Keep it steady!" The Corporal was keeping the ship steady all by himself, if you asked Hodie. He decided Murgott liked to shout orders because it gave him something to obey.

The Princessa pointed to those dark shapes like fists either side of a blur of gray sea. "If we get beyond headlands, I can be free. Free of my father. I will build bungalow outside in sunshine, with biggest green lawn, and flowers of pink, crimson, and blue…"

"A little cottage close to the sea would suit me fine," said Murgott. They both blushed.

Hodie stared at the horizon, hoping it would stop him from feeling seasick. The headlands and beyond made his eyes water. So he glanced down and saw a little puddle… and another…too many puddles to be the squirrel's accidents.

"We might not get past the headlands," he called. "Your father's wind-car has sprung leaks."

The Princessa dropped to her knees and checked. "So. We are going to sink and drown," she said in a matter-of-fact tone.

The wind-ship tilted sharply then just as sharply tipped the other way. Lu'nedda stood up, life-bottles clinking, pulled herself to her full height (very tall and very full—imposing) and faced Murgott. "I will say at this point, it has been great privilege to know you, Corporal Murgott. Such fine steady loyal person. That is all I have to say."

"Er." Murgott seemed to realize that hardly-a-word was not enough of a reply. Hodie agreed—if you were probably about to die, you should choose some good last words. "Er," Murgott said again, "thank you, Princessa. For my part, I have never met so fine a lady." He glanced at Sibilla with some embarrassment. "Except for my little Queen's mother, Lady Helen. And except of course for Her Majesty Queen Sibilla."

"I'm still twelve," Sibilla said, "and not a lady. Please get us through the headlands so with luck we come to shore beyond the Moat. Then I'll have a chance to grow up. Murgott, please, do your best."

She was being very brave and Queen-like now without being bossy. But Hodie saw how tense she was. He hoped he would be as brave when it was needed (which was actually right now). Those waves beyond the headlands would pitch the wind-ship around like a cork from a bottle.

*Chitter!* screamed the squirrel. *Chitter-chit!*

Lu'nedda screamed too. "A Toad! An Ocean Toad! It's dead ahead!"

~

If the Toad had been ahead and dead, it wouldn't have mattered. But it was alive, heading straight for them, three times bigger than the huge Toad in the Zoo, three hundred times more dangerous. It surged toward them, sank down, then surged again. Each time it surged, a terrible stench came with it.

*Chitter!* the squirrel cried again. *Chitter-tck-tck-tck-tck-tck!*

The little Queen uttered the Royal Swear Word. Hodie wouldn't ever want to repeat what Murgott said. Lu'nedda's curses were Um'Binnian and didn't make sense to Hodie, but he wouldn't repeat them either.

The Toad was closer. Lu'nedda and the squirrel were still screaming.

Murgott was trying to manoeuvre the controls. "Start bailing!" he roared.

"What with?" Sibilla cried.

Lu'nedda yanked open a cupboard and found a royal peanut bowl. She threw it to Sibilla and snatched one herself. They began scooping, tossing water through the shattered windows. It would hardly help a drop.

The wind-ship lurched. The Ocean Toad raised its head alongside. It was nearly as big as a small elephant.

The squirrel batted the last full bottle of Roar-juice toward Hodie's boots. Of course! He grabbed the bottle and yanked out the cork. The smell of cabbage and sickly wormwood fought with the stink of the Toad. Prowdd'on obviously found Roar-juice irresistible—it might appeal to other dreadful creatures.

Hodie held the bottle up to a (broken) window. Teasing it away and back, he kept the Roar-juice just inside the wind-ship. The wind-ship kept bobbing. The Toad kept bumping. The puddles on the floor connected as they grew deeper. The Toad watched the bottle. Its eyes were white with a dot of gray—maybe the creature had poor vision. Maybe it hunted by smell. Its nostrils wrinkled. Hodie put his whole arm out the window. He hoped no royal female (nor Murgott, nor squirrel) would scream at the wrong moment.

The Toad's bottom lip stuck out at last. Hodie upended the bottle and glugged Roar-juice down the toadly maw.

The toad dropped back from the wind-ship and licked where it should have had lips. It blinked. After a moment it rolled over to one side. It rolled back. It ducked under the waves, swooshed up, and rolled again. Dreadful sounds of partying boomed from it.

Then the Toad surged right out of the Great Salt Moat with a joyous bellow. It crashed on the roof of the wind-ship, and the wind-sails smashed into the sea. The vessel lurched to starboard. A wave slammed through the broken windows. It lurched to port and back—more water burst in. Murgott held the wind-ship steady but the weight of the Toad pressed it low in the water.

The Toad's smell like rotten onions stung Hodie's eyes and made his nose run. Sibilla coughed and retched. Lu'nedda gripped Sibilla with one hand while her other covered her own mouth. Sweat poured down Murgott's forehead (unless it was sea water splashes). "Horror," he groaned, "horror, horror…"

The Ocean Toad let out a reverberating belch. The vessel shuddered. The roof creaked and threatened to crack. A vast scaly foot with horny toenails scrabbled in near Hodie's head. Sibilla and the squirrel screamed. There was another resounding belch, another lurch, and the Toad slid—oh, only half off.

For a moment it clung to the side, so big its pale scaly belly (with plenty of warts) covered three windows. At last, with a happy Toad-roar, it flung itself into a backwards somersault and disappeared in a monumental splash.

"Thank you!" Sibilla hugged Hodie, which was surprising.

Weak at the knees (from escaping the Toad), he fell onto a seat. Now all he had to do was wait to drown with the lost treasures of Fontania in his satchel.

—

# SWIMMING STYLES OF
# WEARY TRAVELERS

They still had a roof. But puddles sloshed inside the wind-ship. Waves slammed the hull. They'd reached the headlands.

"Check that your life-bottles are on tight!" Murgott yelled.

The tide dragged the wind-ship past the headlands. It scraped on a rock, just missed another, and splintered against a third. Water dribbled in at a fast rate.

"No, no, no!" Sibilla shouted.

Hodie leaped onto the gold throne-chair, stretched up to the hatch in the roof, and tried to slide the bolt. It stuck—he had to bash it several times—but at last the hatch crashed open. The squirrel scrambled out over his head. Hodie grabbed the edge and hauled himself through and onto the roof. He reached down to help Sibilla, but Lu'nedda pushed her up and was tall enough to clamber out by herself. She was also strong enough to help haul Murgott. There was a frightening moment when Murgott stuck. Hodie suggested the Corporal take off his life-bottles, pass them up first, then climb out, and put them back on. Murgott actually said thank you.

They clung to the top, bracing against the twirly golden bits or the broken spars of the wind-sails. The wind-ship swept northeast in the current. There was no wind.

Hodie gazed at the north and wished for clouds foaming, ripe with gale. Sibilla glanced at him then up at the sky. A strong gust swept out of nowhere, caught the last shreds of sail, and pushed the vessel south, out of the current. Another early shred of magic from the Queen? Sibilla blinked and clutched her pendant.

The wind dropped again and the wind-ship bobbed gently. By now they were far from the headlands and Hodie saw the northern coast stretching up and round to the northeast. The southern coast curved southeast, which was where they were heading, if this bobbing about was going anywhere much by now. The sun was maybe an hour from sinking into the Great Salt Moat behind Um'Binnia. It seemed far longer than a single day since Hodie had eaten bacon and raspberry jam at the Princessa's.

Hodie wiped his nose on his sleeve. His life-bottles clinked. He felt surprisingly good considering. The squirrel crept onto his lap, rested its ugly little head on the satchel, and closed its eyes. Lu'nedda, Murgott, and Sibilla were bedraggled, but Hodie thought that added to your charm if you were a traveler.

It would be a shame for them all to drown now. But, just as the sun was lowering, so was the wind-ship into the waters of Old Ocean.

Hodie wondered if this would be a good time to tell Murgott he was carrying the notebook of poems.

The water lapped and sent up teasing drops.

"We'll have to swim," Sibilla said.

"I cannot," Lu'nedda answered. "After my father's stories about Toads, I do not even like a bath."

*Chit*, said the squirrel.

"I've dog-paddled in the Grand Palace pond," Sibilla said.

"Me too," said Hodie. "Between the ducks."

Murgott cleared his throat. "Then you two had better set off."

"And you?" asked the Princessa.

"Pirates don't swim," Murgott replied.

"I'm not leaving you behind," Sibilla said.

"Your Majesty," said Murgott. "I'm not actually your subject either. I only signed up for the Fontanian Army because you were such a dear little girl when you were small. Now I offer my official resignation. May I have a confirmation letter?"

"No," said Sibilla. "Anyway, I'm not swimming either. The Toad might have plenty of friends."

In a moment of silence, waves licked the sides of the wind-ship. A sea-bird called.

"I was dear little girl once," Lu'nedda said into the sunset. "It is cruel fact that nobody is ever as cute again as toddler at two or three."

"You were a cute little boy," Murgott said to Hodie. The surprise nearly toppled Hodie off the wind-ship. "When Dardy and you arrived at the Grand Palace, you'd just turned three. Still cute. You grew out of it."

Hodie decided this was definitely not the time to mention the poems. The right time would never come now.

Lu'nedda and Murgott sat side by side, staring at the land, not talking. Now and then there was a clink from the life-bottles. The wind-ship bobbed lower. A breeze whistled in Hodie's ears, cold and thin, and stole around his hands. He found his fingers on the buckle of the satchel.

"Before the sun completely goes," Hodie murmured to Sibilla, "you must look at this." He opened the satchel, unfolded the bag, and showed the little Queen the pocket where the silver map lay glowing. Sibilla started to shake her head, but glanced at the Princessa's back and then nodded.

~

The last rays of the sun washed veils of color, pink and peach, through the clouds. The little Queen drew out the map. The glow grew much stronger than it had under Hodie's palm. He took in a breath.

"There's the Eastern Isle, where my father will be," Sibilla murmured. "And there's the City of Spires...the Grand Palace where my mother is...where you lived."

Hodie felt a pang round his heart. "It's your Palace. I did the odd jobs."

"It was your home," said the little Queen. "It still could be, if..." She looked at the glowing map again. "In a steamship, we could be at the Eastern Isle in a couple of days."

The wind dropped completely. The vessel bobbed lower, lower, and bumped on something. Hodie felt sick at the thought of another Toad, but there was no surging. The wind-ship simply seemed stuck.

Murgott clambered to his feet with a gruff laugh. "Tide's full out. We're on a sand bank. There won't be a better chance than this. It's a long walk—or a paddle—to shore. But we already got our boots wet. We've got life-jackets of a sort and company." His smile at the Princessa was rather sweet.

Lu'nedda stiffened. "But that piece of coast is Fontanian."

"Upper Fontania, ma'am. The Waiting Lands," Murgott said.

The Waiting Lands? Waiting for what? Hodie couldn't see the name on the map.

Lu'nedda put her chin up, like a Princessa. "Corporal, our countries are at war."

"For goodness sake," Sibilla said. "It's not as if we can arrest you."

She gentled the map back into its pocket in the bag, taking care not to let Lu'nedda see it. Hodie folded the bag into the satchel again, took off the cloak Lu'nedda had given him (so it was useful yet again), and wrapped it around the satchel. The bundle held high, he slipped into the water. His foot only just touched bottom.

The others splashed in with a few shrieks each. Lu'nedda made roars of protest at how wet the ocean was, but at the same time she seemed to enjoy it. She touched the bottom easily and helped keep Sibilla's chin above the wavelets. Murgott made explosive noises (swallowing curses as well as sea water, Hodie supposed).

"We forgot the squirrel!" cried Sibilla.

*Chit*, said something, spluttering.

The life-bottles were a chinking blessing because the sea floor was uneven. It didn't matter how slowly Hodie went in his one-armed dog paddle. It mattered only that he carried the bag to land, safe and dry. They were going well—very well—till the strings of Murgott's life-bottles broke apart. He roared and splashed. Lu'nedda didn't let go of Sibilla and dragged Murgott along too till he found his footing. Royal females seemed pretty good in an emergency. But it was a long paddle before they waded at last onto a beach.

"Welcome home to Fontania, Your Majesty." Murgott collapsed on his back.

Fontania—Sibilla's home, where they might find the dying Dragon-eagle. Hodie hoped so. He untied his own life-bottles and the squirrel's. There was no house visible, not even a road. The stars had started to come out.

Sibilla's face was a pale oval in the evening gloom. "How far does the tide come in?" she asked.

She really should be a Queen—she had a good brain now that it had started working.

Hodie expected Murgott to take charge, but he seemed utterly exhausted. He'd even stopped cursing. The Corporal simply climbed to his feet and began trudging. Soldiers are trained to do so without question.

They reached the dunes. Beyond was open grassland with a few low bushes.

Lu'nedda groaned. "This is far enough for me." She fell to the ground under a scrubby sort of shrub with tiny white flowers that shone faintly in the dark.

Murgott collapsed again onto his knees. "We're still damp," he muttered. "Need to dry out. Have to huddle to keep warm. Even though one of us is at war with the rest of us. It's sensible soldiering."

This was embarrassing. Hodie didn't want to huddle Murgott. And how could he huddle with a royal female? But something crept beside him and said *Chk?* For a small squirrel it was very warm. He was thankful for its company. And at least they were now in Fontania. He just hoped it wasn't too far from this part to the bit where you might come upon a dying Dragon-eagle.

—

# NO CHOICE FOR
# BREAKFAST

The next morning Hodie learned something new about Um'Binnians. Well, not really new. Just something he had hoped would not stay true. When the Great Prowdd'on gave them orders, Um'Binnians didn't dare give up.

The sun rose in the east (the right place). In the opposite direction, over Um'Binnia, three dots appeared. In the dawn sky they looked like seagulls. As they soared nearer over the headlands, they looked like bigger seagulls with more wings (and sharper ones) than usual. They droned close and passed overhead—Hodie's heart raced. Huge barrel-shaped wind-cruisers, bristling with spiky-looking guns and several cannons.

Lu'nedda shook her head. "They must be new battleships, sent to overcome Fontania. But they cannot land. If they do, they cannot get up again. It is very expensive design problem. It is biggest waste of money."

"But…" said Sibilla.

"They cannot see us here, so they will not shoot,"

Lu'nedda said. "Especially if they know it is me. But I think we hide now."

Hodie caught Sibilla's eye and frowned a little. Sibilla nodded, her pointy chin firm. So she too was still cautious about trusting the Princessa.

The flowering shrub was not big enough to hide them properly. Murgott couldn't tuck his feet in. Nor could Lu'nedda (was she trying hard enough?). Hodie peered up through the thorny branches. One of the wind-cruisers passed overhead. A door in its side seemed to be sliding open.

"I don't think it matters that they can't land," he said. He learned that fright squashes your voice high and thin.

One by one, small soldier-shapes began to drop from the cruiser. For a second they fell like stones, then something shot up from the back of each man and a sort of mushroom opened out. The soldiers floated into the hinterland some distance away.

"Um'binni-chutes!" Lu'nedda said. "I heard Gree'sle boast about them. Oh, my father is supremely clever…"

She seemed to realize it was better to shut up. Even from this distance, Hodie saw one of the Um'binni-chutes was purple and gold. Prowdd'on himself was coming down! His heart sank. That was actually very brave of the Emperor. Bundles of stuff started floating down too. Hodie bet that it was military equipment.

The wind-cruisers turned back toward the mountain.

"What shall we do?" asked Sibilla.

"You're the Queen," Hodie said through gritted teeth. "You tell us."

"What about my opinion?" Lu'nedda sat up straight and her ringlets tangled in the branches. "I am Princessa."

"This isn't your country," muttered Hodie.

"Mind your manners, boy," said Murgott.

"Don't speak to me like that, you're not my father!" Hodie said.

Murgott's face went purple-red. Hodie crouched and dug his fingers into his hair. He usually punched only his own head, but right now he would have loved to hit somebody else.

"Er-*hem*." Lu'nedda freed her ringlets (by now most of them looked like whisk brooms). "Let us begin again. What shall we do?"

"Arrest you," muttered Hodie.

Sibilla whacked him.

"Sorry," she whispered at once and rubbed his arm.

Hodie dared to stick his head out and have a look. The distant Um'Binnians were rolling up their chutes and grouping together.

"The advice of a military man," said Murgott, still red in the face, "is stay in hiding."

"These bushes won't hide us very well for very long," Sibilla said.

"The tactic of coward and wise man would be sneak away," said the Princessa.

"You can't sneak in open country," said Sibilla.

*Tck-tck*, chittered something in the middle of the bush.

"The third possibility is stand firm," Lu'nedda said.

"To fight?" cried Sibilla. "What with?"

"Murgott has his pocketknife," muttered Hodie. "We could take turns to stab the soldiers with the corkscrew."

"No more lip from you, boy," Murgott growled.

Soldiers ought to be good at quick decisions. So should ex-pirates. So should Queens and Princessas. Any of these three should be a million times better than an odd-job boy. But Hodie spoke up, a note in his voice he hadn't heard before. He figured it was better to be brave just before you were captured or killed than never at all. "Princessa, are you on our side or not?"

"I am here," Lu'nedda said. "Beside you."

"That wasn't what he meant," Sibilla said. "But you've already called me royal sister so…yes, I will trust you."

Lu'nedda bowed her tangled ringlets. "Good idea," she said. "Remember it through coming trials."

Hodie kept going. "Empty everything we have from our pockets and bags. Let's see if we have anything to help." He couldn't roar like Murgott because he didn't have a man's voice yet. But Murgott, Lu'nedda—even Sibilla—began to empty out their things.

Murgott had the pocketknife, shaving gear, and extra underpants. He set his anemometer carefully on a pillowy grass tuft. He didn't bring out the emerald slipper, and Hodie thought it best to leave it unmentioned. Sibilla said nothing either.

Hodie tried to read Lu'nedda's face as she tipped out her ringlet-comb (unused) and a handkerchief (used). Perhaps she wanted Prowdd'on to catch up. Perhaps she expected her father to believe she'd been kidnapped a second time. Who could understand the mind of a Princessa? Not Hodie, that was for sure.

Sibilla's bag had her pair of bloodied socks, her hairbrush, and that was all.

Hodie realized Murgott and Lu'nedda were waiting for him to open his satchel, back over his shoulder. The only thing in it was the drawstring bag. Slowly he drew it out.

Lu'nedda's jaw dropped. "You snuck that from my cupboard! Such cunning boy! Such...son of your mother!" The Princessa actually looked impressed.

Sibilla was trembling. "You'd better open it," she said.

The squirrel sat up as if it expected to be fed a magic crumb.

Hodie had no idea what Murgott would say about the notebook, right at the bottom with the sooty squashed cup. He opened the bag slowly.

The tangle of seedlings was paler than before. But at the first touch of sunlight a flush of darker green appeared.

"Can we eat that?" asked Lu'nedda.

Sibilla's hair was a cloud of gold in the sunshine. "I...I think it has to wait."

A sweet fresh scent came from the tangle. It looked to Hodie too as if it was waiting for a signal. He didn't know this in his head, and his heart felt too bruised to know anything except that it longed for a true home where you'd have ordinary arguments about whose turn it was to dry the dishes. No—he glanced at the little Queen's worried and resolute face and knew in his bones that Sibilla was right. The green tangle was waiting for some special moment.

The wind breathed in his ear that there was magic in the world, more magic than Hodie had seen yet. But—well, Hodie thought maybe magic was simply science that was still to be explained. And whatever the truth, magic wasn't really meant for ordinary people, not for him.

Lu'nedda reached toward the bag. "Tip it out. I remember seeing a wrench and a book..."

*Cht-chit!* The squirrel's tail expanded to twice its size. Fur stood up along its spine. It pointed one of its paws toward the east.

Hodie shoved the tattered bag behind his back. Striding toward them over the tufts of spiky grass was a squad of soldiers. Four of them carried a sedan chair. The person in it wore a purple and gold helmet.

Lu'nedda looked a bit sick.

And this was all before breakfast. Actually, Hodie didn't think any of them had eaten since breakfast yesterday, except the squirrel which had taken that lick of Roar-juice. Hodie didn't count the peanuts in the royal wind-car, they'd tasted too horrible.

He felt his hand squeezed. Sibilla gave a very small, sweet smile. "We just have to trust," she whispered. "Trust Lu'nedda and Murgott and each other. I trust you, anyway." So that was another good moment.

Then they and the shrub under which they had slept were surrounded by large soldiers from Um'Binnia. Emperor Prowdd'on, Commander Gree'sle, and the soldiers all looked as if they'd managed to eat a hearty breakfast, probably with vast pancakes and oversized sausages.

# THE CHOICE OF
# OCEAN TOADS

Prowdd'on gave a royal jerk of his hand. After a moment, Lu'nedda brushed down her tattered skirt, pushed her battered ringlets behind her ears, and walked to stand beside the sedan chair.

*Families*, thought Hodie. *Stick together, no matter what—except for mine, of course. Ha ha, that was not a bit funny.*

The little Queen stood straight, hands clasped before her.

"Good morning," she said. "You seem to have captured us again, but what is the point? You can't get home."

"That is in splendid control." Prowdd'on patted his mustache (today it was shaped like two pistols). "My army marches this way now with horses and carriage. The Um'Binnian Imperial Navy is sailing here too. Of course we get home. Meantime, I believe you carry something I desire for many years. Something that will mean I can have both Dragon-eagles as well as Fontania."

"Empty out all pockets! Empty all bags!" Gree'sle's eyes were narrow slivers.

"Look around," Murgott said, "already did."

Hodie snuck sideways to stand so the bag of treasures was concealed between him and Murgott.

An officer picked Murgott's anemometer from the clump of grass, smirked, and flicked the lid open. The little wind-speed attachment popped up.

"Nice toy," said the Great Prowdd'on, and grabbed it. "Now toy is mine." The wind-cups turned slowly. He scoffed and dropped the anemometer on the ground beside his chair.

Hodie saw Sibilla glance at the horizon. Another officer grabbed Murgott's duffel bag and upended it. Out fell Lu'nedda's slipper—the emeralds glinted and the chin-fluff of the mountain dove wafted in the breeze. Murgott blushed like a very hot fire. Lu'nedda looked shocked and blushed like an even hotter fire.

From the ground came a faster whirr from the anemometer. Hodie glanced at it, then at the sky. A dark gray roller of cloud was starting to form on the horizon. He heard Sibilla draw in a breath, but now she was staring down to the beach. Several large gray things bobbed in the surf.

"Your turn, boy. What are you hiding?" Gree'sle's eyes went squintier with every sentence. "Show me at once!"

*Chit!* On its hind legs the squirrel danced toward the Emperor as if it longed to bite and scratch. Sibilla gathered it up, held it tight, and glanced again at the northwest sky.

"Fontanian Ties!" Gree'sle hissed. "Give me Ties! I found them for Emperor and I will give Ties to him now!"

Hodie picked up the bag. What choice did he have? The wind blew his bangs into his eyes and made them sting. He put a hand up, and the bag slipped. One shoot of the green tangle spilled out and touched the ground. He jerked the bag shut and tried to seize the fallen shoot, but it had already twisted into the ground and little green side shoots were beginning to twine around the shrub.

Prowdd'on lurched out of his sedan chair. "Just give The Ties!"

Gree'sle snatched for the bag, but the side shoots forced up and immediately become a thick tangle that kept Hodie from him. Hundreds, thousands of green side shoots grew like a platform now—under Hodie's feet, Sibilla's feet, Murgott's. Within seconds, that one scrap of broken shoot had become a cup of vines for them to stand in, leaves round as coins, flowers like sweet-scented stars. Waist-high to Murgott, the cup encircled and supported them, a barrier between them and the Um'Binnians. It raised them up so Hodie saw past Prowdd'on, past the soldiers, down to the beach.

*Chk-chk-chk!* The squirrel screamed in the little Queen's arms. Murgott groaned and turned pale as paper. The gray things in the waves were Ocean Toads, hopping directly for them—three…four…seven Ocean Toads spread out in formation.

The oniony stench of the seven Toads began to drift up from the beach. Lu'nedda, still at her father's side, put a hand to her nose, went stiff as a statue, then turned and saw the Toads coming. She gave a most impressive scream and grabbed Gree'sle's sword.

"Sire!" cried the Commander. "For heaven's sake, look!"

Prowdd'on let out a yell, began to dive back to his sedan chair, then tried to scramble into the cup of vines. It bounced him off. The wind blew a little harder. One moment Hodie smelled a sweet scent from the green tendrils, the next the odor of Toad again was thick and dank.

Officers used pistols and soldiers used their rifles, but the hides of Ocean Toads were thicker than elephant skin. Even their eyelids were reinforced. Bullets ricocheted and rebounded again off the soldier's armored vests. The Toads came on.

The officers drew their swords but they must have known that Ocean Toads can spit many swords' lengths. The solders backed further, further…by now many of them were well behind the cup of vines (and several had run off into the distance).

Again Prowdd'on tried to clamber through the tangle into the cup. It threw him back a second time. Gree'sle grabbed his sword from Lu'nedda and slashed at the vines. They were unbreakable. Lu'nedda edged away from the Toads but stayed close to the green tangle.

The Toads hopped nearer, white eyes blinking. They croaked and snorted, the kind of noise that meant an animal was hopeful about something delicious.

"Let me in!" shrieked Prowdd'on. The Toads were heading straight for him now.

"The Toads are hungry," Sibilla cried.

A soldier hurriedly unbuckled a rucksack, flung out a sandwich, and jumped back behind the cup of vines. The

Toads croaked, sniffed, shuffled, and ignored it. An officer threw them a bun. But the semicircle of Toads kept closing in.

Hodie, Sibilla, and Murgott ducked down inside the vines.

The squirrel batted Hodie again and spat: *Ptha-ptha!*

"Roar-juice?" Hodie said. "We don't have any."

Sibilla jumped up. "Roar-juice!" she cried to Lu'nedda.

"Roar-juice! Of course!" Lu'nedda pointed at Gree'sle's jacket pocket. "Gree'sle! Give them Roar-juice!"

Gree'sle fumbled the gold flask out of his pocket. The Toads drew in, blinking faster. Pleading croaklets tumbled from their mouths. Gree'sle unscrewed the top and shoved the flask into Prowdd'on's hand.

"Not me, fool! I order you to feed the beasts!" screamed Prowdd'on.

Gree'sle stood like an icicle of fright.

"You are creature of feebleness!" Lu'nedda snatched the flask from his hands and poured out the Roar-juice.

With seven croaks, the Toads bumped over the Emperor, Commander, and Princessa. They pounced on the puddle. Every last soldier screamed and ran behind the cup of vines. Every last officer rattled out confusing orders. There were terrible groans from Prowdd'on and Gree'sle as they wrenched themselves up and out from the Toad-huddle.

"Princessa!" cried Murgott. "Princessa!" He scrambled out of the cup of vines, tripped to the ground, and started crawling to find Lu'nedda, but she was clambering out the other side of the Toad-huddle.

A Toad raised its head and sniffed in the direction of the Emperor.

"Keep them off me, stupid woman!" Prowdd'on cried. "Pour them some more!"

"The flask is empty!" yelled Lu'nedda.

The wind blew so hard that the vines around Hodie and the Queen, held by an anchor of roots, began to rock.

"Save yourselves!" came Murgott's voice from somewhere on the ground. "Hodie, save the Queen!"

If the wind blew hard enough... Hodie tugged the rim of the vines nearest the wind. Yes! The cloud was right above now and the wind increasing with a roar like thunder. Hodie tugged again. At last the roots tore from the ground and the tangle rose into the air. It skimmed across the dunes like a runaway nest.

*Chuk!* The squirrel clambered onto the rim and clung tight, fur ruffled every-which-way in the wind. The Great Prowdd'on and his soldiers, along with Lu'nedda and Murgott, were left far behind. In the last glimpse Hodie had of the Toads, it looked as if they might be playing leapfrog.

# THE PROBLEM WITH DISAGREEMENT

The nest skimmed inland, lifted over a forest, flew across a rushing river, then over more forest. Hodie clung on, sweating. Twigs jabbed into his legs. For a moment, the nest stuck in the top branches of a tree and rocked madly. It tore free but stuck in another tree almost at once.

Sibilla's hands were still white-knuckled. "This is definitely one of The Ties," she began.

"You don't have to make conversation," Hodie said, trying not to be actually sick.

The nest lurched and Sibilla let out a yelp.

"Ouch…" Hodie clung as tight as he could and tried shifting to another spot. "If you're being exact," he continued, "this flying nest could be a sort of tumbleweed. It does come from one of the seeds that seem to be part of some treasures. It is unusual, but there is often a scientific explanation."

The little Queen's jaw clenched, probably on the Royal Swear Word. "It is obviously magic. It's more obvious all the time."

The nest was still stuck, high above ground. The tangle grew more prickly with every moment.

"Ouch," Sibilla muttered. It would be awful if she burst into tears. Instead she tried to smile, but it looked fake-jolly. "Well, we can argue about that later. I just hope it takes us to my brother. Jasper will know what to do."

"For goodness sake!" shouted Hodie. "If you're the Queen, you should know what to do at a time like this! What on earth do royal people teach their children?"

She gave him such a filthy look he was sure she'd come out with the Royal Swear Word. But something small flashed past, flashed back, and clattered into the bottom of the nest. A mechanical brass pigeon—one of Jasper's? Sibilla stretched a foot out and gave it a nudge.

Whirring noises came from the pigeon, clacking and a beep.

"Jasper!" she said.

"Get to…" said Jasper's voice. "…too far for me (*clack*) map is lost…(*clack clack*) Sibilla, I believe you're out of Um'Binnia. You have to find the old… quickly as… (*whirr, click, clack*)."

"But Jasper!" cried Sibilla. "Where will I find the old Dragon-eagle?"

"(*whirr*)…you have The Ties, might also have the map … magic is hard to manage but… trust your instinct … the Dragon-eagle will tell (*whirr, clack*)."

"Jasper!" she yelled again. "Just come and get me!"

"…take The Ties, especially… tinder-cup… Mount of the… (*scraunch*)… I'm sailing across the Great Salt…

(*whirr clack*)… Beatrix and the *Royal Traveler* an hour ahead of me… important for you to know… she discovered… Queen's scepter, you know, the (*graunch graunch*)… in two places for safe-keeping… (*click-ick*)… When you save the old Dragon-eagle, come at once, meet us at the foot of Um … (*clank*)."

One wing of the pigeon fluttered up and then collapsed. A puff of smoke rose from where a real bird might have an ear.

The flying nest rocked madly in another gust and ripped free from the tree.

Sibilla's hair was in the worst tangle Hodie had ever seen. "Now do you believe me?" she shouted.

"I believe the pigeon is a poorly made mechanism!" he shouted back.

The nest hurled through the sky for a moment as if someone had thrown it in a fit of temper. Then, at the edge of the forest, the wind dropped and, with a sickening plummet, dumped the nest down beside a roaring river.

~

Within seconds, the squirrel (when it had stopped reeling) hopped out to nose about. Hodie scrambled out too, getting thoroughly scratched, and had a thorough retch into some bushes. When he staggered back, Sibilla was still in the nest, standing up, looking around with her hands in fists.

"Where are we?" she cried. "We're nowhere! I thought… I thought The Ties would spring into life when I needed them. That we were heading toward Jasper."

He shook his head. "It's not a good idea to believe everything will turn out the way you want."

Again she looked as if she'd love to give his shins a royal kick, but she stayed in the nest. "But the Toads came just in time. The wind blew exactly when we needed to escape."

"The first Toad liked the Roar-juice, told its friends, and they sniffed us out at a lucky moment," Hodie said. "Lucky for us, I mean. Bad luck for Prowdd'on. And either the Toads or the Um'Binnians have got Murgott, so it's definitely bad luck for him."

"Sometimes you seem so stupid!" She put her fists to her mouth but it didn't smother the Royal Swear Word.

Hodie tried to calm his temper. "I just know how things work. Watch something long enough, think about it, and eventually you figure it out."

"You are impossible!" She bashed the nest. "Ouch. Get back in—it might take off again."

He stayed where he was and spread his hands. "I think it's people who made the difference, not magic. Special people who keep on trying, who don't give up. I actually think if you get the chance, you'll be a good enough Queen…"

"Good enough?" she shouted. "Good enough's not good enough!"

He nearly strode off and left her. But the wind skirled, waves wrinkled across the river, and Hodie felt his forehead wrinkle too. "Maybe it's true that a special royal person can …um…communicate with magic—if that's another word for nature—and help keep the world safe, so children don't lose their parents and…" His throat hurt with a rush of pain and sadness. "But people do lose their parents. And you're in danger of losing yours too, as well as your brother." He cleared his throat. "Anyway. Since the wind set us down here, come and have a proper look at the map."

She clambered over the edge of the nest, ripping her pajama trousers. He opened the bag for her to ease out the silver map. She held it carefully. The wind was absolutely still, but the map weighed nothing and moved in the breath from their mouths. She made him rest his hand under a corner to keep it steady.

"It's just a lot of scribbles," she said.

"Pass your hand over it," said Hodie.

She flattened her palm and slowly moved it over the silver sheet. The map glowed and seemed more beautiful. The images and names shimmered. There was the Eastern Isle on the right side of the map—the east—where the Dragon-eagles bathed and fed. There were the hills behind the lake, where the Dragon-eagles lived. How far could they fly? Around the entire world if they wanted, Hodie supposed. But even very small non-magical birds—and mechanical ones—could do that.

"Eagles usually built their nests in high places," Hodie said. "Is that what Dragon-eagles do?"

"They don't need a usual nest." She traced the curve of the coastline and mountain ranges. Starting with the Isle, south around Old Ocean, west to the City of Spires, up over the Stones of Beyond to Um'Binnia, to the northern ranges, and back again to the Eastern Isle—together all the ranges made a broken oval. It could almost be the shape of a huge nest.

"There…" Hodie pointed at a spot near the center of the nest made by the curving mountain ranges. It was sort of near the area Murgott had called the Waiting Lands, halfway between Um'Binnia and the Eastern Isle. A low hill was marked there, inland, but it had no name. Sibilla reached out and touched the image with a fingertip.

Tiny green flames flared out of the map then died away. For a brief moment a line of writing curled under the image—*The Mount of the Four Storms*. Four wings appeared in the silver and beat ripples across the whole map. Then the map was still again.

~

Magic at last. The little Queen looked sick and drained. Her lips parted. "How do I get there?" she murmured.

Hodie was practical, not magic. He folded the secret pocket back over the map and looked at the nest. It had put down roots again, huge thick ones. The coin-shaped leaves rustled in the breeze and the flowers sent out sweet scent.

"That's not lifting off a second time," he said. "You can try the rest of the shoots but there's no guarantee they'll grow. And if they do, there's no guarantee the wind will blow in the right direction."

"Don't bring out the shoots," Sibilla said.

He thrust his hand deeper into the shabby bag for the battered cup. "What about this?"

"What about it?" Sibilla asked.

"I thought you'd know by now," said Hodie.

"I don't have a clue!" she snapped.

His last drop of patience vanished. He dropped the bag at her feet. "Nor do I! And it's not my business!" He slung the satchel off his shoulder and held it out. "You'll need this to protect the bag. There's the cup and the rest of those seeds, and the wrench, I don't know why. I'm off!"

The little Queen didn't reach out to take the satchel from him, so Hodie simply dropped that on the ground too and walked away.

"Stop!" she called in a cold and regal voice.

He took no notice.

"You complained that you'd never been paid!" she called more loudly.

"I don't care!"

But he couldn't resist a glance back. The satchel still lay on the ground, but Sibilla had fumbled the drawstring bag over her shoulder and was putting her dressing gown on top.

"You are a wretched stupid boy!" She tossed something. The wrench landed beside his boot.

"I believe you found that useful. You'll be able to find work with it." Her voice dripped with scorn. "I thank you, odd-job boy, for all your help."

~

# WRONG CHOICE,
# WRONG
# WRONG
# WRONG

There was no point in letting an excellent wrench lie there and rust. Hodie snatched it up, stuffed it down his shirt, and marched off. Within moments he was back in the forest. He bashed his fist against a trunk and let out a tirade about which one of them—the Queen or him—was the most stupid. King Jasper and his metal birds had given the Queen false hope. False hope was cruel.

The trees muttered and whispered. He started to walk on but heard a louder roaring from the river. He swung around and, through the trees, made out the shape and colors of a high-speed Um'Binnian warship, smoke rising from its funnels. A small boat had already left the ship and nosed into the riverbank, letting off a group of soldiers. A scruffy squirrel was sniffing about, getting its paws wet, as if it wondered whether to try stowing away.

There on the deck of the warship was a tall, portly figure

in purple and gold. Beside him stood Princessa Lu'nedda in her bedraggled pink frock and the Commander with skinny arms akimbo.

What could Hodie do? Not one single thing.

~

In stories, Hodie had heard that travelers spent the night in ditches and used their bags for pillows. He no longer had a bag and thought that ditches would be damp. A crook of tree roots made a more comfortable bed ("more comfortable" didn't actually mean "comfortable"). He half-hoped the squirrel would turn up and help him keep warm, though perhaps it had hidden on the warship.

Hodie tucked his legs up and pulled the collar of the cloak around his neck. He felt something hard in his top shirt pocket. The last of the seeds. If it hadn't sprouted from being soaked with sea water, it must be a dud. Just his luck. Bad again.

So he curled up alone in the Um'Binnian cloak, wrench down his shirt, and asked if he could have done anything differently. Never have left the Grand Palace in the first place? Not have left Queen Sibilla like that back by the river? Everything had been a mistake. Now he was feeling sorry for himself again—how pathetic.

When morning came, he didn't wake up because he hadn't been to sleep at all. The leaves of the forest grizzled at him. The wind slapped him in a bad temper. The sky was yellowy-gray, the color of misery.

He stood up at last. Walking out of the forest seemed the best idea, otherwise he might go in circles. He followed a stream inland, and it didn't take long to leave the trees behind. The stream dwindled into just a boggy patch and his boots were soon covered in mud. He trudged on till it dried and fell off. The land was fairly flat with still no house in sight although there was a field of cows.

Then more or less south he saw a hill. Just a hill with a flat top, hardly high enough to be the magical (*ha ha!*) Mount of the Four Storms. But that flat top was unusual. From there, Hodie might get more of a view, at least, and see the best road to travel. It might be interesting, too, to see if there was a hill in the distance that could be the Mount of the Dragon-eagles. Whether a boy was somebody or nobody, if he was normal he was expected to be curious.

~

The day continued as miserable as early morning and sent rain in sulky splatters. But it wasn't cold, and though he'd had no sleep and nothing to eat, Hodie didn't feel tired. The wind blew steadily. The lower slope, smooth at first, soon thickened with bushes. He found a way through easily enough.

Around midday the thin clouds thickened and the wind dropped. Hodie could have sworn he heard horses whicker and a jingle of harness. There must be a road, but he was hiking over stones and clods of dirt. He suddenly felt furious. He'd tricked himself into believing that magic was real after all, but... His foot slipped.

Down he plunged, crashing through bracken, nothing to break his fall. Then the air thudded out of him and he found himself at the foot of a steep bank, on his back, cramped between a rock and a stout tree root. He struggled, but his own weight simply wedged him deeper. His shoulders and arms were trapped by the cloak. He could kick a little with one leg and move one arm from the elbow, but he couldn't grip on anything or wave for help. Not a single person in the world knew where he was.

The jingle of harness sounded again, further off. He tried to call out but couldn't draw breath. But the wrench jabbed into his chest. He fumbled it out with his free hand. If he could just ease the wrench between his shoulder and the root—it would bruise but all he needed was some leverage. He squeezed his eyes tight with the effort.

When he opened them again a silvery-green glow surrounded him. He could sit enough to get the elbow beneath him and raise himself up. His lungs filled again with air.

On one end of the wrench a faint curving image had appeared. He rubbed it, but the image didn't get any clearer and, after another moment, faded away. The green glow had faded too. *I was just feeling faint*, he told himself, then *No*, and he whispered aloud, "There is magic." He tucked the wrench back between his shirt and undershirt and hauled himself out of the hollow.

"Thank you," he breathed, to luck, to quick thinking, desperate thinking, and to the wrench, to the merest shred of magic that had touched an ordinary boy and saved him from dying alone.

His arm where the wrench had levered was sore when he touched it, which meant the best thing was not to touch it. He fought up another ledge of bush and scrub, grabbed a branch and swung himself the last strides up the hill.

The top of the hill wasn't flat. It sloped down like a shallow bowl, so it might once have been a volcano. But Hodie didn't have time to examine it further. Arriving further around the rim were three military carriages pulled by horses. Hodie ducked behind a clump of grass and hoped the green Um'Binnian cloak would work as camouflage.

Out of the carriages stepped Prowdd'on, Lu'nedda (still in yesterday's ruined pink dress), soldiers, Sibilla (still in the hospital dressing gown), and Murgott (arms cuffed behind his back). Something seemed stuck on the top of the last carriage—a scruffy bird's nest? It lifted its head and waved a tail—it was the squirrel. And there, surrounded by a scattering of broken branches, in the center of the shallow bowl, lay the dying Dragon-eagle.

～

# SOMETIMES YOU JUST KNOW—
## AT LEAST,
## YOU HOPE SO

The Dragon-eagle was slumped on a few broken branches as if it had tried to build a nest. Its coronet of feathers was limp and dull. There was no sign of the silver-green glow Hodie remembered from the Palace garden. Its eyes were half-closed. The air was so still that Hodie heard a dull metallic rustle as the scale-feathers lifted and settled.

Prowdd'on gave a shout of triumph. His commander echoed it (of course) and the Dragon-eagle raised its head. For a moment Hodie saw how strong and beautiful it must have been when it was young. Although it was weak now, it was still magnificent. It reached a lion-like paw toward another branch, sunk its claws in, and dragged it closer.

Emperor Prowdd'on shoved Commander Gree'sle. Gree'sle urged an officer toward the Dragon-eagle. The officer took three steps, the Dragon-eagle half-reared up, and the man faltered.

Then Prowdd'on elbowed Sibilla. In the strange stillness

of the bowl, Hodie heard every word. "You said you had to come here. If you capture it for me, then maybe I let you go."

"There's no point in capturing it just before it dies." Sibilla sounded close to tears but angry too.

The Dragon-eagle slumped again.

Prowdd'on gestured to Gree'sle, who gestured to a soldier to fasten manacles on Sibilla. She held her arms out, wrists together, and gave the soldier a tiny royal nod. The soldier bowed before he clicked the handcuffs on her. None of them had noticed Hodie yet.

With a rough grip on the little Queen's arm, the Emperor pulled her to stand just below the rim. Sibilla looked only at the Dragon-eagle in a way that twisted Hodie's heart. She wrung her hands, and he heard the faint chink of handcuffs like an echo of the Dragon-eagle's scales. How must she feel? The young Dragon-eagle was caged inside the mountain with a broken wing, and the old Dragon-eagle here... Hodie finally believed in magic utterly, and he was looking at it dying.

The silence in the bowl began to fill with a faint buzzing and Hodie knew that this place was not quite part of the real world. An ordinary boy had no place here. But he stayed where he was.

The Dragon-eagle eyed Sibilla beneath its drooping lids. It moved its paw, moved it again—what was it doing?

Sibilla raised the handcuffs in front of her and stepped down into the grassy bowl. The buzzing increased and pulsed, and it seemed the air was waiting.

"What can I do?" she asked.

The creature bowed its head.

"You want more branches?" asked Sibilla. "I can't lift much with my hands like this…"

There was a small green flash and the manacles chimed as they fell from her wrists. She looked astonished, as if she was waking from some long dream. "Oh…" She bowed to the Dragon-eagle. "Thank you." The creature nodded and slumped again.

"More handcuffs!" said the Emperor.

Commander Gree'sle clicked his fingers. A soldier pulled another set of manacles out of his pocket.

Princessa Lu'nedda snatched them from him. "Father! Give little Queen her chance."

Prowdd'on shrugged. Hodie supposed the Emperor knew he'd won, whatever happened.

Sibilla glanced at Lu'nedda. She didn't smile, but the glance said thank you. Lu'nedda bowed a little. Sibilla tugged at a broken branch, heaved it beside the Dragon-eagle, and brushed her hands.

"But this won't be enough," she said.

The creature's eyes closed. Sorrow seeped from its coronet of feathers like a dull mist, like the green of shadows in moonlight just after the sun has sunk out of sight when color begins fading from the hills and the evening wind's deciding what to do.

*Green, of course*, thought Hodie. *The Queen needs to use the green tangle. She'll think of it, any second.*

Sibilla's head lifted, and she glanced in his direction. She looked so relieved it hurt his heart. She flung the dressing gown away so she was just in the tattered pajamas and slipped the bag off over her neck.

"You didn't check what she had with her?" Prowdd'on shouted at Gree'sle.

"I have told you for years, Gree'sle is useless except for carrying Roar-juice," Lu'nedda said.

Sibilla drew the bag open. The pale green tangle sprang out into her hands. The Dragon-eagle raised its ancient head and sighed.

The mist swirled in tendrils and that sweet scent filled the air. Ropes and coils of mist floated like nooses around Prowdd'on and his Commander, covering their mouths, surrounding the soldiers—it looked as though they couldn't move or didn't dare. But Sibilla walked in a circle around the Dragon-eagle, strewing strands of the green tangle into the few branches and twigs beneath the creature. The tendrils twisted and darkened at once. She brought out the pouch and scattered the remaining seeds as well. Roots thrust down into the soil. Within moments the Dragon-eagle was surrounded by a living nest that grew white flowers like roses, glowing and fragrant.

Hodie's heart began to hammer. Those roots looked so tough that even the strongest gales couldn't carry this nest away. How would the Dragon-eagle escape?

Slowly, painfully, the creature sank down in the center of the nest. Sibilla stretched out a hand and the Dragon-eagle raised its head to touch her fingers with the tip of its mighty beak.

Mist settled around the nest, around her feet, like a

carpet of silvery green feathers.

~ *Queen* ~ the Dragon-eagle said ~ *it is time* ~

"I'm not really a Queen," Sibilla said. She didn't look it either, a lonely scared figure in torn pajamas, hair a dull and tangled mop.

The Dragon-eagle tipped its head to look at her. ~ *Royal baby, royal girl, and royal woman* ~ chimed the voice.

Emperor Prowdd'on wrested his head away from the rope of mist with a laugh of disdain. "A Queen has a crown!" The mist muffled him again.

The Dragon-eagle eyed the Emperor. Without taking its gaze off Prowdd'on, it touched its paw to the side of the tattered bag in Sibilla's hand. There was a tearing sound, and the silver map was in its grasp.

The creature beckoned Hodie with its lion's paw and held out the map. ~ *Fold the crown* ~ rang the voice.

Hodie found he'd stood up from hiding.

~ *You are the Queen's Companion and Guardian of The Ties* ~ the creature said.

Hodie stumbled with shock. Even if he hadn't known he was the Companion or Guardian? Even if he was nobody, and it had happened by accident, and he'd been trying to head south all along? Well—he didn't dare make any objection to such a creature at such a time.

Trembling, he walked down into the bowl, close enough to take the map, to feel the soft metal feathers on the Dragon-eagle's paw, to see the silver claws and feel its breath on his forehead. His hands shook so much that he thought the silver map would rip to pieces, but he folded it in half, in half again lengthways, then half again, and again to make a long strip. He folded one end over the other so it made a tiny peak like the top of a star.

~ *Well done* ~ chimed the voice that was no voice.

Hodie held out the circle. The creature breathed on it and there, in its claws, was a crown of silver etched with feathers.

The Emperor struggled against the ropes of mist but they held firm. Up by the carriages, Murgott stamped in a piratical dance of pure excitement. "You wanted magic, now you're seein' it!" he cried.

The Dragon-eagle held the crown out for Sibilla, but she took a step back.

"It's yours, Sibilla," called Lu'nedda.

Sibilla seemed to have a little argument inside her head and then she bowed. The crown floated from the Dragon-eagle's claw and rested on her tangled hair. Hodie was very afraid he might cry, so he bit the inside of his cheek till the feeling passed.

The buzzing in the air grew more intense.

~ *Now* ~ said the Dragon-eagle. With a terrible effort, the creature raised a paw and clawed at its chest over its heart. It plucked a feather and held it out. On its glowing point was a drop of jasper-red blood.

Sibilla hesitated again as if she was listening to a voice inside her. She reached into the bag and brought out the rusty old cup. She dropped the bag and took the feather from the Dragon-eagle, held it up, and bowed to the creature. Then she stuck the quill into the cup.

When she drew it out, a tiny flame of green burned at

the tip. She held it high. The air was still and the flame soon brightened.

~ *Trust me* ~ rang the ancient voice of the Dragon-eagle.

"Trust me," the little Queen echoed and touched the green fire to the nest.

There was a great cry from the Dragon-eagle. It spread its wings. Flames raced around the circle of the nest. Hodie flung an arm up for protection, but even as he backed away he realized the flames reached only upwards. They made a fiery crown, branches of green fire, gold fire, silver, so high they scorched the edges of the clouds.

~

## THE ONLY CHOICE POSSIBLE

The shape of the Dragon-eagle crumpled and flaked like paper, diminished to ashes. Shreds of black edged with red sparks flew about like fiery moths. Hodie saw Sibilla shuddering, her face wet with tears. Hodie was shaking too, crouching on his hands and knees in the rough grass.

"Wait," he heard the Queen say to him, her voice hoarse. "Wait." She wiped her face on the sleeve of the pink pajamas.

The roar of the flames died down. The nest was nothing but a blackened twist. No embers glowed.

"This is wrong!" bellowed Prowdd'on on the rim of the hill. "I wanted it! I have one but I wanted two!"

Hodie knew down to his bones now what was coming.

Another roar began to build, up, up. It was the roar of the four winds, which pounced and plunged over the rim from every quarter and breathed on the nest.

In the ashes one silver ember flared, then seven, then more, like tiny stars. The winds dropped to gentle breathing. Sibilla's hands lifted to urge the new flames on. They glowed and came together in a fiery flower of silver, blue and green, gold, that grew larger and larger. Something started to form in the petals of flame—a curve like wings, a shape like a coronet, a spreading tail. A young Dragon-eagle lifted from the fiery flower into the sky. A little unsteady, supported by four now-gentle winds, it circled the hill on its new wings, silver voice in a chiming song.

For a moment, Hodie thought everything would be all right.

But the ropes of mist around the Um'Binnians were beginning to break up.

"Shoot it!" Prowdd'on bellowed. "Gree'sle! Kill it! Capture it! Shoot the Dragon-eagle down!"

"Make your mind up!" cried a soldier.

"Rebel!" Gree'sle pointed his sword as well as a pistol. "Under arrest! Court martial!"

The Dragon-eagle opened its beak and sent a green flame to scorch Gree'sle's hat. The Commander ducked. A squirt of flame nearly hit Prowdd'on. But the Dragon-eagle was too new to have much control yet. It tried again and there was only a spark.

The Princessa struggled down from the rim of the mount. Hodie readied himself to shove her back, but Lu'nedda took Sibilla's arm exactly like a royal sister. "Call the Dragon-eagle down," she said. "You have to hurry."

The wind tugged Sibilla's hair. Her pajama trousers flapped. "Call it down? I can't! They'll kill it!"

"For goodness sake. You are Queen Sibilla." Lu'nedda said it with a strange stern look (very much like Ogg'ward, actually) and gave her royal sister's arm a shake. "Call the Dragon-eagle. Hope that it is strong enough to rescue its companion, your brother, and his fiancée. If you do not, my father will rule your country as well as mine. Is that what any sensible woman or man wants?"

"Definitely not," Sibilla said.

Hodie scrambled out of the way fast. The little Queen called up to the Dragon-eagle. With a chiming of feathers, it soared down beside her. The winds tossed Sibilla's hair about and gusted with such force that it was impossible for Hodie to hear what she said, though the new crown stayed on tight. The Dragon-eagle let out a fierce cry then lowered its head to Sibilla.

She ducked away and snatched up the drawstring bag. Why? None of The Ties were left in it.

Before Hodie could call out to her that Murgott's notebook was not a treasure, Sibilla was back beside the Dragon-eagle. It scooped her onto its back. She grasped the feathers at the base of its neck, and the wings started to fan out behind her. The Dragon-eagle tipped its head as if it asked for her encouragement. She stroked its neck.

The winds roared, the Dragon-eagle rose up. In a few beats, the creature had swept the little Queen so high in the smoky sky that all Hodie could see was a blur soaring in the direction of Um'Binnia.

—

# OH PLEASE,
# NOT ANOTHER BAD CHOICE

In the bottom of the bowl, the air was still. The mist had disappeared though a sweet smell lingered along with drifts of ordinary smoke. Hodie crouched again behind a clump of grass and watched the Um'Binnians regroup. The Emperor snapped out orders. Gree'sle handcuffed Lu'nedda and thrust her into the biggest carriage and the Emperor climbed in after her. The officers shouted to each other about wind speed and air-lift and took wrenchs to some mechanism beneath the carriage.

Murgott, still manacled, lay on his belly in the long grass. He jerked his head, and Hodie wriggled over to him.

"They're sending Prowdd'on directly to Um'Binnia," Murgott growled. "They say if the wind holds, they can lift from here and reach a speed at least as fast as the Dragon-eagle." He struggled onto his side. "My pocketknife, boy. Get the cuffs off me. Use the lock-pick."

By the time Hodie had freed the Corporal (fast), the carriage had been transformed into a wind-ship (equally fast).

"So you believe in magic now, boy." Murgott rubbed at his wrists and flexed his hands. "But the fight's not over. Let me tell you straight, from the heart of a man who has lived with the most evil set of villains you could wish to avoid, from a man who has drunk the dregs of bad behavior and relished each drop—I tell you, hope is the source of magic. Hope's a gift, boy, from a generous and loving heart. The little Queen has such a heart. She's had it since she was two years old. And a generous heart is better than the most vast of treasure hoards the world could hold."

The Corporal's words made Hodie wonder why his poetry wasn't better.

"I thank you, boy, for your service to the little Queen. And now…" Murgott took back his pocketknife. "Goodbye, sir." Murgott crawled off as if he was a large spy beetle.

So—Hodie had been called "sir" and yet the Corporal had dismissed him. The little Queen had not even said goodbye. It felt like a kick in the stomach—but only if he let it. It was all right. He'd done a good job, even if it was mostly by accident. And Queen Sibilla had come into her magic, or as close as she ever might. Hodie wondered if she'd be satisfied. He would hear news of her as he lived his quiet life. He hoped she would succeed in this last bit of the struggle. But yes, his part in it was done. He'd found out about his parents—all three of them, which had been a surprise. He might never altogether forgive his mother, but he figured that was fair enough. He might actually miss her a bit, but he had always coped.

So now he was on his own, free to go south. To go anywhere. To find work. Find a place to call home. It was Queen Sibilla who was unlucky. She still had jobs to do: join her brother and the injured Dragon-eagle in Um'Binnia, deal with the war, and rule with her brother— that is, if the Fontanians won. But that was her set of problems. Not Hodie's.

The military carriage was ready for takeoff. The wind-sails were hoisted. Any second the wind would pick it up and send it soaring for Um'Binnia.

If somebody wanted to, they could stow away. If somebody thought his arms were strong enough, he could cling to the carriage axle. He'd have to cling for at least an hour of land, then over the Great Salt Moat. It would be unwise for a boy scared of heights. It would be the most foolish thing that any boy could do.

But if he was a Companion and a Guardian, there was actually a big job still to be finished.

Hodie stood up and looked south. The sky was eggshell blue and sunshine painted the hills with a golden wash. Then he turned and sprinted for the wind-carriage, kicked a leg over the back axle, and hunched into the wheel well.

*Chuk!* said something tucked at the other end of the axle.

Hodie had lost count of the number of times he'd been impressed by that squirrel. He hoped it was holding on with every claw. Perhaps it had a serious job to finish too.

~

## HOW TO FIND SOUTH

When Hodie dared look down, the wind-carriage was soaring over wild lands. The Great Salt Moat soon lay beneath, crinkled with waves. His hands cramped. So did his knees. Then at the foot of Um'Binnia he saw the Fontanian flagship the *Excellent Eagle*, moored beside a small sailing vessel. Her sails were furls of green, the hull painted in segments—orange, yellow, red, and purple. The *Royal Traveler*. Just as the second metal bird had told Sibilla, King Jasper and Lady Beatrix had each arrived. There would be a battle ahead.

Hodie couldn't bear to see the approach to the wind-garage. He closed his eyes against the sting of the wind till he felt a bump. He tumbled off onto the cavern floor, too cold to move. Something furry rolled after him—*ch-ch-chk!* He managed to wriggle with the squirrel into shadows behind a workbench.

Gree'sle, the Emperor, and six officers jumped from the carriage. The Princessa stumbled out last, handcuffed and forgotten.

THE QUEEN AND THE NOBODY BOY

At the rear of the cave was a turmoil of silver feathers, flashes of swords and daggers, the crack of pistols. There were so many Um'Binnians, so few Fontanians. King Jasper, in a helmet and metal jerkin, shielded the wounded Dragon-eagle. Fresh blood trickled down its side. Its broken wing dragged on the floor. There was Lady Beatrix, the King's fiancée, one of her arms red with blood as well, wielding a sword as if—well, as if it were a heavy sword. Hodie's mother was there, too, in the cluster of Fontanian soldiers. She was alive and fighting too! Allana swung a short sword with both hands as she held off two Um'Binnian officers.

Near Hodie there came a roar of fire. On his side of the cavern stood the new-born Dragon-eagle, wings half-spread, staggering a bit because it was so young. Sibilla still clung to its shoulders. Another flash of fire came from its beak, but it was unable to get closer to the fighting. And how could it use its flame when it might kill the King or Lady Beatrix?

"Surrender," Prowdd'on shouted. "Everything is mine! Fontania, treasures, all things!"

An Um'Binnian officer blew his trumpet. The fighting quieted.

Both Dragon-eagles swung toward Prowdd'on. His shoulders stiffened.

The wounded Dragon-eagle spoke and the air in the cavern rang with a long chime ~ *Magic must be given freely* ~

Prowdd'on laughed, though it seemed rather put-on.

There was another rush of wind into the cavern and Hodie's bangs blew in his eyes. A second military wind-carriage landed. From behind its rear axle tumbled the big shape of Murgott. So he had been stupid too! In a second, the Corporal was hidden behind a pile of crates near Hodie.

But now officers were leaping out of the carriage and standing with Prowdd'on, pistols aimed at King Jasper, Lady Beatrix, and Lady Allana.

Hodie felt more hopeless than he'd ever felt in all his life.

Jasper lowered his sword and raised a hand, palm up, to Prowdd'on. "Think about it, Emperor. Your city is full of rebels. Do all your people want you to destroy the last chance to preserve magic?"

"You're hardly older than a boy and your beard is a joke," said Prowdd'on. "Your sister is a ragamuffin brat in stolen pajamas."

Lu'nedda called out. "Father! Listen to King Jasper! For once, think of something besides selfish self!"

Hodie saw Murgott's head pop up. Pocketknife out, the Corporal was sneaking along the side of the carriage to release Lu'nedda's handcuffs. For a moment, Jasper too was distracted by the movement. Gree'sle lunged for him and caught King Jasper was in a death grip, sword at his throat.

The wounded Dragon-eagle reared up and threatened Prowdd'on with a flame.

Nobody moved.

Except Sibilla. She let go of the silver feathers of the new Dragon-eagle's neck and slid to the cavern floor, an arm's length from Hodie. The drawstring bag slid off too and fell apart completely. On the floor lay Murgott's notebook, open. Tiny silver shapes of words began to float

THE QUEEN AND THE NOBODY BOY

up from the fluttering pages. Sibilla blinked at them. Hodie recognized them as they shimmered and curved in the air. It was the poem Murgott had written about the little Queen when she was two, the day she and her brother had been crowned—words about her generous heart and loving soul.

For a moment Sibilla pressed her head to the new young Dragon-eagle's side. Then she stepped into the center of the cavern.

Hodie's hand flew to grasp the wrench in his shirt—it was all he had left with which to defend her.

"Emperor Prowdd'on," cried Sibilla. "King Jasper. Lady Beatrix, Princessa Lu'nedda, everyone! Please listen. I'm willing to share what I have—it isn't much. But, for instance, now I have two crowns. I've got one at home already. The Dragon-eagle made this one—well, Hodie helped. Emperor, tell the Commander to let my brother go, and I'll give you this crown."

"It is only silver," Prowdd'on said. "I will have gold."

Gree'sle's grip tightened on King Jasper's throat.

Sibilla's hand went to her neck too—she gripped the pendant. "I have this!" she shouted. "It's the oldest gold!" She yanked it off her neck.

This was the moment to distract Gree'sle. Hodie leaped on top of the workbench. "There's this too!" He pulled out the wrench and raised his arm.

In the same moment that Sibilla tossed the pendant, he threw the wrench. Glittering, they whirled toward Prowdd'on. The Emperor jumped back. The pendant and wrench collided with a flash of green—the air around the two vibrated and glowed as the pieces fused. A clash of music rang and echoed and swelled throughout the cavern.

There, on the floor, lay a golden scepter. It shivered and shimmered and grew three times larger as everyone watched. It was richest, brightest gold.

Prowdd'on bent to pick it up.

"No!" cried King Jasper.

~ *The Queen's scepter!* ~ cried the re-born Dragon-eagle. ~ *Only the Queen of Fontania must touch it!* ~

Jasper kicked out then and Gree'sle staggered and let go. The standoff, if you asked Hodie, was at a standstill.

~ *Queen, take up the scepter* ~ said the wounded Dragon-eagle.

~ *Take it up* ~ said the other, the newborn, the fire-born. ~ *Queen, take it up* ~

King Jasper and Lady Beatrix whispered encouragement. Hodie heard his mother urging too. Lu'nedda and Murgott, both very bedraggled, looked at the little Queen, waiting. Hodie held his breath.

~ *There is more to magic than anyone knows* ~ said the wounded Dragon-eagle. ~ *The scepter is proof that you have come into your magic, Queen Sibilla* ~

She brushed her dirty hands on the even dirtier pajamas, stepped over, and took up the scepter. It seemed heavy.

The wounded Dragon-eagle spoke again. ~ *First I must ask you to heal my wing. Then you may grant one wish to one person. It may be to any person present* ~

Sibilla raised her head and walked slowly to the wounded Dragon-eagle. With the golden token she touched the broken wing. Sweet-scented mist rose around her. Then she stepped back. The Dragon-eagle carefully flexed its wing, flapped both wings hard enough to make a breeze run around the cavern, and lowered its head to her in thanks.

~ *True Queen* ~ sang two silver voices.

For a moment the very air seemed a blur of silver. A murmur trickled through the crowd—Sibilla's grubby pajamas had disappeared and she was dressed in a green and gold tunic with green leggings and what looked like nice soft boots. Her face and hands were clean. Under the crown of folded silver, her hair was glossy, thick, and honey-yellow. (Hodie saw her squint sideways and give it a pat.)

"Now I have to grant a wish?" she asked. Hodie could tell how nervous she was. "To anyone? And I choose?"

The Dragon-eagles lowered their great heads and seemed to smile.

"Then I grant it to Prowdd'on," she said in a shaky voice. "Of course it can't be to rule Fontania. But he's really an unhappy man, and I hope he will have what his heart truly desires and be content."

Prowdd'on gave a delighted snort.

"It is a trick, Magnificence!" cried Gree'sle.

"Shut up," said the Emperor. "This is finally promising."

~ *Think carefully* ~ chimed the re-born Dragon-eagle.

~ *Very carefully indeed* ~ rang the voice of its healed companion.

"I have best brain in Um'Binnia," said Prowdd'on. "My wish is this—that I am surrounded forever by what I most love."

Sibilla raised the scepter. "Are you sure?"

"Never question me," the Emperor said.

So Sibilla touched the scepter to Prowdd'on's shoulder. Hodie saw her arm tremble as if sparks ran through it.

A fresh flask of Roar-juice flew out of Gree'sle's pocket. It arced through the air, flattened, then with rattling and clattering multiplied into many mirrors. A complete lattice of little mirrors formed around the Emperor, taller than he was—a glittering container, bars of mirrors facing him.

"What's this?" Prowdd'on bellowed. "Take it away!"

Through the gaps in the mirror lattice Hodie saw a thousand bellowing reflections of the Emperor.

~ *We said be careful* ~ said the healed Dragon-eagle.

~ *We said be very careful* ~ said the other.

"Get me out!" Prowdd'on roared inside the cage.

A soldier with a crowbar started toward him.

"There has to be another treasure! This isn't fair!" the Emperor cried.

"There's nothing else," said Sibilla.

Hodie fumbled with the button of his shirt pocket. "There is," he called. "I'd forgotten. But it's just the last seed."

"Give it to me!" Prowdd'on stuck his hand out through the lattice. The soldier with the crowbar bowed and waited.

Hodie shuffled over. It was awful being the center of attention. The Emperor wiggled his fingers for him to hurry. Hodie held the seed up then drew his arm back.

"I think it's a dud, but it might still be dangerous," he said. "I'm not sure…"

Something gray streaked over the cavern floor and tripped Hodie up. The seed soared through the air, the squirrel caught it with one deft paw, scampered up the network of mirrors and dropped the seed into Prowdd'on's palm.

"I've got it!" shouted Prowdd'on. "Now what do I do?"

"Don't eat it!" cried Sibilla.

"You mustn't eat it!" Hodie cried at the same moment.

There was a split second of silence, then Prowdd'on chuckled. "Another trick," he said.

Through the grille, Hodie saw him lift his hand to his (very big) mouth and pop in the seed.

Silence again. The Emperor coughed and spat the seed out.

Too late. It was growing already, sending roots and purple shoots and twirly gold tangles around his head. It threaded through the mirrors, stronger and more flourishing each moment, so fast there was nothing anyone or any Dragon-eagle could do about it (even if they'd wanted to). The squirrel chittered and danced and leaped around the cavern walls, screaming with glee.

Lu'nedda took a step toward the glittering tumbleweed that encased her father. "Oh dear," she said.

Sibilla wiped her nose on her green and golden sleeve and glanced out at the sky with a look of shock. A moment later the wind began to whistle into the cavern.

It was an insistent wind, very particular. It whirled around the cavern, chose the shining tangle with Emperor Prowdd'on in the center, and whisked it out into the air, up and away until it wasn't even a dot in the cloud free sky beyond Um'Binnia.

Lu'nedda's face was wet with tears, but she turned and bowed to Sibilla. "Royal sister. My first announcement as Empress is that I declare the war officially off."

Soldiers and officers on both sides cheered.

Lu'nedda took Sibilla's hand. "I am sure you would like to go home as soon as possible to your lady mother." She bowed to King Jasper. "Royal brother, you and Lady Beatrix are welcome to rest here in my city before you leave."

Jasper bowed too. "It seems that Um'Binnia has a new ruler."

"Actually," a voice cried from the rear of the cavern, "some of us want Ogg'ward for President!"

Lu'nedda raised her head. In her tattered pink gown, Murgott's best (scuffed) boots and ratty ringlets, she walked to the center of the cavern and looked more of an Empress with every step. "I will consult with the rebels!" she declared. "I honestly promise!"

So it looked like a pretty happy ending, if you asked Hodie.

Silvery mist still feathered around Sibilla. Her brother and Lady Beatrix each went and hugged her then hugged each other.

Gree'sle was looking fairly sick and trying to sneak off.

Allana stopped him—a short stern woman, a tall uneasy man. She beckoned to an officer who looked very pleased to lead Gree'sle away in manacles.

Allana dusted her hands then threaded through the

THE QUEEN AND THE NOBODY BOY

crowds, hunting for something—oh, Hodie realized—hunting for him.

"My brave son," she said in her husky voice.

"My brave mother." His voice had gone husky too.

"I can go home at last," she said. "Where I belong. I hope you…" She stopped. It was one of those tricky family moments.

But Murgott's heavy hand landed on Hodie's shoulder. "I knew the little Queen could do it."

"Me too," said Hodie. "With or without magic, actually. But it is better with."

"Attention!" Murgott saluted Sibilla, true Queen of Fontania, who was walking toward them in her magic tunic, magic leggings, magic boots.

"Hodie, thank you," she said. "Just a little thank you right now. We'll have a ceremony back home, a really huge one where you'll sit between me and my brother, and I'll thank you properly. With a medal or the key to your own palace or probably both. But what we really need now is some breakfast. I'd like pancakes cooked by Murgott, down in one of our own ships—the normal kind that floats."

"Sausages," said Murgott. "Pancakes definitely, and bacon, in the *Royal Traveler*. It has the most comfortable kitchen I've ever known."

"Hodie, will you join me there with your mother?" Sibilla asked.

For a moment he didn't know what he wanted. "I was going south," he heard himself say. "To become somebody." He bowed and tried to step away.

Sibilla took hold of his hands and shook her head. "You're somebody already. The Dragon-eagle said. You guarded The Ties. You're the Companion. Anyway—" her eyes looked mischievous—"the *Royal Traveler* is moored on Um'Binnia's south side."

Hodie felt like someone suddenly realizing he was home at the end of a difficult journey. He blinked and felt a smile grow from deep inside. Home where he belonged. Because, after all, the Grand Palace in the City of Spires was south from here too.

"Your Majesty," Hodie said. "I will be honored."

THE END

## Postscript 1

The Royal Swear Word: *Brisket*. (It sounds very effective indeed if you clench your teeth as hard as you can before you say it.)

## Postscript 2

### Emperor Prowdd'on's Mustache Wardrobe

The double spear
The circle with circles
The six circles
The rising sunburst (or embarrassed sea anemone)
The double pistol

## Postscript 3

### Um'Binnian Cabbage Cream

This is not the dessert served at the banquet in Fontania. It is the one Lu'nedda serves in her apartment. (If your grandmother made it for you, you'd have to say you liked it. But it would be best not to be too effusive or she might make it every time you visit.)

Find a cabbage as big as your head.

Cut it in half (yes, dear, I mean the cabbage) and put both halves in a pot of cold water.

*Continued overleaf…*

Put the pot on the stove and let the cabbage cook for 15 minutes. (Watch that it doesn't boil over. If it does, you're the one who has to clean up the mess.)

Pour off the water. (Don't let any cabbage slither into the sink.)

Fill the pot again with boiling water from your kettle.

Boil it for 20 more minutes.

Drain the cabbage dry then chop it into very little bits.

Put the bits into a bowl, add three big knobs of butter, and sprinkle in 12 dessert spoonfuls of brown sugar.

Add a heaped teaspoon of cinnamon and half a teaspoon of nutmeg.

Stir it all up.

In another bowl beat three fresh eggs and half a cup of cream.

Stir the eggs and cream into the cabbage.

Put it all into a baking dish.

Bake the dish in a medium oven until the cabbage is brown on top. (No, no, you can do it in a small oven or a very big one. I actually mean a medium temperature, which is about 350°F.) It should take about 20 minutes.

~

I don't think it is actually very nice. But try it with ice cream if you like. Your choice.